AMETHYST

ROJO GEMS
BOOK TWO

CEE BOWERMAN

Professionally edited by Chrissy Riesenberg
Cover created by Sweet 15 Designs

Please follow Cee on Facebook, Instagram, and Twitter. Also, for information on new releases and to catch up with Cee, go to www.ceebowermanbooks.com

Cee Bowerman Master Book List

The Rojo, Texas Universe

Texas Knights MC
(completed)

Home Forever
Forever Family
Lucky Forever
Love Forever

Texas Kings MC
(completed)

Kale
Sonny
Bird
Grunt
Lout
Smokey
Tucker
Kale & Terra (Novella)
John & Mattie
Bear
Daughtry
Hank
Fain
Grady
Stoffer
Luke
Clem

Conner Brothers Construction
(completed)

Finn
Angus
Mace
Ronan
Royal
Tavin
Chess

Rojo, TX
(completed)

Rason & Eliza
Atlas & Addie
Jazmyne & Luc
Kari & Levi
Noah & Tallie
Nick & Cindy
Marcus & Reagan

The Tempests
(completed)

Wrath
Creed
Loki
Styx
Thorn
Freya
Sin

Lonestar Terrace
(in progress)

1005 Alamo Way
2011 Texas Drive
2012 Texas Drive

Rojo PD
(in progress)

The Dark Side

Rojo Gems
(in progress)

Emerald
Amethyst

Rojo Kings
(in progress)

Lucky

Texas Queens MC
(in progress)

Lark

Cee Bowerman's Stand Alone Series

Time Served MC
(completed)

Boss
Hook
Chef
Preacher
Captain
Bug
Santa
Kitty
Rodeo
Stamp
TS in NY
Hammer
Soda

Time Served MC: Nomads
(in progress)

Sugar
Dub

The Four Families
(in progress)

Rico Romano
Zach Campana
Luca Russo

Springblood
(in progress)

One More Day
Fly Away with Me
I'll Stand by You - COMING SOON!

The Donovans
(in progress)

Drink It Up
Pull It Up
Pretty It Up
Curl It Up
Build It Up
Whip It Up

Mereu
(in progress)

Bear Witch Me

The Rojo, Texas Universe In Chronological Reading Order

Home Forever: Texas Knights MC, Book 1

Forever Family: Texas Knights MC, Book 2

Kale: Texas Kings MC, Book 1

Sonny: Texas Kings MC, Book 2

Bird: Texas Kings MC, Book 3

Grunt: Texas Kings MC, Book 4

Lout: Texas Kings MC, Book 5

Smokey: Texas Kings MC, Book 6

Tucker: Texas Kings MC, Book 7

Finn: Conner Brothers Construction, Book 1

Kale & Terra: a Texas Kings novella

John & Mattie: Texas Kings MC, Book 8

Angus: Conner Brothers Construction, Book 2

Bear: Texas Kings MC, Book 9

Lucky Forever: Texas Knights MC, Book 3

Reading Order for the Time Served MC Series

Boss: Time Served MC, Book 1

Hook: Time Served MC, Book 2

Chef: Time Served MC, Book 3

Preacher: Time Served MC, Book 4

Captain: Time Served MC, Book 5

Bug: Time Served MC, Book 6

Santa: Time Served MC, Book 7

Kitty: Time Served MC, Book 8

Rodeo: Time Served MC, Book 9

Stamp: Time Served MC, Book 10

Time Served In New York: Time Served MC, Book 11

Hammer: Time Served MC, Book 12

Soda: Time Served MC, Book 13

Reading Order for the Time Served MC: Nomads Series

Sugar, Book 1

Dub, Book 2

A NOTE FROM THE AUTHOR

Dear Reader,

If you've read my Time Served MC: Nomads series, you might recognize that the prologue of this book stems from the epilogue of Dub's book. That's going to be the case for quite a few books going forward - one event will be able to be seen from many different angles and spawn so many others.

I hope you enjoy reading about Amethyst and Tiny - although she absolutely refuses to call him that, or does she? Join me in checking in on the rest of the Rojo family. I'm glad to have you on this adventure and want you to know there are many more to come.

Happy reading,

Cee

AMETHYST

"Seriously, Amy, we've gotta move away from Rojo," Bella said for at least the third time in as many hours. She wasn't even looking at me while she spoke. For that matter, she wasn't looking at any of us who were seated at the table with her. Instead, she was craning her neck around so she could look at the men scattered around the yard. "The men at home don't look like this."

My sister knew how much it upset me to think of not having my friend close by and chided, "There you go, threatening Amethyst again."

I tried to ignore the pang of anxiety the thought of Bella moving away caused and said, "Others might disagree, but we can't see it because we're either related to them or have known them since birth. Although, I must say that there are some very handsome men here. Why haven't we ever seen them when we've come to visit?"

"The groom belongs to an MC near Dallas. I think most of these men do too."

"That explains the biker look," my sister said. She had always been attracted to more refined-looking men, whereas the rest of us seemed to gravitate toward the bad boy because that was the type of men we were raised around. "There are some cuties, though. Did you see that big one over there talking to the birdbrains?"

Wren laughed at her description, considering Diamond was referring to her brothers who were also named after different types of birds, and then asked, "How could anyone miss him? He's huge!"

"Who is that? He doesn't look like a biker," Bella said wistfully. "He looks like Lucifer Morningstar from that television show."

"Oh! Do you mean the guy from the cooking channel?" Gracy asked. "Look at them next to each other. I think they're father and son."

"Looks like they could be," Bella said. "The younger one doesn't need a cooking show to be delicious. Ba-dum-dum."

"Lame," Diamond muttered.

"He might be just the guy to get you out of your love slump," I said hopefully.

"Isn't that a book trope?" In a breathless voice, Cydney said, "They met at a wedding, and it was love at first sight."

"I'm not quite there yet," Bella insisted. She tried again to make a joke and said, "I am hungry, and it looks like his dad cooked up a fine meal."

"Please stop. You're embarrassing yourself," Diamond said with a roll of her eyes. "What is wrong with you people?"

"What's this 'you people' malarkey?"

"There aren't any children around, and we're four

hours from home. Just say the word shit. Just once. Please," Wren begged. "I know you can do it, Amy. *Please.* For me."

"Shi . . ." I drew the first vowel out for a second or two and then finished with, "Lamalamadingdong!"

Wren's head fell forward in shame, and the rest of the women around the table groaned and scoffed in disapproval, which just made me smile. The man I couldn't keep my eyes off of was staring at me openly now, his expression intense and almost angry, but when I smiled, he smiled back. It was almost as if the clouds had parted to let the sun shine through. It was only for a moment, but it brightened my day even more than the disdain from my friends.

And since irritating them with my refusal to curse fed my soul, that really meant something.

TAMA'I

"It's the original location. You want to be part of that legacy, don't you?"

"How much fucking snow do you get?" the man on the left asked. He looked at me and said, "We get snow, but they get *snow*. Believe me. I used to live here."

The men continued bickering about whose tattoo shop was better, and I looked at the guy standing next to me and smiled as he shook his head in embarrassment. I knew that he was about my age and one of their relatives, but I wouldn't be able to remember his name if you had put a gun to my head.

When my friend Dub invited me to his wedding, he assured me it would be a casual thing. As a matter of fact, I distinctly remember him saying, "We're going to have a cookout with some family and a few friends. No big deal. Swing by on the way to your sister's."

Because it made complete sense to ride up to Colorado on the way from Las Vegas, Nevada to Texas. But he'd found the woman of his dreams and invited all of his club brothers to witness their faaipoipoga. Even though I'd rather get my teeth pulled than attend a wedding ceremony, I made the drive anyway.

However, his idea of "no big deal" and "casual" were vastly different from mine. There were at least a hundred people here, if not more. Between my brothers from the club and their old ladies along with their children, the "few" in his description was blown out of the water. When you added in all the people I didn't know, who must be his new wife's family and friends, it was a full-fledged party complete with a live band, enough food to feed my old platoon, a dance floor with more square footage than most homes, and enough people to populate a small town.

The people in attendance were all from different walks of life too. Earlier, I was joined at the table by a doctor who asked if he could do a CT scan on my brain to see if it was in proportion to my body. Another doctor sitting at the table was appalled at the first one's question and just sat there shaking his head. I listened to the men bicker, like only family can do, when we were joined by *another* doctor who just happened to be their sister. Her play-by-play of their argument was hilarious and kept me amused through dinner. The woman was the whole package - gorgeous and funny with razor sharp wit, a sarcastic mouth, and an attitude that was so damn sexy, I nearly proposed to her on the spot.

Everyone at the table was pleasant and personable, even polite and inclusive, which I thought interesting considering that most people avoided me on principle. The fact that I was closer to seven feet tall than six made people look twice, the tattoos that sleeved my arms and came up to my jaw was enough to make people stare, and I'd been told more times than I could count that my face looked menacing even when I was happy. All of those characteristics combined generally made people uncomfortable, but not the ones who I happened to end up eating dinner with. They took it all in stride and involved me in their conversation as if they'd known me for years.

But then, a man I thought I'd never see again walked up and said hello, which led me to this moment right now which wasn't quite uncomfortable but not exactly pleasant either. There was no way having two grown men arguing over who could 'have me' wouldn't be awkward, especially when they didn't feel I need to be included in the decision-making process.

Finally, Hawk, a man I'd taken a few college courses with in prison, walked over and handed me a beer. "So, how's the argument going? Do we have a pool started yet?"

"Let's start one. I've got some cash," I offered.

"You can't go in on it. You've got to make the final decision," the other man scoffed.

"When I introduced you, I had no idea they'd know your name," Hawk said with a laugh. "Look at the shit you've stirred up, man. You'd fit right in at either Tempest Tattoo shop."

"Speaking of introductions, can you go over all that again? I've met so many new people today that all of their names are just one big jumble," I admitted.

The other man laughed before he said, "I'm Crow, this guy's brother."

"And who are these men again?"

"The one on the right is Wrath. He owns the Colorado Springs shop. The man on the left is his brother Fain, and he owns the shop in Rojo."

"And why are they arguing about where I'm going to live when I've already said I'm going to Texas?"

"They're not really arguing," Hawk said confidently. "They're just discussing things vigorously."

"What's the point? I'm not moving to Colorado, I'm moving to Rojo."

"Yeah, but that's not going to stop them from arguing about it. They might even come to blows," Crow said hopefully. "Who are you taking?"

"You want me to bet on two brothers throwing down over something they have no control over?"

"Absolutely," Hawk said cheerfully. "I think I'll take Fain. He's scrappier, probably from his time in prison."

"I think Wrath can take him. He's older and meaner."

"What are we betting on?" another man asked as he walked up beside Crow.

"If Wrath or Fain would win in a fight," Crow replied.

"That's a hard one. Who are you taking?" the man asked me.

"Oh, Nix, this is Tiny," Hawk said. "Tiny, this is my youngest brother, Phoenix."

I shook his hand before I said, "I've got no skin in this game, but I'm going with the older brother."

"Why?"

"He looks devious. The younger one is probably tougher, but I'd guess the older one is meaner."

"I think you should hit him," Hawk encouraged the men.

"Which one are you talking to?" When Hawk shrugged, I shook my head. He just laughed, so I said, "You guys are nuts. You know that, right?"

"It's a family thing."

"How are you related to them?" I asked, watching the two men who were walking away - still arguing over me even though they'd left me here.

"Fain is married to our aunt."

"Okay," I said as I nodded. "What about that table of doctors?"

"Not blood, but still family," Crow explained.

"And that table of women over there? None of them are related to you, are they?" I asked as I nodded toward a group of beautiful women, one of which had been watching me for at least ten minutes. "How do you know them?"

"Let's see. Starting with the one in purple and going clockwise, you have Bella Conner, Cydney Stoffer, her sister Gracy, our sister Wren, and then Diamond and Amethyst Hamilton."

"Diamond and Amethyst? Sisters?" I asked. The women looked close in age, and even though their skin tone looked more like mine than most of the people here, there was enough difference in their features that I wasn't sure if they were related.

"Yeah. Their other sister is named Emerald. She's the pregnant one at the table you were sitting at earlier."

"How do you guys know Dub?" I asked.

"We're friends with Elizabeth. We've known her for ages. As a matter of fact, she used to work at the bar our cousin runs," Hawk explained.

"She seems really nice."

"She's good people," Nix said with a smile. "We've missed her since she moved to Colorado, but we come up here a lot to visit family, so we'll see her often."

"How did you meet Dub?" Hawk asked.

"We belong to the same MC. I joined when I got out, but then became a Nomad when I moved to Vegas."

"Time Served MC? They're from Tenillo, right?"

Phoenix asked. When I nodded, he said, "I've met a few of them before and even more since we got here yesterday."

"Most of the men in our club are spread out all over the place, but we couldn't miss this."

"When are you coming to Rojo?" Hawk asked. "I guess you've got a job if you want one."

"I'm going to take it too," I said with a laugh. "Talk about luck. What are the odds that I'd meet a shop owner here when I figured I'd have to pound the pavement looking for a booth?"

"From the way they were arguing, it looks like you wouldn't have had to do that for long with your reputation," Crow pointed out.

"My work has been in a few magazines," I said vaguely.

"You were on that tattoo show, weren't you?" Phoenix asked. When I nodded, he said, "I knew I recognized you from somewhere."

"I did, too, but I thought you just looked like that player from the 49ers. Forest? DeForest? Something like that," Crow said thoughtfully. "I can't remember what his name is because that's not my team."

"I've heard that before too," I admitted.

"Tiny. That's a helluva name for a man your size," Phoenix said as he exaggeratedly leaned back so he could look at my face. "Not sure Rojo is big enough for you, man."

"I'll find a way to fit in. I always do."

And it was beyond perfect.

Who is in charge of our HR department? Do we even have one? When you find out, let me know. I'd like to file a formal complaint against Amethyst. It's absolutely none of her business what I'm packing downstairs.

Text from Terran to Spruce

AMY

"I need you to take this into the bathroom and fill it up to at least that bottom line, okay?"

My patient looked at me like I was nuts, but I smiled at him and then rested my hand on his shoulder to nudge him toward the door, hoping he'd take a minute or two so I could talk to his mom. Once the bathroom door closed, I stepped back into the exam room and smiled at the concerned woman.

"I'm going to look at the tests, but I have to say that I'm almost positive he has another UTI."

"Again?" When I nodded slowly, she whispered, "Shit."

"We need to address this because it's becoming an issue."

"I don't know what else to tell him! He's six, and neither of us feel comfortable with me . . . you know."

I shrugged a shoulder and said, "Circumcision is still an option. It doesn't just happen when they're infants."

"I need a man."

"I'm right there with you, and we can commiserate about that later, but right now, we should . . ."

The woman burst out laughing and said, "No. I need a man for him to talk to! I know he won't be comfortable talking to you about his penis."

"You're right. Let me go get one of the other doctors so he can have a man-to-man discussion about penis things."

"Would they be willing to do that?"

The exam room door opened and Jacob reappeared with an empty specimen cup. Before I could ask him why he didn't bring me a sample, he said, "I flushed the toilet before I tried to pee, and it was working fine, so I didn't have to go in the cup."

I cleared my throat so I didn't laugh and smiled at his mom before I said, "I'll go grab him a bottle of water and talk to one of my associates."

Jacob's mother had her lips pulled in between her teeth to hold back a grin as she nodded. Once I was out in the hallway, I looked at the digital board and found that my next patient had canceled. I might actually have time to eat lunch. However, Spruce and Terran were both with clients, so rather than interrupt them I went on the hunt for my cousin, Roscoe, the OB/GYN in our family clinic. I found him in his office studying something on his computer monitor, so I knocked on the door frame to get his attention.

"I have a bit of a strange question," I warned when he looked up.

"No, I have not forgiven you for telling my girlfriend I was born with a tail."

I burst out laughing and said, "That was years ago!" When he glared at me, I laughed even harder and said, "I'm surprised you even remember that!"

"I ran into her at the gym the other day, and the trauma of that time in my life resurfaced." I bit back a laugh, and Roscoe narrowed his eyes and glared at me before he said, "She told all her girlfriends who told *everyone* else, and that fall during the football season, all the guys kept pretending they weren't staring at my ass in the shower."

"Did I ever apologize for that?"

"No. You didn't."

"Can we get to my request yet?"

"You still haven't apologized."

"I'm aware of that."

"You're still not sorry at all, are you?"

"No. Now, my question?"

"What?" Roscoe asked grumpily as he lifted his bottle of water to take a drink.

"Are you circumcised?"

Roscoe started coughing and water came out his

nose. I snatched a few tissues out of the box on the corner of his desk and handed them over as I tried my hardest not to laugh.

"Why . . ." He blew his nose and coughed a few more times before he was able to choke out, "Why do you want to know that?"

"There's a six-year-old boy that I've treated for a UTI at least four times in the last year. He needs some instruction on how to clean himself and hopefully avoid more UTIs in the future."

"You're his doctor."

"And I'm a woman. I know the science behind it and the steps he needs to take, however, he's six and probably not too keen on having that discussion with a woman."

"Is there not a man . . ." Roscoe's voice trailed off and he pushed his chair back so he could stand up. "Not my business."

"From what I understand, his father isn't in his life, so she's sort of flying blind."

"Shit. I'll go talk to him."

"Are you qualified to talk to him?"

"I have a medical degree, too, you know."

"I know that, but I'm asking if you're circumcised. If you are, then maybe I should ask one of the other guys if they can do it."

"How do you know if Spruce and Terran are?"

Roscoe asked hesitantly.

"Ew. I *don't* know, so I'll have to ask them."

"Look, I'll go get started with the little guy. You find Terran and Spruce and ask them if they might be more qualified to do this."

"I guess that answers my question about your anatomy, but you're still a man, so you'll do in a pinch. Will you take him a bottle of water, please?" Roscoe laughed when I explained the urinalysis sample fiasco and assured me he'd explain that, too, so I said, "Thank you, Roscoe."

"Not a problem, Amy." I turned and walked into the hall with Roscoe just a few steps behind me. I motioned toward the exam room where my patient and his mother were waiting just as Roscoe said, "Are you ever going to apologize for that tail bullshit?"

"Maybe someday if I ever feel remorse for it," I said with a grin. "Love you, Dr. Hamilton!"

"I hate you, Dr. Hamilton," Roscoe growled as he walked away. As he reached for the door with his left hand, he flipped me off with his right and then scowled when I started giggling. As he pushed the door open, he mouthed, 'Fuck you!' and then shut it behind him.

Jewel Parker, a general practitioner who I had worked with since I got my license, came out of her office with an empty leftover container in her hand, most likely going to the breakroom to rinse her dish.

"What's got you so amused?" Jewel asked.

"Are your brothers circumcised?" I asked.

Jewel's expression didn't change, but she did blink a few times before she asked, "Why do you want to know that?"

I explained what was going on with my patient and then told her that Roscoe had suggested I find out if Spruce and Terran might be better qualified. When I told her that he was cranky about it and still pissed at me about the tail comment, she looked thoughtful for a minute before she said, "And you never apologized to me for turning my hair that horrible shade of orange."

"In my defense, that wasn't my idea." Jewel's blank expression was a little disconcerting, so I felt like I needed to explain, "The birdbrains dared me to do it, and your brothers are the ones who told me how."

"I have no idea if either of them are circumcised, so you'll have to ask them."

"Thanks, Jewel," I said pleasantly before I turned back to look at the board.

From the note updates, which were displayed in code so we could keep their information private, I could tell that Terran was just getting started with his patient but Spruce was almost finished and ready to dispense the patient's medication. Since we insisted our nurses take a full hour for lunch, it was our responsibility to take care of all the patients' needs while they were gone, which was something that we'd voted on in the hopes that our nurses felt they were treated fairly. It would also keep us humble, unlike many doctors we knew. I was sure that Spruce wouldn't have a problem quickly completing that task himself, so I leaned against the counter across the hall from the exam room where he was working and pulled out my phone to check my messages while I waited.

I wasn't sure how long I'd been standing there when I heard a man's shout and then a loud noise. Just as I put my hand on the door, I heard Spruce pleading with his patient to calm down, so when there was another thud, I threw the door open with the worry that he might be in danger.

I took in the scene and then stood there in shock when I saw the patient standing behind the chair that was usually in the corner of the room. That wasn't the most shocking part, though. He had one hand on the back of the chair as if he was trying to use it as a shield and the other trying to pull up his pants that were unbuckled and hanging down near his knees.

"I know it's out of your comfort zone, but I promise it's not going to hurt," Spruce said calmly. "It will take less than three seconds, and then we'll be finished."

"Nope. Can't let you do that," the big man said firmly as he shook his head, his eyes wide with fear. "I thought I could go through with it, but I can't."

"Tiny, I promise it's not . . ."

"I don't give a fuck," the man interrupted. "I'm just gonna have to die of high cholesterol."

"Do you want me to get the nurse who took your blood at your last appointment? You seemed to have a rapport with her and . . ."

"I managed to hold my shit together while she took all my blood, but I thought that was it. I didn't know you'd want me to do this shit on a regular basis."

"Tiny, come on. She just took a few vials. You know she didn't take all of it."

"Seemed like she did."

"This medication will help, and it's just one shot every six months."

"Nope!"

"Is there something I can do to help?" I asked quietly. I studied the man's face when he looked at me and realized that I knew him from somewhere. Suddenly, it struck me where I'd seen him before. "You're from Colorado."

The man visibly calmed as I smiled. He finally said, "I saw you at the wedding. You're Amethyst Hamilton."

"How do you know my name?" I asked as I walked farther into the room. When I was standing beside Spruce, I stopped and stuck my hand out. "It's only fair that I learn yours. What's your name?"

"Tiny."

I burst out laughing and said, "No, it's not."

The man glanced at Spruce and reluctantly let go of the chair so he could shake my hand. "I'm Tama'i Fuamatu."

"Tama'i? That's a beautiful name."

"Thank you."

I considered the man's features and size before I asked, "Is that Polynesian?"

"My family is from Samoa."

"I bet it's beautiful there?"

"It is."

"What brings you to Rojo?"

"I moved here to watch over my sister's kids while she's deployed."

"Really? When is she due back?"

"She'll be home in six months, but her husband should be back well before then."

"That's so sweet of you," I said sincerely. "What a great uncle."

He looked down at his feet and frowned. I could see by the color in his cheeks that he'd just remembered his pants were still halfway down his legs.

"Are you afraid of needles, Mr. Fuamatu?"

"Tiny."

I laughed softly and said, "I can't call you Tiny in good conscience."

"Why not?"

I ignored his question because if I answered it, I'd be the one blushing. At first, I'd noticed that the hem of his boxer briefs were straining around his muscular thighs, but then I let my gaze travel just a little higher. Now the only thing I could think about was that I was suddenly well aware that this man hung to the left and quite substantially so. As a doctor, I understood the biology of the penis and that its size really had nothing to do with the height of a man although it was affected by a man's weight. However, in Mr. Fuamatu's case, the size of his member was most definitely in proportion with his large frame, and his thighs weren't the only thickness being constrained by his black boxer briefs.

Considering that the man was under stress and not at all aroused, the fact that his penis hung down his leg was almost terrifying, not from a medical professional's standpoint, but from a woman's point of view.

Tiny was most definitely not a word I'd use to describe any part of the handsome man in front of me, even if he was a 'shower and not a grower' as my friends and I had joked. Most men would have to claim that they were a 'grower' to justify the size of their flaccid member, but Mr. Fuamatu didn't have to say any such thing. On behalf of the woman in his life, I hoped that he didn't grow *too* much because even as a medical professional, I couldn't figure out how exactly that might work.

Get it together, Amethyst! Here you are thinking about the size of the man's dick when he's mortified because he's half-dressed and terrified of needles. You're a doctor for goodness' sake! Act like one!

"Would you be more comfortable if I gave you the shot?" I asked.

Mr. Fuamatu looked confused when he countered my question with one of his own. "Why would that make a difference?"

"You never know. It might. Would you like to sit down and talk to me for a few minutes while you mull over your options?"

"I have a little time," he conceded.

"Well, you're in luck. So do I. However, I do need to speak to Dr. Parker in the hall for just a second, okay?" The man nodded, and I smiled at Spruce. "A moment, please?"

Spruce handed me the syringe he'd been holding and held the door open for me. Once he'd closed it, he said, "Thanks for the save, but he really needs this."

"I'll talk him into it, but first, I have a question."

"Ask away?"

"Are you circumcised?"

TAMA'I

The second the door shut, I yanked my pants up and buttoned them, scoping out the room to see where it might be possible to create a new exit since I didn't want to be here. At this point, my fear of needles was the least of my worries. It was the mortification of quite literally being caught with my pants down by a woman who was so fucking beautiful that she'd been dancing through my dreams since I saw her last month. The embarrassment made me want to bust through one of the walls and run out to my bike so I could leave town forever.

At this point, I was so fucking humiliated that I probably wouldn't even bother going home to pack my shit. I'd just hit the highway and ride until the wheels fell off, hopefully while I was going Mach Five so I wouldn't feel the impact. That was probably the only way to get over one of the most embarrassing moments in my life, and I'd had more than a few.

Honestly, anyone who'd been locked up could list at least twenty just from their first few days in prison. By the end of the first week, every prisoner seemed to lose the ability to get rattled. You had two choices - get over it or not, but either way, things were happening that you never thought you'd experience. That became perfectly clear the first time you had to take a shit on a toilet just a few feet from your cellmate who usually didn't even pretend he couldn't hear the havoc that the crappy prison food was wreaking on your intestines.

Right now, shitting in front of a crowd paled in comparison to looking like a pussy in front of a woman that hot.

"Get it together, man. What the fuck is wrong with you?" I muttered to myself as I paced in the small room.

I heard laughter in the hall and wondered if Spruce was really a man I could trust. I'd gotten that impression from him, and my friend Hawk insisted that he was a good man, but if he was out in the hallway laughing at me, I had my doubts. And since he was laughing, that meant the beautiful woman was laughing at me, too, which was not something I wanted to deal with anytime, but especially now, when my heart rate was just slowing down after my fight or flight kicked in at the sight of that needle in the doctor's hand.

"I don't know why you think that's so darn funny, Spruce," Amethyst said as she opened the door. She shut it firmly with a huff and then smiled at me before she said,

"Sorry about that. Just between you and me, Spruce can sometimes be a bit of a smash-hole."

"It only makes sense that he'd be laughing at me," I admitted grudgingly.

"Oh, he wasn't laughing at you. I asked him if he was circumcised, and one of the nurses overheard me as she was walking out of the breakroom and ended up bumping into the doorframe. He's always been the kind of guy who finds humor in the strangest places." I didn't know what to say to that, so I nodded, still processing why she might want to know about his dick. "Anyway, Mr. Fuamatu, let's talk about something else. How has your day been - well, up until Spruce tried to attack you with a sharp, pointy weapon?"

"Um. . . well . . ."

"Don't worry. I won't ask you personal questions like that."

"You can if you want to," I assured her, which made me want to drop my head in shame and make that second exit before I embarrassed myself even further. Hopefully, when I busted out of this joint like Lawrence Taylor going through the defensive line, I'd end up with a head injury and this entire day would be erased from my memory. "It's been a day, ma'am. That's all I can say."

"Tell me about it."

I scoffed before I said, "You don't really wanna hear about my shit; you just want me to quit being a pussy and get out of here so you can bring in the next patient."

"Your mind-reading skills need some work, Mr.

Fuamatu, because that's not at all what I'm thinking."

"Tiny."

"I sincerely doubt it." It was her turn to be mortified because she realized the implication of what she'd said and started sputtering. "I mean . . . I wasn't . . . I'm sure . . . Ugh. Great googly-moogly. I need to invent a surgical procedure to install filters on people like me."

I burst out laughing and assured her, "If you figure it out, I'll be your guinea pig."

"Don't make me a promise you won't keep, Mr. Fua . . . I just can't bring myself to call you Tiny. I have no idea why calling you by your nickname is so abhorrent to me considering that until my little brother was born, I had no idea my father's name wasn't Lout."

"That's his nickname?"

"I think it would be considered his road name, which is the biker version of a nickname, I guess."

"Your dad is a biker?"

"He is."

"Do you like motorcycles?"

"I do. Some of my favorite memories of my childhood are riding with my dad to get ice cream."

"So just short trips?"

The doctor laughed as she shook her head. She explained, "When my dad would ask one of us if we wanted to take a ride to get ice cream, he didn't mean he was going to take us to a local place. That meant he wanted to take a long ride, make a circle around the lake, and then stop for the treat in a little town about forty-five minutes away before we took the same winding route home."

"Must be some good ice cream."

"It's just a Dairy Queen, but that wasn't ever the point of the ride. We've got a Dairy Queen in Rojo, but it's more fun to take a ride with someone you love while you decide which kind of Blizzard you want."

"Butterfinger every time."

"How boring is that? You should mix it up, Mr. Fua . . . Darn it. Tell me your name again."

"Tiny." The doctor smiled as she rolled her eyes. "Call me Tama'i."

"Thank you, Tama'i. Anyway, life is all about experiencing new things. Speaking of which, why don't we work on some breathing exercises so that you can stay calm while I give you the injection you need."

"I'll take the shot on one condition."

"What's that?"

"You'll take a ride with me and then help me decide which Blizzard to get when we get to our destination."

"That's blackmail."

"It is," I agreed, hopeful that she wouldn't be offended and that I hadn't just given myself something else to lament about later.

"I'm not above that myself, actually."

"Well, what do you think?"

"In the interest of your health and the fact that I never say no to ice cream, I'll take a ride with you if you let me give you a shot." The doctor put her hand up and gave me a pointed look before she said, "But . . ."

"There's always a 'but,' isn't there?" I asked petulantly.

"I'm not going to get on a motorcycle with a man I just met. That's reckless for more than a few reasons, the main one being that I don't know you well enough to trust you with my life in more ways than one."

"I'm a safe rider, it's the assholes driving with their phone connected to their fucking noses that are the problem."

"I don't disagree with that, however, you're still a stranger and riding off into the great beyond with someone who may or may not be a serial killer goes against everything my parents taught me."

"I didn't go to prison for murder," I assured her, not sure why I felt the need to explain myself. Suddenly, I realized I might have just shown more of my hand than this burgeoning friendship could handle, so I said, "I guess the cat's out of the bag."

"That you've been to prison? Was that supposed to be a secret? Motorcycle clubs aren't a foreign concept to me. I know that the only way you can become a member of the Time Served MC is to have actually served time." When I nodded, she said, "The fact that you were convicted of a crime does give me pause, but that's only because I don't know what you went in for."

I shot my shot again, this time in the hopes that she might give in. "I guess that will give us something to talk about on our first date."

"Which will be in a well-lit and populated place."

I smiled because I took her stipulation as confirmation that my luck was changing for the better. "It doesn't bother you that I'm an ex-con?"

"That depends on the crime. What really bothers me is the fact that you got caught."

I burst out laughing and asked, "*That* is what bothers you most?"

"You'll come to understand why if you ever meet my family."

"That's an option?"

"Let's get through our first few dates before we start planning for that encounter," Amethyst said hesitantly. "My family is *a lot*."

"A lot of what?"

"Practical jokers. Overprotective uncles and cousins. A father and younger brothers with no filter who have made it their mission in life to harass every man my sisters and I have ever dated until they're a shell of their former self, and a mom who is not afraid to stand on a chair and go nose to nose with anyone who deserves to be put in their place."

"Sounds like a fun challenge."

"But you have to fulfill your end of the deal in order for us to take that first step and exchange phone numbers." I tensed, and Amethyst rested her hand on my arm. "Just focus on what I'm saying, not what I'm doing."

"Okay." That was harder to do than she could imagine, considering that I felt warmth spreading up my arm from where she was still touching me. "I'll try."

"Good job, big guy. Now . . . drop your pants."

I have to say that self-care is important to me. If your feet look like you could use your toenails to scale a tree or start a brushfire by rubbing your heels together, there's not a chance in hell I'll be interested in touching any part of you. Ever.

Text from Amethyst to Tama'i

TAMA'I

"What does your schedule look like today?" Pearl, the artist who had a station next to mine, asked over the buzz of the tattoo gun in her hand.

"I've only got consultations today, and I have to go pick up Tameka from school since the boys will be in practice."

"I love that girl. Are you bringing her back to the shop or taking the evening off?"

I leaned back in the chair as I rubbed my irritated eyes. I'd been looking down at the lit drafting table for at least an hour now, and I could feel a headache coming on. Finally, I answered, "I have a consultation at four, so I'll bring her back with me."

"If you don't have any plans this evening, would you like to do some touch-ups and maybe a tattoo?"

"Yes to the touch-ups, but what size tattoo are we talking about?"

"I don't know. It's my mom, so there's no telling what she wants."

"She doesn't know?" I asked, not thrilled at the prospect of tattooing someone who hadn't already made what I considered a life-altering decision. Some people didn't consider that a tattoo was forever, and since I'd started tattooing, I'd made it my policy to remind them of that, especially when they wanted something stupid that wouldn't stay vibrant or was some sort of passing fancy. "If she has no idea what she wants, then why is she getting it now?"

"She has a blank space," Pearl told me with a shrug as she sat up straight and wiped the tattoo she was working on. She studied it for a second and then dipped her needle into a color well before she bent back over her client's leg. As the machine buzzed, she explained, "She's been considering a new one for a while, but when I told her that you started working here, she got serious about it."

"What does she need touched up?" I asked.

"Some of her older ones need a refresh, and she scraped her arm pretty badly working in the garden with Gamma, so she wants that fixed now that it's been healed for a while."

"What's your mom like?" I asked, trying to imagine my own mother covered in tattoos. As far as I knew, she didn't have a single one, which was saying something since she was career military. On the other hand, my father had more than a dozen - one for each country he'd been stationed in during his own career in the Navy. "I take it she doesn't disapprove of your chosen profession."

Pearl laughed, and it reminded me of my sister, who I already missed. It wasn't that I didn't love my sister, but we hadn't lived in the same town in years. My guess was that I probably only missed her because she'd left me with her three teenagers, two of which I'd already had problems with even though she'd only been gone for a few weeks. I knew that they were great kids who were just trying to test their new boundaries, but if they didn't cut their shit out, I'd have to not so gently remind them who the matai of our little tribe happened to be, just like Tutu had when she was raising me and my sister.

"My mom is not your average middle-aged . . ." She stopped talking and gasped before looking around the shop as if someone was about to jump out and attack. She hissed, "Do *not* mention that I used those words."

Pearl's client laughed along with me when the other artist who worked with us popped his head out of the breakroom and said, "I heard that!"

"Mom is unique and awesome in every way you can imagine," Pearl said, ignoring Stone's laughter as he walked to his station.

"You don't have to suck up, Pearl. She's not here."

"I'm not sucking up. Tell me I'm wrong."

"I couldn't describe her better myself," Stone agreed as he opened a cabinet and started sorting through ink bottles. As he pulled out the ones he wanted, he said, "She's a hoot, Tiny. You'll love her."

"You will, but let me warn you right now that she's gonna love you," Pearl drawled as she looked up and smiled at me. "Just remember, she's married to my father, so whatever she happens to say when she's surfing the tattoo endorphins doesn't really count, okay?"

"I'll keep that in mind," I promised. "Your parents are friends, right?"

"They are. Our moms are really close, and our dads grew up together," Stone explained.

"Your brother-in-law knows them," Pearl added.

"Oh, really?"

"Yeah. When they were in high school, Bart dated my sister Di, so he's met our entire family. So has your nephew Aleki since he's in the same class as my youngest brother, Onyx. He is probably friends with my sister-in-law Mercy, too, even though she's a year or two older than him."

"Small town connections, I guess."

"The population makes it sound like a big town, but it seems like everyone knows everyone. Was your hometown like that?"

"It's on an island, so it's definitely got that small-town feel."

"When did you move to the States?" Stone asked.

"We moved from Samoa to Hawaii when I was really young but then transferred to California when I was in middle school. The summer before I started my senior year of high school, we moved to Florida."

"That had to suck," Pearl commented.

"The same thing happened to my sister right before her senior year. That was when we moved to California. That's why she asked me to come stay with the kids instead of dragging them away from their friends."

"How long is she going to be gone?"

"She'll be gone for another six months and then home for good. My brother-in-law is retiring and will be back sooner than that, though."

"And then what will you do?" Pearl asked curiously. "Will you leave or stick around and work here?"

"My Tutu is here so . . ."

"Tutu?"

"That's our word for grandmother," I explained. "Since my parents are still on active duty, they can be transferred at any time, so Rojo is going to be our new home base, even though it's nowhere near the coast."

"Your parents are in the Navy, but your sister is in the Marines?"

"Yeah. She and I were rebels and joined the Marines instead of following in our parents' footsteps and joining the Navy."

"How long were you in the Marines?" Stone asked.

"I did four years and then got out. I should have listened to my mom when she insisted that military life was not for me."

"I couldn't do it," Pearl admitted. "I don't take well

to people telling me what to do."

"Pfft," Stone said. "That's an understatement."

"Make sure you don't ever end up in prison then because for people like us, that's a living hell."

I walked up the steps to the school and wondered how the office staff would react to my appearance today. They'd been informed that I was the guardian for my sister's kids when she got all the paperwork in order, but seeing that in print was much different than meeting me in person. I was aware that I could be . . . Okay, I was almost always an intimidating guy, considering my size and apparent inability to control my facial expressions. Knowing that didn't make it any easier when people stared at me or cowered in fear.

In certain instances, I was perfectly fine with people thinking I was more menacing than I really was, but I tried very hard to avoid those times since I got out of prison. I hadn't been completely successful, but at least I'd never gone back. I counted that as a win.

However, parenting teenagers, even if it was for a short time and I had Tutu's help navigating the choppy waters of hormones, emotions, and rebellion, might very well put me behind bars again. Not that I'd ever harm a child or intentionally hurt anyone in my family, but if things kept going the way they had been for the last week, I might commit a crime just so they'd send me away.

I'd thought about it, and prison seemed to be the only reasonable excuse I could use to make my escape. Considering I'd already lived that hell on earth for nine years, one month, three weeks, and one day, it was definitely telling that I was thinking about prison as a long-term solution.

If my eleven-year-old niece, Tameka, had another screeching fit and slammed her bedroom door one more time, I was probably going to lose my shit and go knock off a convenience store for chump change and a second felony. Same with Kai and his attitude. The urge to knock that boy down a peg or two had been almost overwhelming. Lo and behold, he'd apparently encountered a teacher who felt the same way I did.

I walked through the front doors of the high school and passed a few groups of twittering young women before I finally found an adult and asked them how to find the office. The second I walked through the glass doors, I heard Kai yelling. My day was even shittier than I thought, and my nephew's was getting worse by the second.

Without even thinking about it, I walked around the desk, past the middle-aged woman who was looking at me in complete shock, into an office where I found my nephew with three women.

"What in the fuck is wrong with you that you'll speak to an adult so disrespectfully, Kai? I better not *ever* hear you take that tone with a woman again," I roared as I walked into the room. I slammed my hand down on his shoulder and forced him to sit in the nearest chair. Kai looked up at me in shock, and I leaned down so we were almost nose to nose before I growled, "Have you lost every bit of fucking sense, *boy?*" Kai didn't respond, and I noticed that he didn't even squirm beneath my hold, so I gripped his shoulder even tighter as I looked up at the women and asked, "What's going on here?

"I don't appreciate your language, Mr. . . . Who are you?" The woman who asked that question looked like she'd just sucked on a lemon as she slid to the side and reached for the phone on her desk, probably to call the law to fulfill my fantasy of late.

"I'm Tama'i Fuamatu, this little asshole's uncle. I'm his guardian while his parents are away."

"Mr. Fu . . . Fua . . . um . . ."

"Fuamatu," I said slowly. "Again, what's going on?"

"This is bullshit," Kai said from his seat as he squirmed under my grasp. "I'll tell you . . ."

"Shut your fucking mouth until I give you permission to speak," I barked. I looked up at the women and asked again, "What happened?"

The one who I guessed may be Kai's teacher didn't look nearly as intimidated as the one I assumed was the principal and was more than happy to spill the story. "We had a pop quiz today, and I caught Kai using his phone to look up the answers. When I asked him for the phone, he refused to give it to me, so I ordered him to go to the office. He wouldn't leave his seat and called me a racial slur before he threw his test paper at me."

"Did you do that?" When it looked like Kai was going to argue, I said, "One of two words will be acceptable in this case: yes or no. Did you do that?"

"Yeah."

"You were cheating?"

"Yeah," he said petulantly.

"Give me your phone."

"What? But I . . ."

"If I have to take it from you, it's gonna hurt really fucking bad," I warned. Kai held his phone up, and I let go of his shoulder to take it. I held it with both hands and snapped it in half, ignoring his cry of outrage and their expressions of shock and then handed the pieces back to him before I looked at his teacher and said, "Problem solved. No more using his phone to cheat on tests. Now, what do you suggest I do to get rid of his attitude because I've got a few ideas, and every one of them is right along those same lines."

"For every drop of paint you get on the floor, you owe me a lap around the track," I warned before I turned my stool around and looked at my niece. "Take your homework into the breakroom and get started but feel free to come get me if you need help, okay?" Tameka glanced at her brother and then back at me before she swallowed hard and nodded. "You can grab a drink and a snack out of my bin in the fridge but don't mess with anyone else's stuff."

"Yes, sir," Tameka said before she slung her backpack over her shoulder and walked toward the back of the shop.

I watched her go and saw Kai look over his shoulder at her, so I barked, "Focus, Kai. That wall ain't gonna paint itself."

"I didn't realize that hiring you meant I got free child

labor," Fain said as he sat down on my table. He smiled at me and said, "I see parenthood agrees with you."

When I scowled at him, he laughed. Pearl walked by and asked, "Did my dad publish a parenting book and not tell me?"

"That is definitely a punishment Lout would use," Fain said as he watched Kai dip the Q-tip I'd given him into the bowl of paint and then dab it against the cinder block wall in front of him. "Is he gonna do that whole wall or . . ."

"Every fucking inch," I interrupted. "He'll be here with me for the rest of the week."

"Damn," Pearl whispered. "That boy done fucked up."

"If he thinks my punishment is bad, just wait until I tell his mama what I fucking heard today."

"That bad, huh?" Fain asked. When I nodded, he put his hands together as if in prayer and looked up at the ceiling. As the bell over the front door sounded, he said, "Thank you God for letting me get through parenthood with my sanity intact and giving me the opportunity to have grandchildren who act just like their fucking parents so they can understand the hell they put me through."

I heard a man say, "Preach it, brother."

"Hallelujah!" a woman cheered. "That's every parent's prayer."

I turned my head and found a couple walking across the lobby, both of them heavily tattooed and very obviously Pearl's parents. The man had skin almost the same color as mine with a shaved head and a permanent scowl that was also a lot like my own. The woman, however, was white with a shocking swath of dark purple hair that swooped up as if she'd been in a windstorm, barely contained by the black bandana she had tied around her head. She was covered in tattoos ,and I admired the work as she walked closer while also admiring her athletic body and outgoing personality.

"Oh my goodness! What do we have here?" the woman asked as she tried to walk closer to me.

The man holding her hand frowned as he kept her from walking any closer and said, "Down, girl. I'm right fucking here."

"Hi. What's your name?"

"Tiny."

"I sincerely doubt it," she retorted. When the man next to her growled, she turned and smiled at him. "You're still the handsomest man I've ever seen, and I love you the most, Cocoa."

"Blech," I heard Pearl snort. "Mom, leave poor Tiny alone. He's probably defenseless against your powers."

"Aren't we all?" Stone asked cheerfully. "Hi, Aunt Willow. Lout."

I stood up from my stool and watched Pearl's mother's eyes widen and her father's frown intensify. I stuck my hand out toward the man first and introduced myself, and after he shook my hand, I nodded at his wife before I smiled and said, "Are you ready for some ink?"

"Yes, please," she answered before she let her husband's hand go and walked across the room to look at my nephew's progress. He looked at her over his shoulder when she asked, "Wow! How bad did you screw up?"

When he didn't answer, I said, "That's my nephew, Kai. He's not allowed to talk for a while because he's practicing the skill of keeping his fucking mouth shut."

Out of the blue, Willow asked, "How old are you, Tiny? Are you married? Dating someone? Single?"

"I'm thirty-six, and yes, I'm single."

The woman's beautiful face transformed into something almost ethereal before she said, "That's perfect!"

"Let the games begin," Lout muttered as he walked past me toward Pearl. As he pulled her into his arms for a hug, I heard him say, "Call your sisters and give them a heads-up that your mom is plotting."

"Where's the fun in that?" Pearl asked as she smiled up at her dad. "I'm going home. Please keep her in line."

"Where's the fun in that?" Lout mimicked as he let his daughter go. In his normal voice, he said, "As if I could anyway."

I decided to let them have their drama . . . or amusement. I wasn't sure exactly what to call it. They acted as if this sweet woman was rabid or something, but I could tell she was a fun person to be around, which I needed in my life. Well, at least in small doses.

After just a few minutes of discussion and then a few more minutes of sketching, I had what Willow proclaimed was the perfect flower to add to a small gap in her sleeve and then looked away as she stripped down. When she was standing in front of me in the same clothes I'd seen other women wear at the gym - a tight cropped tank and matching shorts, I looked over her other tattoos and explained what I could do to touch up the coloring and clean up the outlines that had faded over time.

After a little discussion, we decided to start by touching up the color on the bows on the backs of her thighs, so Willow got comfortable on my table while I chose the ink I would use for the color and shading. Lout sat down in Pearl's tattoo chair and leaned it back before he propped his feet on her stool and closed his eyes for a nap. I appreciated the fact that he wasn't hovering over me, considering his gorgeous wife was my canvas this evening.

I had been working for a few minutes when Willow asked, "I know you said you're single and new to town, but have you met anyone you're interested in yet?"

I knew that keeping my clients talking helped take their mind off the pain I was inflicting, so I made sure to converse with them as much as possible if they started up a conversation. Since she seemed like a personable lady and was interested, I answered honestly.

"Actually, I met a woman today and got her number."

"Oh, really?" Willow asked but didn't seem nearly as excited as she had been before. I chalked it up to the tender area I was tattooing but then it dawned on me that she was disappointed because she had a woman in mind. "Three of my daughters are single and close to your age."

I avoided her obvious attempt at a set-up and asked,

"How many daughters do you have?"

"Five."

"Holy shit," I mumbled. "Pearl mentioned that she has brothers too. How many are there?"

"I have four sons."

"I have to say that you do not look like you've given birth to nine children."

"Thank you! Technically, my three oldest daughters are my bonus kids, so I only had six pregnancies."

"Well, you look fantastic," I told her. I heard a deep grumble and looked up to find Willow's husband glaring at me. I shrugged and asked, "What? Do you want me to lie?"

Willow burst out laughing at the same time Stone yelled, "Holy shit!" Lout's gaze never wavered, but it went from a scowl to a grin. I took that as a win, considering I'd spoken without thinking and really didn't want to throw down with my co-worker's father and one of the club brothers of the shop owner.

Through her laughter, Willow said, "I don't know your type, but I've got three single daughters. Surely, one of them would be perfect for you."

"I don't know about all that, but don't call me Shirley."

Willow started laughing again while Stone and Lout chuckled and snickered. I was glad I'd broken the tension my compliment had caused. I gave in and confided, "Actually, I did ask a woman out this morning, but she partially shot me down."

"Partially? Is that a thing?"

"She said she wanted to exchange phone numbers and talk before she agreed to meet me in a well-lit and crowded place just in case I'm a serial killer."

"Good call on her part," Lout said cheerfully. "Sounds like a smart girl."

"I would say so. She's a doctor."

Willow had been laying on her stomach but pushed up so that she was resting on her arms as she craned her neck to look at me. "A doctor?"

"Yes, ma'am. I had an appointment this morning, and she . . . Well, I'm afraid of needles." When laughter broke out again, I interrupted, "I know, I know, it's stupid because I'm covered in tattoos and I work with needles everyday. I'm not saying it makes sense, but it's true. Anyway, she talked me off the ledge, and I let her give me a shot in exchange for her phone number."

Lout scoffed and Stone rolled his eyes, but Willow just smiled. "So, what do you think about this doctor you met?"

"Other than the fact that she's obviously very smart, she's beautiful and funny. She's got absolutely no filter, which is refreshing now but might make things uncomfortable at some point, and she's cautious about who she dates, which is something I appreciate."

"Have you called her yet?" Willow asked.

"Honestly, I'm rethinking the whole thing," I blurted. What the fuck was wrong with me? Yes, I talked to and engaged with my clients, but I didn't usually pour my heart out to them. It was usually the other way around. Most people couldn't stand silence for any length of time, so they filled it with mundane chatter that usually ended up telling me more about them and their personality than they realized.

"Why?"

And just like before, I suddenly started baring my heart to this woman I'd just met. "Because she's a white-collar professional, and obviously, I'm not."

"So what?" Willow asked.

"Doctors are snooty country club members, and I'm . . . Well, the first time I saw her was at a biker wedding in the mountains."

"Oh, at Dub and Elizabeth's wedding."

"Yes." After a few seconds, I admitted, "There seemed to be something there, but maybe she's just that kind of person."

"What kind of person?" Willow's husband asked.

"Electric. That's the only way I can describe it. Maybe she's the kind of person who is good at connecting with people, and the spark I felt was just her being friendly. It just felt like something else to me."

"Hmm," Willow said as she turned back around and started typing on her phone. "So, you're not going to call her?"

"I don't know. Maybe if it's not too late when we get out of here, I'll call."

"You really want to take her on a date?"

"Yes. I'd love to see her again, but this time, I want to be on more even ground. There's a spark there, at least on my part, and I guess if it's meant to be, it's meant to be."

"Remember earlier when Pearl said this was a small town?" Stone asked.

"Yeah. Why?"

"It just got smaller."

THREE

It's not that I don't like people, it's just that they do things that irritate me. Like breathing. And talking. The way some people blink pisses me off. Sometimes, I think it's better for everyone involved if I just stay home alone.

Text from Tama'i to Amethyst

AMETHYST

"Do you remember that big biker we saw at Elizabeth's wedding? The one that was so hot, it was hard to look at him too long without feeling like you were about to combust."

My sister, Diamond, laughed. "There were more than a few men like that at the wedding, but then again, that clean-cut guy Bella was talking to was also pretty hot."

"You're going to have to be more specific," Opal said as she used the palm of her hand to push my head to the angle she wanted. "Which big hot biker are we talking about here?"

"The man makes Dad and his friends look regular-sized. Are you this rough with your clients or just me?"

"The frowning islander guy with the tribal tattoos?" Diamond asked.

"Yeah. That guy."

"I remember him," Opal said dreamily, ignoring my question. "He was a big bowl of deliciousness covered in a liberal serving of bad boy. Just my type."

"What about him?" Diamond asked as she lifted her hand up to blow on her wet fingernails. "What do you think of this color?"

"I like it," I assured her. "Will you do my toes while she finishes my hair?"

"Sure," Diamond said before she used the spray can of quick-dry that was on the table in front of her. "Give me a minute."

"Back to Mr. Hot Colorado," Opal redirected. "Have you been thinking about him? You should call Elizabeth and ask for his info."

"He was at the office for an appointment this morning and asked me for my number."

"Here in Rojo?"

"No, dummy, Mars," I retorted and then winced when Opal pulled a little too hard on the section of hair she was parting. "How many braids do you have left to do?"

"A dozen or so," she replied. She pushed my head again and said, "It would help if you'd be still. Jeez."

"He came in to see Spruce, but I helped with his treatment and . . ."

"What did he come in for?" Diamond asked.

"You know I can't tell you that."

"It was worth a shot," Diamond retorted. "Put 'em up."

I shook off my flip-flops and adjusted myself in my chair so I could get my feet onto the table and winced again when Opal pulled my hair to adjust the angle of my head to her satisfaction.

As Di removed my old polish, I said, "He asked me out, but I told him we should exchange numbers and get to know each other first."

"Good call. He might be new in town, but at least you can call Elizabeth and get the scoop on him just to make sure he's a nice guy."

"He belongs to the same club as Elizabeth's new husband," I replied.

"They're all ex-cons, right?" Opal asked.

"Yeah. That's sort of a requirement since it's in the name of the club."

"Time Served does say it all, doesn't it?" Diamond asked. "Does Dad know him?"

"I'm not sure. I haven't asked because you know how he gets."

"He's really mellowed out over the years," Opal said cheerfully.

"It's taken a lot of hard work to get him to this point," Diamond told her. "You're welcome."

"What the hell should I be thanking you for?" Opal

asked.

"We've gradually broken him down, and he's a lot more passive now when we tell him we're dating someone new," I informed her. "Emerald kick-started his training, and me and Di have continued it. So, you're welcome."

"That's probably true. Now that I think about it, the last guy I went out with didn't even get threatened with death. I mean, he did mention beating him half to death but never once said anything about burying him somewhere."

"He's come so far," Diamond said proudly.

"He has, but then again, it's not like Mom's easy on the girls the boys date," Opal said, referring to our younger brothers.

Our sister Emerald was a little more than ten years older than me, but Diamond was just a year younger than I was, while Opal was three years younger than her. Our sister Pearl was born two years later, and after her birth, Mom and Dad had a boy every other year until our youngest brother Onyx was born when I was fourteen.

Emerald, Diamond, and myself were sisters who our parents adopted soon after they got together. Our adoptive father was technically our biological uncle, but I'd grown up calling him Dad since he took me in when I was just two. From what little we knew about our biological mother, information I'd heard from the few times Emerald and our parents had mentioned her, Diamond and I understood just how lucky we were to be considered our uncle's children.

Our parents had never shown any favoritism for their biological children, which was unfortunately something I'd seen happen more than a few times in my practice as a pediatrician. I hated to witness it, but luckily, that wasn't the norm. Because of my experience as an adopted child, I'd made a decision at a very young age to continue that cycle and adopt. I wanted to have at least two children naturally just so I could experience pregnancy and childbirth, but then I planned to adopt siblings and give them the same loving family my parents had provided for me and my sisters.

"Are you going to go out with him?" Diamond asked.

"Hold on. You're talking about the big guy who looks like an angry Polynesian god, right?"

"Yeah."

"He's friends with Hawk. I heard him telling Brighten that they took classes together or something."

"Hawk went to college in prison, so that means this guy did too. I wonder what he does for a living."

"I don't care about his profession as long as he's got a job," I said honestly. "And doesn't live with his parents."

"Also a no-go for me unless there are extenuating circumstances," Opal agreed.

"Should I put on another coat?" Diamond asked as she looked at my toes. "What do you think?"

Just as my text notification sounded I said, "I love it, but yes, they need another coat."

I leaned to the side to pull my phone out of my back pocket, and Opal took that as an invitation to commit a violent assault on my person that threw me back into my childhood memories of my mom who was a take-no-prisoners kind of braider. Obviously, she'd been training Opal.

"If you pop me with that clucking comb one more ducking time, I'm going to do things to you that . . ."

"You are like a walking version of auto-correct, Amethyst, and I don't know a single person that *likes* auto-correct," Diamond chided. "Just say 'fuck' like a normal person."

"If she doesn't start letting it out, she's going to explode someday," Opal agreed.

"The only way I'll explode is when I jump into action to beat you like a dirty rug because *you keep hitting me with the comb!*" I yelled. Opal didn't care at all and snorted as she used the point of the comb to part another section of my hair. As I opened my texts, I asked, "Do you treat all of your clients like this?"

"I know, right?" Diamond asked.

"Not the ones who pay me," Opal answered. When we didn't respond, she sniffed and said, "That's what I thought."

"Mom's getting a new tattoo," I told my sisters after I read my text. "She asked if we'd come down and keep her company when we're finished here."

"I'm starving, so tell her we've got to pick up some food first. See what she wants, and get Pearl's order too."

"Pearl had a thing with Worth this evening, so she's not there," Opal informed us as she finished the second coat.

"Then it's probably Stone doing it for her. You know Uncle Fain doesn't like to work in the evenings anymore," I reminded the girls. "I'll ask Onyx to pick it up and bring it to us. He owes me big time."

"What did he do now?" Opal asked.

"I can't talk about it," I said without thinking as I typed out the reply text to my mom. I realized that Opal's hands weren't moving anymore and Diamond was frozen, too, when a drop of clear topcoat dropped onto my foot. "What?"

"He's sick, and you're not telling Mom?" Opal asked.

"Oh, God. Did he get an STD? He did, didn't he? After all of Dad's preaching about 'no glove, no love,' the boy got an STD."

"He did not . . . as far as I know. It's something else."

"If it's not medical, then what is it?"

"I can't talk about it."

"I will snatch you bald," Opal threatened.

At the same time, Diamond said, "Tell us or I'll tell Mom you're hiding something, and then we'll both sit back and enjoy the show." I reached up and made the motion to zip my lip and throw away the key. Diamond gasped. "Oh my god! Did he get a girl pregnant? Oh no. Oh no no no no."

"Why are you always gloom and doom?" I asked my sister. "Cheese and rice, Di. You always jump to the worst possible scenario."

"That way, when it's not as bad as I first thought, it's actually good even if it's bad. Do you know what I mean?" Diamond asked.

"No," Opal and I said in unison.

As she cleaned the drop of clear polish off my foot, she said, "It's not pregnancy or an STD, and his grades are good. I know that."

As Diamond pondered all the worst case scenarios, Opal asked, "You're never going to share what's going on, are you?"

"You know I'm a vault."

"You are. That's come in handy for us more times than I can count."

"And I'll do the same thing for Onyx."

"Is that really necessary?" I asked Diamond when she waved at a passing motorist. "They're going to think they know you or something."

"I know," Diamond said with a grin as she waved at the next car. "Right now, every person I've waved at since we left the salon is wondering how they know me and kicking themselves because they didn't honk and . . . Oh! I got one to wave back. Now *she* is wondering who the hell I am!"

"How much food can Stone really eat?" I asked as I lifted my shoulder to keep my purse strap up since my arms were overflowing with bags of takeout containers.

"We should have had Onyx deliver it straight to the shop," Diamond whined. "Get the door, Opal."

"Let me just grow a third arm real quick, and I'll . . . Well, hello!" Opal said when a very tall and handsome teenage boy opened the door and held it for us. She walked through and called out her thanks. I was smiling at him about to do the same when Opal yelled, "Soup's on! Come and get it!"

"What do we have here?" Diamond asked as she stopped in front of me.

I wasn't paying attention and bumped into her back which made my purse fall to my elbow. "Move your badonkadonk, hoe."

"Watch out!" my mom called out. "That was *almost* a curse word."

"It depends on the context. Technically, a hoe is an inanimate gardening tool that . . ." My voice trailed off as I stepped around my sister and saw who was bent over my mom's prone form with a tattoo gun in hand. "Hi." The man met my eyes with shock, and he looked from me to my mom and then back. "I brought dinner."

"I carried a watermelon," Diamond mumbled in a falsetto voice behind me. She yelped when I intentionally stepped back and stood on her toes. "Get off me, fatass. You better not have messed up my polish."

"Or what?" I snapped without thinking.

"Ladies," Dad called out in that menacing tone he used to try and curtail a fistfight. It didn't always work, but this time Diamond didn't respond, so he probably considered that a win.

"Hi, Dad," Opal said as she breezed past him toward the breakroom. "Come get your grub on."

"My, my, my. You are a big one, aren't you?" Diamond said as she smiled at Tama'i. "I'm Diamond."

"It's a pleasure to meet you."

"Oh my God, that voice!" Diamond whispered over her shoulder before she followed my dad toward the breakroom. "Let's do this. I've got places to go and people to see."

"Since when do you go places or talk to people on purpose?" my mom yelled at her retreating back.

"The newest episode of that firefighter show she's in love with dropped today," I tattled.

"That makes more sense. Tiny, can we . . ."

Tama'i swiped the paper towel over her fresh ink one last time as he interrupted, "Let's take a break."

"Can I . . ."

Tama'i interrupted the young man and said, "Did I hear something come out of your mouth? At this point, if it happens again, the next thing that comes out will be your teeth."

I felt my jaw drop in shock as I looked from Tama'i

to the young man, but before I could say anything, a young woman appeared and said, "Help me sort out our food, Kai."

The young man didn't utter another peep. Instead, he walked past Tama'i into the breakroom.

As Tama'i helped my mom get up from the table, she said, "Don't get all worked up, Amy. He's got his reasons, and he's doing things his way."

"Do you often threaten children with bodily harm?" I asked, ignoring my mother.

"Only when they get suspended from school for bullying their teachers and running their mouth like they're the baddest man in the room," Tama'i said angrily. He huffed out a breath and said, "Although, I will admit that the teeth comment might have been over the top."

"Just a bit," I agreed as my mom walked away. "There might be other alternatives to that like . . ."

"He's a head taller than everyone at that school, teachers included. He needs to learn that there might not always be someone bigger, but there will always be someone meaner. That person is going to be his mother when she finds out the shit he's been doing."

"That bad, huh?"

"Unacceptable," Tama'i said firmly. "Fa'aaloalo is one of our culture's most valued traits, and I won't have him dismiss that."

"What is that?" I asked.

"Young people should respect their elders because

they hold knowledge that we haven't yet learned."

"I like that," I admitted.

"Is the soy sauce in your bag? They better not have forgotten it because there's no telling how old the stuff in the refrigerator here is," Diamond said as she walked toward me. She took the bags from my hands before she smiled and said, "I'll take those. You two get to know each other. Planned pregnancies are much easier to handle, although I do love a good surprise."

"Go away, sea cow."

"You're adopted, and your parents don't love you," Diamond hissed.

"If your face was on fire, that would be an improvement," I snapped back as I glared at her. When I looked back at Tama'i, I said, "We brought dinner."

"I see that," Tama'i said as he watched Diamond walk away and then looked at me. "Do you think she's going to do something horrible to our food?"

"Why would she do that?"

"I mean, you obviously aren't fond of each other."

"What makes you say that?" Tama'i just stared at me blankly, and I felt like I should explain, "Diamond's not just my sister, she's one of my best friends."

Tama'i blinked a few times and then asked, "How do the two of you talk to people you *don't* like?"

"We smile a lot while we consider the three hundred

and eleven ways we can make them disappear."

People who don't put their grocery cart in the bay after they unload it should be drawn and quartered. It might sound harsh to some people, but I'm a firm believer that actions should have consequences.

Text from Amethyst to Tama'i

TAMA'I

"Oh! Is that chicken curry? Gimme, gimme," Opal demanded as she extended her arm across the table and used her chopsticks to take a piece of my chicken. She popped it into her mouth and then moaned, "Oh, that is delish. You've gotta try that."

I wasn't sure which sister she was talking to, but Diamond took her advice and dropped a piece of her food on my plate and picked up a bite of mine as she said, "Here, I've got General Tso's. Have some."

"That looks yummy," Amethyst said before she took a bite from her sister's plate. She leaned over and got a bite off her father's, and I heard him sigh as he stared at her. Amethyst didn't seem to care one bit and picked a dumpling up from her plate and put it on her father's before she stole another bite. "Dad's got Kung Pao beef."

"I need some of that," Opal said before she took some herself. "Here, Dad, have some noodles."

The urge to pull my plate closer to my body and hunch over it to protect my food was almost overwhelming, but I was able to resist.

"Have a shrimp roll, Tama'i. They're so good!" Amethyst dropped one on my plate and then paused to look at me before she gave me another. "Why aren't you eating? Do you not like what you ordered? I'll trade."

"Why are you staring at us like that?" Opal asked.

Before I had a chance to answer, Lout said, "Because he's wondering why in the hell you think he should bother trading his plate of food with you since you're eating off it anyway. Not every meal is a goddamn buffet, ladies."

Willow cleared her throat and looked down at her plate, which I noticed she had picked up and was holding close to her chest as she relaxed against the back of her chair, probably to keep her food far enough away from the table to protect it from the scavengers.

"Here, Dad, have another dumpling," Amethyst insisted as she dropped one on his plate. As if he hadn't just snapped at them about sharing food, he picked it up and took a bite. "Aren't they good?"

"They are," Lout agreed before he picked up the other dumpling she'd given him and ate it too.

Amethyst smiled at my niece and asked, "Did you get enough to eat, Tameka?"

"Yes, thank you."

"Kai? What about you?" Amethyst asked. "Tameka, I've got more dumplings. Would you like to try one?"

Tameka looked at me and then back at Amethyst before she shrugged. When she looked back at me, she asked in Samoan, "Can I do that, Uncle? Wouldn't it be rude?"

"It's rude to speak in another language in front of people who don't speak it," I chided. I smiled at Amethyst and translated, "She asked if it would be rude to take your food because in Samoan culture it's rude to have seconds once you finish the food on your plate."

"You can't take seconds?" Diamond asked.

"Really?" Opal asked. "What if it's really good and you're still hungry?"

"We don't follow the rules all the time when we're at home, but my mom likes us to honor them when we're in public."

"Mom's not here," Kai snapped.

I swung my head around and looked at him before I said, "I'd be happy about that if I were you."

Kai narrowed his eyes and started to say something but thought better of it when I raised my eyebrows in question. He huffed out a breath as he stared at me intensely, and I heard one of the women laugh softly before another said, "It's like watching someone glare at themself in the mirror."

Kai was the first to look away, and I turned back to my niece and said, "If you're still hungry, take the dumpling she offered."

"You're still hungry?" Opal asked. She picked up her plate and scraped a portion of her food onto Tameka's and said, "Here, have some of mine."

"This is so good," Diamond told her as she gave her a few spoonfuls of her food.

Before long, Amethyst was sharing hers and even took a bite of beef off her father's plate to share. The women realized Kai had finished his food, too, and without asking, started piling more onto his plate. I saw him looking at my chicken curry and sighed before I gave him half of what was left.

When I looked up, Willow was smiling at me and winked before she reached over and put her hand on her husband's arm. He was staring at me, too, but didn't look nearly as aggressive as he had before. Instead, it seemed like he was taking my measure - hopefully, not as a threat since I knew he was Amethyst's father. I'd do my best not to bump heads with him in the future. I wasn't a fortune teller, but I had lived enough life to realize that sometimes dreams were the only way to keep hope alive. I sincerely hoped Amethyst was as open and honest as she seemed to be because if that was the case, I'd like to get to know her much better. If she was as wonderful as she seemed with all of her brains and beauty, then she was the kind of woman I'd always dreamed about.

It seemed like Lout could read my thoughts, which was also something I didn't quite believe in, but the look on his face was taking steps to change my mind. He seemed to be studying my interaction with Kai and Tameka, and from his relaxed demeanor, I thought he might like what he was seeing. I saw his eyes move from me to Amethyst, and I glanced over to find her watching me. She smiled brightly, and I smiled back before I looked at her father.

That murderous look was back in his eyes, and as I

watched, it was like shutters slamming closed over his emotions before he smiled at me. Considering what Amethyst had told me earlier about smiling at people she didn't like, watching her father give me that very expression was more than a little bit terrifying.

Someone knocked at the front door, and I stood to answer it, leaving my plate for the scavengers. I knew it had to be my other nephew, Aleki, since he was supposed to pick up Tameka and Kai, but was surprised to see two other young men with him.

"'Sup, Uncle?" Aleki asked as he walked through the door. "Are they ready?"

"Are my parents still here?" one of the young men asked. He sniffed the air and said, "Are they eating?"

"I smell curry," the other young man said before he walked away, heading straight for *my* dinner.

"Uncle, this is my friend Jett," Aleki said as he motioned toward his friend. "Jett, this is Tiny."

"It's nice to meet you," the young man said. "The rude guy who's more interested in food is my brother, Flint."

"Oh! I've heard of you. Your parents and sisters are in the breakroom."

"All of them?" Jett asked warily.

"Um . . . How many do you have again?"

"When they're all talking at once, it seems like there are at least a dozen, but technically, I have five."

"Pearl is gone, but there are still three of them here."

A woman's laughter rang out, and then it was joined by a few others. The young man recognized their voices and said, "Di, Amy, and Opal?" I nodded, and he said, "And they've got food? Hell, yeah."

As Jett walked toward the breakroom, Aleki asked, "What did he do now?" I released a frustrated sigh before I explained to my nephew about today's drama with his brother and watched his eyes narrow in anger before he said, "That little shit wouldn't be acting like this if Mom or Dad were here."

"I think he's pissed that they're gone, and I'm paying for that."

"He better not get an attitude with Tutu," Aleki warned.

"She can hold her own, believe me," I assured him. My grandmother was a veteran at child-rearing since she'd raised her own children and then helped my parents raise me and my sister. Now she was living in Rojo and helping me care for my niece and nephews, but considering her age, I was more than willing to take the brunt of the responsibilities. "However, if your brother turns his poison on her, I'll put him in line."

"Once he wakes up after I kick his ass, you're more than welcome to," Aleki threatened. "But I guess that's for another day. Right now, I'm starving. What's for dinner?"

AMETHYST

"The step stool is underneath the front passenger seat," Tama'i called out to his nephew as they walked through the front door. "Make sure she eats something before she goes to bed or she's going to be hungover in the morning."

"Yes, sir," Aleki responded before the door shut behind him.

"Does your girlfriend drink too much often, or is this a special occasion?" Diamond asked nosily.

"Do you drink too much?" Tama'i asked me with a grin as he looked at me over my mom's back where he was touching up a tattoo just below where her workout tank ended, ignoring my sisters not so subtle fishing.

"I'm not your girlfriend yet," I said haughtily. "I still have to make sure you're not a serial killer."

"You said 'yet' which is a step in the right direction," Tama'i teased before he explained, "My Tutu . . ."

"That's what they call his grandma," Mom interrupted to explain.

"Yeah. Tonight she went to play bunco with some ladies from her seniors group, and they get a little wild sometimes."

"I know they do. My Gamma and her best friend play bunco, but we don't call them seniors."

Apparently, listening to us bicker was having a horrible effect on Tama'i. He winked at me before he said,

"Your sister had a meltdown earlier when she said your mom was middle-aged, so I guess the whole family has a problem with getting older."

"She said *what?*" Mom asked menacingly.

I grinned when Stone put his hand over his mouth to stop himself from laughing. I slid my stool closer to the table and leaned in so we were almost nose to nose before I whispered, "Did you just throw my sister under the bus?"

When Mom shifted so she could start typing on her phone, he leaned even closer and whispered, "No. I just flung her into oncoming traffic in the middle of rush hour."

"That was mean!" I couldn't stop the evil giggle that escaped, which just made Tama'i smile even harder. I put my fist out to bump his and then remembered he was wearing gloves and wouldn't be able to touch me. He stuck his elbow out so I could bump it instead. "You're horrible, Tama'i."

"It's part of my charm, but it seems like that's going to come in handy as a self-preservation technique when I'm around your family."

"I love it," I whispered. I schooled my features and cleared my throat before I said, "Wow, Mom, I can't believe Pearl would say such a thing about you."

I glanced up at Diamond who was standing behind Tama'i and saw her grinning. She pretended she was holding a mug with one hand as she mimed stirring it with the other as she added, "That's better than the time Pearl referred to you as elderly, right? Do you remember that, Opal?"

"I do. As a matter of fact, I think Emerald is the one

that encouraged her to say it," Opal added.

"I distinctly remember that," I added. "Ungrateful children, I swear. It's a good thing you have us."

"Are you wearing boots, Tiny?" Mom asked.

"Yes, ma'am. Why do you ask?"

"Because the shit's getting deep in here. They act as if I haven't watched them do this little dance their entire lives. I have vivid memories of Di and Amy banding together to pick on people from a very young age. Granted, it was mostly the boys in the family who probably deserved it." My dad didn't open his eyes but started laughing from where he was reclining in the chair across the room. "As the other girls came along, Di and Amy enlisted them into their army, but the infighting was what really kept us on our toes."

"For a few years, we wondered if any of them would make it to adulthood," Dad added. "They tried their best to kill each other every second of every day, but when an outsider crossed one of them, it was like watching the hounds of hell attack."

I shrugged and told Tama'i, "They're my sisters, so I'm the only one allowed to pick on them."

"Ditto," Opal and Diamond said at the same time.

Diamond pinched Opal's arm as she chanted, "Pinch, poke, you owe me a coke."

"Ouch! Are you trying to break my fucking arm?" Opal yelled before she reached out to pinch Diamond back. Diamond slapped her hand away, and that turned into a slapping fight that would soon end up with one or both of them throwing punches.

Mom saw the inevitable just like I did and used the tone that every person under the age of thirty recognized as law and barked, "Enough!"

I stifled a laugh when I saw Tama'i press his lips together and sit up a little straighter as he glanced around the room. Dad must have seen it, too, because he burst out laughing and said, "Down, girl. You're scaring the big guy."

"Oh, honey, that wasn't aimed at you," Mom said sweetly before she gave him a big smile. "You've got wonderful manners, and I'm sure you know how to behave in public."

"Burn," I whispered and got a glare from my sisters.

"And now that they're adults and we don't have to pay their medical bills, we *usually* just let them run free," Dad said as he settled back in to continue his nap. "Vanilla, you know if you don't let them take out their frustrations on each other, they'll draw in some poor unsuspecting victim, and we'll end up having to post bail."

"I can't go to jail because I could lose my medical license."

"That's why it's important not to get caught," my dad reminded me.

Tama'i burst out laughing and said, "You were right. I get it now." When Dad lifted his head and stared at Tama'i with his eyebrows raised, he said, "She told me that it was going to be a while before she let me meet her family but warned me about all of you anyway."

"I think we should take the warning labels off of everything to help weed out the weaklings," Dad said for at least the millionth time. "Natural selection."

"Your dad is a god among men."

"You don't have to suck up," I whispered.

"I've never sucked up to anyone in my life, and I'm not about to start now," Tama'i warned. In a louder voice, in answer to my father, he said, "If someone looks at a table saw and thinks, 'That sharp thing seems to be going really fast. Maybe I should touch the spinny part,' then we should let them try it."

"I bought one of those sun shields for the front window of Vanilla's new ride, and the first time I opened it, I happened to notice the tag on the thing. You know what it said?"

"I'll bite. What?" Tama'i asked.

"Do not use while driving." We all started laughing, and Dad just shook his head in wonder. "The damn thing is a quarter of an inch thick and made out of reflective material with the express purpose of keeping out the sun, so what sort of dipshit is going to try and drive with it in their window?"

"Somebody had to have done that or that warning label wouldn't exist," Mom mused.

"It was probably one of our cousins," Opal said with a sad shake of her head. "They're pretty but not all that smart."

"Hawk is your cousin, right?" Tama'i asked.

"Yes. He's one of my sister's kids. Growing up, they were what some people might consider feral, and that hasn't really changed much with age."

"Mom and Dad didn't have to worry about us because we were angels," Diamond boasted.

"I distinctly remember Amethyst blacking Squid's eye at one point, and that wasn't even the worst damage they did to each other."

"She knocked out my tooth!" I yelled.

"Squid?" Tama'i asked.

"Her name is Cydney. She's my best friend now, but we went through a short adjustment period when we were younger," I explained.

"They fought each other like honey badgers going for the last piece of meat on the planet," Mom explained.

"Honey badger don't give a shit!" Dad said happily.

"Have you ever seen that video?" Mom asked Tama'i.

When he shook his head, Mom picked up her phone to search for it as I said, "They're freakin' awesome. The girls and I have always joked that they're our spirit animal."

"Do you have a honey badger tattoo?" Tama'i asked.

"Nooo," Mom drew the word out and then grinned at Tama'i.

"You said you wanted a flower in that empty space,

but it might just be the perfect home for a honey badger," Tama'i suggested.

Diamond gasped. "Mom! That's the perfect tattoo for us!"

"It is!" Opal agreed. "What do you think, Amy?"

"I want it," I said firmly. "Can you draw one up and then do them for us?"

"I can do that."

"It needs to be cute but deadly," Mom insisted.

"Just like my girls," Dad boasted. "Hell yeah."

"Dad, you need one too," I suggested. "Not a cute one, though. The dad honey badger."

"Let's do it," Dad agreed.

"Not today!" I said when I saw Tama'i glance at the clock on the wall. "Draw it, and let us tweak it, and then we'll come in when you've got time."

"Okay. That sounds like a plan," Tama'i agreed. "I do have one question, though."

"What's that?" I asked.

"Have you spent enough time with me to decide whether or not I'm a serial killer?"

"If you are, then you hide it very well."

"I'm not trying to put you on the spot or anything but

. . ."

"Really?" I asked as I looked around at my sisters and parents who were watching us expectantly.

"Can I take you out on a date, Amethyst?"

"I suppose," I teased. "But it still needs to be in a well-lit and well populated area."

"I'll make sure of it."

FIVE

How many times do I have to remind you ladies to keep my name out of your mouth? I just got a text from Mom, and I want you to remember that pregnancy hormones have been successfully used as a defense in a criminal trial.

Group text from Emerald to her sisters

AMETHYST

"It's becoming a day," I said as I walked past the nurses' station toward the bathroom.

"Technically, it's been daytime since the sun rose this morning, so you'll have to be more . . ."

"Terran, I've had to pee for the last hour, and if I have to stop and argue with you, I'm going to pee on your shoe."

"What makes you think I'll stand still when you start to pull down those horrific scrubs you insist are something a medical professional should wear?"

"Wait right there while I go to the bathroom. I might have time to choke you with your tie before they bring my next patient back," I threatened.

"Nope. You've got a patient in Exam Four," Matilda Duke, one of our newest RNs, said as she breezed past me on her way to the supply room.

I glanced at the monitor and said, "Where's the info?"

Matilda shook her head and said, "There isn't any."

"I kind of need to know what I'm walking into here," I said testily.

Matilda pulled her lips between her teeth before she said, "Trust me on this, Amy. I'm pretty sure this is going to become Roscoe's appointment, but they did ask for you. Either way, I'm gathering what I think you may need right now."

"We have protocols for a reason," Terran said grumpily.

At the same time, I said, "Who is it? What's going on?"

"Go pee before you have an accident," Terran ordered.

Usually, I wouldn't appreciate being told what to do and would shoot back a sarcastic retort, but since I had abandoned my path toward the bathroom to go toward the exam room, I realized Terran was right. I needed to take care of myself, which wasn't something I always did very well, so I could focus on my patient.

By the time I came back out to the desk, True Stoffer, my best friend's little sister and one of our nurses here at the clinic, had a stack of papers for me to sign - mostly referrals and a few prescriptions that couldn't be called in to the pharmacy.

I walked into the exam room and was shocked to find

my brother there with a young woman I didn't recognize. He looked terrified, and she was crying as she clutched at his hand so tightly that his nails had gone completely white. Suddenly, my heart dropped when I remembered that Matilda had told me this was going to become Roscoe's case, which meant this young woman was going to need an OB/GYN.

"Oh, great googly moogly, Lazlo," I muttered as I shut the door behind me and then leaned against it as I let my head fall forward with a sigh. I stared at the floor, bracing myself for the answer, as I asked, "Honey, when was your last period?"

"No! It's nothing like that!" Lazlo said urgently.

I looked up suddenly and asked the girl, "You're not pregnant?"

"Oh no! I could be!" the girl cried before she sobbed loudly. "Oh my God. What have we done?"

I heard my brother gulp, and then he got so pale that I was afraid he might pass out, so I used my foot to push the rolling stool his way. "Sit down before you fall down."

Lazlo sat down with a loud thump, never letting go of the girl's hand, which he probably couldn't anyway because she had such a tight grip.

"Before I ask too many questions, I need to know how old you are," I informed the young woman, who, now that I was a little calmer and able to focus, I could see wasn't quite as young as I'd originally thought.

"Jesus, Amy! What sort of man do you think I am?"

"I'm a pediatrician, numbnuts. I have to assume that if she's here to see me, she's under eighteen, which would become an entirely different conversation, considering you're twenty-two."

"I'm twenty-three, Amy."

"Excuse the French toast out of me, little brother," I said sarcastically.

"I'm twenty-seven," the woman said proudly. With an airy giggle, she said, "I'm a cougar, huh?"

"Rawr," I said before I thought better of it. "Okay, that means I don't have to call your parents, but that doesn't explain why you're here. Tell me what's going on."

"I lost it," Lazlo mumbled.

"Lost what?"

"The condom."

I pinched the bridge of my nose as I tried my hardest to maintain a professional demeanor. I was having a difficult time considering this was my younger brother, and I'd rather walk barefoot through Walmart than imagine him having sex. However, I knew this situation was probably going to become comedy gold . . . someday.

"Did it fall off or . . ."

"It broke and part of it . . . Well, it ripped I guess, and all that was left was the top part . . . The ring, you know?"

I cleared my throat before I got myself together and asked, "The top part that you roll down to the base of your penis?"

"Yeah, that part," the woman confirmed. "That was all that was left. I saw it on there right before he started freaking out."

"And you can't find the rest of it?"

"No."

"Did you try?"

"Yeah. So did Lazlo." My brother's head dropped in embarrassment. Suddenly, the girl wailed, "What if it's way up there? What if it's in my intestines?"

I blinked a few times and wondered if this woman knew *anything* about her reproductive organs, but then the realization hit me that there was a distinct possibility she wasn't talking about her vagina in the first place.

"Oh, sweet baby Harambe on a moped," I muttered to myself before I asked them, "Were you having anal sex?"

"No!" she replied with a horrified look on her face. "Why would you think that?"

"Okay. Alright," I said as my heart started beating again. I put my hand up to calm her down before I explained, "Your intestines are in no way connected to your vagina, so that's not going to be an issue. However, if there is a foreign object inside your body . . ."

"It's not a foreign object," she argued. "It's just a condom."

I stared at my brother so hard that I was sure he could

feel it. I knew he could when he closed his eyes tightly and said, "Just say it, Amy. I know you're thinking it."

"Look at me, Lazlo," I said menacingly. When he finally opened his eyes, I looked deep into them in the hopes that I'd suddenly develop telepathy since I obviously couldn't lose my shit in front of this strange and very, very ditzy woman. "Do you *really* know what I'm thinking right now?"

"That I will owe you until the day that I die," Lazlo said painfully. "Just fix it, Amy. Believe me, this morning has been an eye-opening experience, and I have seen the error of my ways."

"Are you on birth control?" I asked before I suddenly realized I didn't even know this woman's name. "Hold on. Before we get into all the specifics and stuff, let me introduce myself. I'm Amethyst, this guy's sister."

"But you're black!" the woman exclaimed in confusion.

"I am? Are you sure?" I asked sarcastically. I looked at my brother and asked, "Does Dad know?"

I almost lost it when the woman nodded but managed to hold it together as I looked from the woman to my brother. I raised my eyebrows at Lazlo, and he winced.

Finally, he looked at the woman and said, "Now is not the time to discuss my melanin or lack thereof. Yes, Barbie, Amethyst is my sister."

"Barbie?" I sputtered.

"How does that work?" she asked.

"How does what work?"

"Your skin is very dark, and his isn't."

"Our mom didn't leave him in the oven long enough for him to become beautiful melanin perfection like the rest of us," I answered sarcastically.

"Your mom put you in the oven?" she asked in shock. Finally, she scoffed and giggled, "Of course she didn't put you in the oven. She must have meant you were premature."

"Speaking of premature, please, for the love of all that is good in this world, tell me that you realized the condom was ripped before you finished." Lazlo nodded, and I let out a relieved sigh before I asked her, "Birth control?"

She smiled brightly before she said, "I totally forgot I have an IUD."

For a second, I thought I heard angels singing, but then I realized it was just someone laughing out in the hallway.

"Can you just get it out?" Lazlo asked. "Please, Amy."

"Can't do it. That's Roscoe's area of expertise."

"Amy, come on! Don't bring Roscoe in here."

I smiled at the woman and said, "Roscoe is another doctor in our practice, and he just happens to be our cousin. Don't let his skin tone shock you."

"Amy, please," Lazlo begged.

"As a pediatrician, I haven't been trained in condom search and recovery, so I'll have to leave that to the professional."

"I asked to see you so that no one else would find out."

"I know you did, but it's not shameful that the condom ripped, Lazlo."

"That's not what I'm ashamed of," he said through gritted teeth.

"At least you've got that going for you, little brother."

As I pushed away from the door and started to turn and reach for the handle, I said, "I think *Uncle Terran* should come in for a consult too."

"Why do I need two doctors?" Barbie asked.

"Oh, no, honey. Terran's a neurologist, and I think that when he hears about this case, he's going to want to do a scan of Lazlo's head and see if there's anything in there."

"Do you think the condom went up into his penis?" Barbie whispered in horror.

"Not that head, honey. The other one."

"You have gotten so big since the last time I saw you!" I exclaimed when I saw Ethan, a tow-headed little boy who had an adorable dimple in each cheek when he smiled at me. I looked at his mom and said, "I guess I don't need to ask you about his appetite!"

"It amazes me how much that boy can eat," his mom said in exasperation.

"Prepare to be amazed for the next twenty years or so then because my parents are still in shock about how much my brothers can pack away, and they're almost all adults now."

As I did the well-check on the toddler, I asked his mom about milestones that he'd met so far and others he might still be working on and was surprised when she kept interrupting me with details concerning the various bruises and scrapes on his legs.

"And I think he got that one when he tripped on the way out to the car, but I'm not sure. To be honest, I'm not sure about a few of them, but I just want you to know that no one gave him those bruises. He's really an . . ."

"Active little boy who is going to crawl up on any and everything and then jump off of anything that is still long enough for him to fly," I interrupted. I handed the little boy a tongue depressor and started a game of swords to get him comfortable with the object before I let him take mine away so he had one in each hand. I quickly pulled another one from my pocket and unwrapped it so I could look into his mouth while his hands were full and he was entertained. What I saw was concerning, so I asked, "When he eats, does he ever have any problems?"

"Oh my gosh, yes! I have to cut his food into pieces so small that it's almost mush. Otherwise, he gobbles it down so fast that he chokes."

"Has that been happening for very long?"

"A month or so. It started right after his last growth spurt. I just figured that he was trying to pile on the calories so he could outgrow the clothes and shoes I just bought."

"That's probably part of it, but I think there's more to it than that."

"You do?" his mother asked in alarm. "What's wrong with him?"

"I think his tonsils missed the memo that said they could take a break occasionally. They're way too large for his body."

"What does that mean?"

I kept one hand on the toddler's knee to keep him still as I leaned to the side and pulled the rolling tray closer so I could use my free hand to work the mouse. I quickly scrolled through his patient file and then frowned, wondering if I'd missed something when he was here six weeks ago for an ear infection - the latest in a string of infections that he'd been having since he was an infant.

"What's wrong? Why are you frowning?"

I knew better than to admit I might be at fault, so I said, "In looking at his chart, it seems like he's been having ear infections since he was about seven months old."

"Yes. Almost monthly!"

"I think his tonsils might have something to do with that."

"Okay, so how do we fix them?"

I turned back so that I was facing the little boy who was picking up on his mother's anxiety and starting to fidget. I booped him on the nose with my pointer finger and then poked his fat little belly. Finally, he smiled at me, and when I did it again, he giggled.

I looked at his mom and said, "He needs to have his tonsils removed sooner rather than later."

"Okay. Can you give me a referral? My insurance requires one and . . ."

"By sooner, I mean today."

"What?"

"His airway is too narrow for me to safely let this go any longer. I'll make some phone calls and see which one of my associates has time for the procedure."

"He needs emergency surgery?" she asked as tears filled her eyes.

Her son sensed her distress and started to tear up, too, so I booped his nose again and got him to smile as I said, "Emergency is a big, scary word. In this case, I'd rather just say that for his health and safety, I'd feel better if you let me get this taken care of today. While you get him dressed, I'll make some calls and get everything in order for you."

"Oh my goodness! Did I do something wrong?" She gasped and then said, "All those times I told him to chew his food better so he wouldn't choke, it was really his tonsils? I'm horrible!"

"No, no, no," I said as I reached into my pocket and pulled out a handful of lollipops. I held them out and gave him his choice as I said, "If you had a medical degree and looked into his throat and *then* said he just needed to chew better you'd be horrible. But we're both doing just fine because neither of us did that." I held my hand out toward her, and without thinking, she picked up a sucker and pulled off the wrapper. I dropped the leftovers into my pocket and then opened his before I gave it back to him. "While I'm working out the details, I need you to call someone that will be able to sit with you during the procedure. They're probably going to want to keep him overnight, so you'll need to plan for that, too, just in case."

"Okay," the woman said before she sniffed and put her lollipop in her mouth.

"You know what? It's been a rough few minutes for both of you, and I've had quite the morning myself," I said as I pulled the lollipops out of my pocket again. I opened one and put it in my mouth before I extended my hand toward the mom. "I think this is definitely a two-sucker day, don't you?"

What's the difference between the bird flu and the swine flu?

One requires tweetment, and the other requires an oinkment.

Text from Tama'i to Amethyst

TAMA'I

I looked up from the paper I was holding and studied the young woman in front of me before I asked, "If you like tigers, then why don't you just get a portrait of one instead of writing the word out like this?"

"Oh! That would be cool if you could put a little tiger with his name!"

"With whose name?"

"My boyfriend. His nickname is Tiger."

"Hmm," I said as I looked back down at the paper. "How long have y'all been together?"

"It will be three months tomorrow!"

I heard Pearl clear her throat and saw she was biting her bottom lip as she slowly shook her head.

"How old are you again?" I looked back down at her

information sheet and read the details as I said her name, "Tiffany. You're barely eighteen."

"I know."

"Tattoos are forever. You know that, right?"

"Yeah."

"It's your body and ultimately your decision, but I'd be an asshole if I didn't point out that it might be a little soon in the relationship to start inking each other's names on your skin."

"But I love him."

"And I love mangos and papayas, but I don't have them tattooed on my body," I pointed out.

"As if you don't have anyone else's name on you," the young woman scoffed. She looked over at Pearl and saw the scrolling font on her bicep and said, "She's got a name tattooed on her!"

"I do. It's my grandmother's name, and do you know why I have her name on me?" The girl narrowed her eyes, and I smiled before I said, "Because I'm absolutely positive, without a doubt, completely sure that she'll *always* be part of my life."

"My tattoo is my daughter's name," Pearl said cheerfully. "Also a relationship I will have until my dying day."

"Now, I know you're pissed because you don't like for people to tell you what you can and can't do, and you've got your heart set on getting ink today. I get it. I really do.

And, even better, I *really* want to give you a tattoo today. However, I'd rather give you one that you can be proud of in six months, six years, or sixteen years from now. I do not want to give you a tattoo that you might regret."

"Does he have *your* name tattooed somewhere visible on his body?" Pearl asked.

"No."

"Okay then. My suggestion is that you and . . . Tiger?" The girl nodded, so I continued, "Make an appointment with me today to come into the shop and celebrate your five-year anniversary. When you come in together, I will ink your names on each other free of charge."

"You will?"

"Absolutely." I stuck my hand out, and she took it. As we shook on the deal, I asked, "Is there something else you might like to get a tattoo of this afternoon?"

"Can you do something on my toe?"

"Your toe?"

"Yes. I want a toe ring."

"That is definitely something I can get behind, Tiffany."

It didn't take long at all to give her a tattoo she could enjoy for years to come. She'd be much happier with that than she'd be if she looked back in six months and wondered what the fuck she was thinking when she got a guy's name inked on her body. Once she was gone, I started cleaning my station for my upcoming appointment and found Pearl watching me.

"What's up?"

"That was very noble of you, Tiny."

"I don't know about noble, but it made sense."

"That too," Pearl agreed. "What would you have done if she had insisted you tattoo his name on her wrist like she wanted?"

"I would have told her to find a different artist and sent her on her way. What would you have done?"

"The same thing."

"If she finds me in five years, I'll honor her and Tiger's wishes and ink the fuck out of 'em, but until they've got some miles under their belt together, I'm not touching anything like that."

"A lot of artists out there would have just done it and taken her money."

"That's why you've got me here and not some random artist you found on Craigslist."

"Obviously, we got lucky when we found you," Pearl said cheerfully. "Bonus points because you're not a total asshole."

"Well, thank you, Pearl. I think you're a sweetheart too."

"I didn't go that far," Pearl said with a grimace. "By the second day your nephew was here painting the wall with a Q-tip, I knew your soul might be a little darker than I'd first thought."

"You can tell by the look on his face that he's not exactly a beam of sunshine," Stone said as he looked up from the drawing he was working on and smiled at me. "No offense, Tiny, but you give resting bitch face a whole new meaning."

"It keeps the smart people away."

"What about the dumb ones?" Stone asked.

"There's something about me that makes them flock to me in droves. Before I know it, they're talking about sunbeams."

Opal burst out laughing, and Stone grinned. "Okay, you got me on that one."

"You and my sister are gonna make a great couple," Opal said as she leaned a little closer and smiled. "How's that going?"

"I prefer to keep my private life separate from my professional one, which will be very difficult considering she's basically related to everyone I've met since I moved here."

"We're not blood relations," Stone pointed out.

"But you're family all the same." When Stone nodded, I said, "My new boss has known her since she was born, Pearl is her sister, I've got an appointment with each of her siblings and her parents to give them matching tattoos . . ."

"Oh, I love that idea. I can't wait!" Pearl interrupted. She glanced over at Stone and said, "Onyx is pissed because he has to wait a year to get his."

"Technically, your parents can sign off on that."

"Texas law says the only legal way to tattoo a minor, even with their guardian's consent, is if you're covering up an existing offensive or drug-related tattoo."

"True, but . . ."

"You can do it if he really can't wait, but I can't risk it. I've got years left on my parole, and I'm not going down for a misdemeanor."

"You say that like there are things you'd do even if it risked your parole," Opal said without looking up from her sketchbook.

"Of course there are. I'd repeat the exact scene that got me sent to prison if I needed to without a moment's hesitation." I could tell by the look on their faces that they were dying for me to elaborate about the crime that got me incarcerated, and since it was easy to find with a simple Google search, I didn't consider it a secret, so I said, "I beat a man half to death. My sentence was twenty years for attempted manslaughter, but I got out after nine and have to serve the rest of my sentence on parole."

"Did he deserve it?" Opal asked.

It didn't give me any satisfaction to admit, "He earned every single scar I gave him."

"Well, none of us would dare risk being the reason you have to go back, so my baby brother can wait until he's eighteen to get his tattoo."

"I like that idea," I agreed.

"You're really not going to tell me how things are going with my sister, are you?" Opal asked.

"I'm about to meet her for lunch. When I get back, you can text her and get the scoop."

"I was already planning on it."

The next hour was spent gathering up what I'd need for my afternoon appointments and taking care of some final details after my move. By the time I left the shop to meet Amethyst, I was more than ready for a dose of sunshine and glad she'd chosen a place with outdoor seating.

I spotted her the second I pulled into the parking lot. She was sitting at a picnic table twirling one of her braids around a finger as she scrolled through her phone. She frowned at the screen just as I made my way to her.

"When you said well-lit and populated, you weren't kidding," I joked. When she looked up at me, I asked, "I'm not late, am I?"

Amethyst's smile was almost blinding when she said, "You're not!"

"I was raised in a military household where ten minutes early is considered late."

"Tardiness is one of my pet peeves," Amethyst admitted as she started to stand.

I put my hand out to stop her and said, "If you'll give

me your order, I'll get our food while you save our table."

"That's sweet," Amethyst said as she sat back down.

Once she'd given me her order, I got in line. I was pleasantly surprised that it didn't take long for them to make our food even though I'd ordered my usual amount, which sometimes posed a problem at food trucks. I carried the trays back to the table and then sat across from her as she stared at everything I'd brought with wide eyes.

"Is someone joining us?" she asked.

"I'm hungry."

"Is that a basket full of hamburger patties?" When I nodded, she asked, "Do you have a gluten sensitivity?" Before I could answer, she exclaimed, "No, because you've got some . . . oh! You got the diablo shrimp taco!"

"I got three of them just in case you want a bite or two."

"I'm glad you don't mind sharing."

I laughed uncomfortably before I said, "When we were eating with your family the other night, I don't think I had much choice."

"It doesn't bother you, though, does it?"

"It's not my favorite thing," I admitted.

"We really only do that when we're eating takeout so we can all have some of everything," Amethyst assured me.

"We do the same sort of thing in my culture, but we

don't eat off of other people's plates. If you're having dinner at someone's house, you take a bit of everything offered so you don't offend the host."

"That's not really the same thing at all," Amethyst argued. "

"I'm just not used to it."

"I'll leave your food alone."

"I don't think I'll mind sharing with you."

"But not the rest of my family."

"I'm quickly coming to realize that it's going to take some time for me to adjust to the way your family is involved in each other's lives"

"If this lunch goes well," Amethyst insisted with a sly grin.

"Exactly. We're still in the trial phase. I get it."

"Well, you're a quick learner seeing as how you bought me a taco. I can resist most types of bribery, but tacos . . ." Amethyst hummed in pleasure before she said, "Tacos are a currency all their own."

We took the food from the trays, and I tried not to be embarrassed when she ended up with one basket and I had four, but a few minutes later, I was glad I'd ordered plenty because she'd forgotten her proclamation that she wouldn't take food off of my plate. I couldn't help but smile as I watched her savor a hamburger patty that was covered in melted pepper jack cheese. I didn't think she'd need one, so I had only brought one fork, but that didn't stop her.

Watching her lick her fingers was enough to make me think I might always forget utensils just to see that show again and again.

"You know, this isn't bad at all. I prefer my burgers with a bun, some condiments, a few veggies, and enough grilled jalapenos to set my soul on fire, but this is simple and delicious."

"Generally, I don't eat this kind of protein, but that's all they had."

"What do you usually eat?" Amethyst asked before she started to take another bite of the patty. Before it touched her lips, she said, "Please say steak. Please say steak."

"I want it thick-cut, medium rare, with lots of garlic butter and a good sear."

"You're singing my song," Amethyst said with a groan. Once she'd finished off her patty, she said, "Can I tell you something that not many people know?"

"What's that?"

"I always order more steak than I can eat so I have leftovers for the next morning."

"That's reasonable.

"And then I stand in front of the open refrigerator and devour it cold, ripping it apart with my teeth like a caveman."

I imagined her doing that and nodded. "I've never considered that, but now I have to try it."

"If your cholesterol is high, you should probably eat

less fatty meat and increase your soluble fiber intake."

"I only eat like this after specific workouts."

"How often do you work out?" The way she was looking at my arms made me wonder if she was about to take a bite out of *me,* and the thought made me smile.

"Six days a week, but I only do intense workouts three of those days."

"Do you run?"

"Twice a week."

"I'm training for a mud run with a few of my sisters and some of my cousins."

"That's good."

"No, it's not. I'm a firm believer that the only time running should be necessary is when the ice cream truck is getting away or I'm being chased by an axe-wielding psycho."

I burst out laughing before I asked, "Then why are you training for a marathon?"

"Because Pearl said I was a lard ass who couldn't keep up."

"She said that?"

"Those weren't her exact words, but that's what she meant," Amethyst hedged.

"My sister and I were never really competitive with

each other, but neither of us are willing to back down from a challenge either."

"Have you talked to her about the problems your nephew is having in school?"

"He's an asshole at home too. It's not just school." I wiped my mouth and pushed the remnants of my lunch aside before I said, "He's an all-around ray of fucking sunshine."

"Because he misses his parents?"

"Honestly, I'm not sure that's the problem. I know he misses them, but this isn't the first time they've been deployed at the same time. I think he's just pissed that they put me in charge and didn't leave him with Tutu instead."

"But your grandmother lives with you, doesn't she?"

"Yes. She's lived with Kiki since she divorced her first husband, and that's not going to change even after my sister retires. They're having a cottage built for her at the edge of their property."

"That's nice. Will you still live with them after your sister and her husband come home for good?"

"God no," I said with an exaggerated shudder. And then, without even thinking about it, I clarified, "The only children I'm ever going to live with full-time will be my own."

"You want children?" Amethyst asked as she reached over and plucked a shrimp from my basket.

"Of course. Family is important, and children are a

divine blessing." I thought about it for a second before I shook my head and added, "I think that falls by the wayside when they become teenagers, though."

"I guess your nephew has been a real handful."

"I left him at home with Tutu today because she had chores for him to do around the house. Hopefully, he won't be disrespectful to her, but I'm not really holding out much hope."

"What will happen if he *does* disrespect her?"

"When I go home this evening, I'll find him cowering in the corner with his thumb in his mouth, rethinking every bad life decision that got him to that place."

Amethyst burst out laughing and said, "Your tutu sounds an awful lot like my gamma. She doesn't have to lay a hand on you - although she will if it's warranted - for you to know you've messed up."

"This morning, Kai said something to me over breakfast that gave me a little insight into why he doesn't respect me as the matai with his parents gone."

"Matai?"

"The leader of the family."

"What did he say?"

"When Tutu said he needed to get his shit together or he'd end up in trouble with the law, he said, 'Then I can be just like Uncle!' It's not any secret that I've been to prison, but I've never had anyone in my family throw it in my face so blatantly before."

I was surprised that Amethyst didn't ask about the crime I'd committed that landed me in prison. Instead, she said, "Obviously, you've served your time, so there's really no point in bringing it up."

"You don't seem to care at all."

"I know that whatever you did isn't something that would put me or my family in danger."

"How do you know that?"

"Because if that were the case, then Hawk wouldn't have anything to do with you."

"Are you close to him?" I asked. "How exactly are you related?"

"Our moms are sisters, and our dads have known each other since they were kids."

"And your fa'a is large? I remember Hawk talking about his family and saying that there were too many people to count."

"That's true, especially considering that my mom and Hawk's mom, Summer, have so many kids between them. That's not even counting my aunts and uncles on my mom's side or my aunts and uncles on my dad's. Hawk has even more than I do, and that's saying something."

"Are you close to the rest of your family or just your siblings?"

"I'd say we're pretty close. As a matter of fact, I work with two of my cousins, two of my uncles, and one of my aunts."

"Really?"

"Spruce is my uncle."

"He is?" When Amethyst nodded, I said, "I met Spruce at Dub's wedding when I sat at the table with him and his brother and sister. They're a hoot."

"My gigi had two sets of kids. My mom belongs to the first set she had when she was very young. Spruce, Terran, Jewel, and Petra are part of the second set that she had years later."

"Your mom said you were one of her bonus kids."

"I think it's cute when she calls us that. She and Dad adopted us when I was just a toddler. Our birth mother is Dad's sister, so we're his nieces genetically, but he raised us as his daughters."

"It's good that your family takes care of each other."

"Like you're doing for your niece and nephews?"

"Of course. Since they were born, it has been my job to look out for them, and that will never change . . . even when they're little assholes."

"That's true in my family too. Even though I want to choke them out half the time, there's not a chance I'd ever let anyone else do it."

"That's how it should be."

Amethyst looked down at her watch and grimaced. "I hate to eat and run, but I really should get back to the office. I've got a full schedule this afternoon."

"Thank you for having lunch with me. Can we do it again soon?"

"I'd love that."

"Have I proven myself yet so that you'll let me take you on an official date?"

"Isn't that what this is?"

"You know what I mean."

Amethyst made a face before she asked, "By official date, I hope you don't mean that you'll be taking me somewhere that I have to dress up because formality is against my religion."

"Good because I don't want to go anywhere that I'm not comfortable, which means I'll never take you somewhere that requires me to wear a tie."

"No country club dates then. I'm fine with that."

"So, that's a yes?"

"Yes, Tama'i. I'd love to go on a date with you."

"Can I pick you up at seven on Saturday and wow you with my entertainment choices?"

"I can't wait."

"Neither can I."

SEVEN

Did you know that a person who loves tattoos and piercings is called a stigmatophile?

Now you do.

Text from Amethyst to Tama'i

AMETHYST

I was yanked out of a very pleasant dream by the ringing of my phone and grumbled as I reached for it. I opened one eye and saw that the call was from our after-hours service, so I hit the button to put the call on speaker.

"This is Dr. Hamilton," I croaked.

"I'm sorry to wake you, Dr. Hamilton, but we got a phone call from the emergency room. One of your patients was injured in an accident, and his father insists that you are the only one who can treat him."

"Who is it?" I asked as I sat up and put my feet on the floor. As the woman gave me the details, I set the phone back on the nightstand and ran my hands over my face before I eased my silk bonnet off and let my braids fall around my shoulders. "Thank you. I'll take care of it."

I dialed the number to the nurse's desk in the ER as I trudged to the bathroom and calculated the correct dosage of a sedative I knew would help calm my young patient.

After a short wait on hold, I spoke to the charge nurse and explained my patient's diagnosis and instructed her as to the best way to give him the medication he needed before I assured her that I would be there as soon as I could.

Since I'd showered last night after my training session with my sisters, I pulled on a scrub top that depicted a jungle scene and found a pair of scrub pants that would match before I pulled on socks and a pair of Crocs that also matched the theme for today.

Within just a few minutes, I had my backpack over my shoulder and was walking out the door. I only realized what time it was when I opened my garage door and saw that it was still dark.

It didn't take very long to get to the hospital, and I parked in the doctors' lot before I hurried to the entrance of the ER. The second the doors opened, I could hear my patient and winced when I realized that he'd probably been screaming like that since he had arrived.

As I passed the triage nurse, I reached into the side pocket of my backpack and pulled out a handful of the caramels I was never without and dropped them onto the desk in front of her. She smiled at me, and I winked before I pushed the swinging doors open and went in search of my patient. It wasn't hard to find him, considering his yelling directed me straight to his room. As I walked in, his father looked over, and I watched relief transform his face.

Without a word of greeting to anyone, I hit the button on my phone to start the song I'd already pulled up and then jumped into action and did something I knew would draw my patient's attention just like it did every time. By the time I'd completed the first verse, he was smiling, and then he joined me for the chorus as he started clapping.

I reached over and pulled one of the nurses in the room to my side and then waved another one over and instructed them, "Just dance. Come on! Let's get this party started!"

The second they joined me, my patient saw them in a new light and even smiled as he held his injured hand against his chest and continued singing. By the time the song was over, there was a completely different vibe in the room. When the next song started, I started swaying slowly to the calmer music as I approached my patient and brushed his hair back so I could see blood seeping down his forehead.

As the music played, I gave instructions to the nurses while we got to work. I planned to sing and dance as much as necessary to help him. I loved my job and my patients. If singing and dancing was what it took to help them feel better, I was more than happy to perform regularly. The smile on the little boy's face, even though I knew he had to be in pain, told me that every off-key note was worth it.

It didn't take long for us to get him all set and on his way home with liquid stitches on his small forehead cut and a brace for his sprained wrist. I decided to grab a cup of coffee and make my rounds before I went on to open the office.

Visiting the newborns in the nursery was one of the favorite parts of my job, and I made sure to leave a handful of candy on the desk for the nurses. I knew that some doctors were hard to deal with so I made sure that I was never one they dreaded being on duty with. If anything, I wanted them to feel comfortable around me so they wouldn't hesitate to tell me their thoughts on a patient.

In my experience, nurses were the key to good patient care since they had far more interaction with the patients than I ever did. Not a lot of doctors acknowledged that, but it was something my associates and I never forgot. We made it our mission to stay humble and never turn into the kind of physician that nurses hated.

After doing a newborn assessment on my newest patient, I popped my head into the room where her mother was sleeping and found her father awake and playing on his phone. Without waking her, I motioned for him to join me in the hall where I gave him the all-clear to take their baby home to join their family with instructions to make an appointment for her next check-up in two weeks.

Since I still had almost three hours before the office opened, I pondered my options. If I went home and tried to get a little more sleep, I'd probably just be groggy for the rest of the day, but if I went and had another cup of coffee and some pastries, I could surf a caffeine and sugar high until my lunch break when I could take a power nap.

Of course the carbs and caffeine won out, and soon, I was knocking on the door of my favorite bakery.

Janis Grissom was a good friend of mine. We had grown up together as club family since our fathers belonged to the Texas Kings MC. She was known for being temperamental and difficult to get along with while I was much more cheerful and upbeat, so many thought we were an odd pair.

I knocked on the glass as hard as I could but knew she probably couldn't hear me in the back, so I pulled out my phone. Before I had a chance to call her, I saw movement out of the corner of my eye and looked up to find her standing on the other side of the glass. She unlocked the door and pushed it open for me and then locked it again as I greeted her cheerfully, something I knew would set her off.

"Why are you awake, and what do you want?"

"I set my alarm to wake up *hours* before I had to work just so I could come visit you, my sweet friend," I teased.

"Bullshit. You got called out, and now you're going to come bother me instead of going home to sleep like a normal human."

"Okay, I'm busted. You're right," I admitted as I walked around the counter to make myself at home. As the espresso machine did its thing, I found the syrups I wanted and put a few pumps into a large cup and then started steaming my milk.

"It's a health department violation for customers to just walk in and start serving themselves."

"I never pay anyway, so am I really a customer?"

"I'm going to go bankrupt feeding all of you asshats who show up and steal my stuff," Janis grumbled. I knew she didn't mean it, and I also knew that everyone who came in and 'stole' baked goods and drinks pinned cash to the corkboard just inside the kitchen to make up for what they'd taken. Janis changed the subject abruptly when she said, "Tell me about this Polynesian god I've been hearing about."

"What have you heard?"

"Just rumors since you haven't said shit," Janis grumbled. "You know I live vicariously through all of you, so it really hurts my tender feelings when you hold things back."

I heard one of Janis' employees snort and looked

around at the same time she did. The two people who worked under her had been with Janis since she opened, so they knew about her quirks and moodiness all too well. They also knew that the glare she was aiming their way was just for show because when it came to the people she cared about, Janis was all bark and no bite. The people she *didn't* care about should be terrified of the woman, but luckily, I was one of her favorite people.

"Do you mean the guy I've been talking to?"

"Duh. This is the middle of the damn country . . . far, far away from any ocean. How many other islander hotties do you think are floating around here?"

"True."

"I guess my burning question is can he eat a papaya like those guys on the video?"

"What video?" I asked curiously. Janis pulled her phone out and started scrolling through one of her apps before she held it out to me. I watched a short video of shirtless men with their hands behind their back drawing the seeds out of papaya halves and had a full-body shiver when I imagined Tama'i doing something like that to me. "Oh my. That's interesting."

"How have you never seen that? I'm sure at least three of the girls have put it in our group text."

"I ignore the group text until the red dot on my screen starts to get on my nerves. I try to scroll through to see what I've missed but usually get bored and just close it out and go about my day. If someone really needs to talk to me, they'll have to send me a message because I don't have time for all that chatter."

"That is why you and I are friends," Janis said with a smile. "You're secretly an introvert just like me."

"It's never been a secret that you're a grumpy recluse. I just prefer to keep my digital communications to a minimum." I walked down the long counter, perusing the selection of pastries, baked goods, and donuts before I picked one and took a bite. Through a mouthful of deliciousness, I mumbled, "This is the best one you've ever made."

"Maple bacon is a customer favorite. You're lucky you got here when you did because they're usually the first ones to sell out." Janis grabbed a box from one of the tall stacks on a side table and said, "I assume you'll want to take a box to the office."

"Yes, please."

As she started selecting various things for me to take, she said, "Talk while I work."

"His name is Tama'i, but everyone calls him Tiny." Janis scoffed, and I smiled because I knew exactly what she was thinking. The man was *huge*, but I understood how nicknames went, especially in the biker world. However, I thought his given name was unique and beautiful, so I would forever call him Tama'i and let everyone else use his handle. "He's really nice and . . . I can't think of how to describe him."

"Excellent kisser? Gainfully employed? Good in bed? Isn't a homeless thug who is looking for a sugar mama?"

"Haven't kissed him, he works with my sister at Fain's shop, don't know about all that, and he moved here to live at his sister's and take care of her kids while she and her husband are deployed."

Janis stopped in her tracks and looked at me with raised eyebrows as she asked, "He uprooted his life to move here and take care of her children?" When I nodded, she smiled and said, "I like him already."

"He was in the military and has also been to prison."

"So, one way or another, he has something in common with at least half of the men we grew up around."

"He doesn't seem afraid of my father at all."

"Really? I've known your father my entire life, but there are times when he gets that look that makes me remember he's not one I'd ever want to cross."

"That's saying something, but you know Dad is just a big softie. He's just got a very crunchy exterior. Like . . . um . . ."

"Like a complete and utter psychopath?" Janis suggested.

"No! He's like a s'more. Crunchy but filled with ooey gooey sweetness that everyone loves."

"Are we still talking about Lout?"

"Yes!"

Janis laughed as she shook her head. "I know that most people, at least most outsiders, can't see it, but my dad is the same way. So are the rest of the men in our family. I wonder if your big islander is a sweetie too."

"I think he might be. He's smart and funny. Respectful too. Not just to me, but also toward Mom and Dad."

"You haven't even kissed him, but you've already introduced him to your parents?"

I told her about Mom calling me to the shop while she was getting tattooed, and she smiled before she said, "What's your mom going to do when she runs out of skin to tattoo?"

"I have no idea, but the possibilities are terrifying."

"So, what has you out and about before the crack of dawn this fine Thursday morning?"

"One of my patients had an accident, and they needed my help calming him down in the ER."

"Oh, no. How did he get into an accident in the middle of the night?"

"He's an artistic little guy and likes pushing the boundaries his parents have put in place to protect him. Occasionally, that manages to get him into trouble like he did while they were sleeping and he crawled up onto the counter to reach the treats he'd seen his mom hide in the cabinet above the refrigerator."

"Hmm. Artistic. You mean autistic, don't you?"

"No, I mean he's artistic. He sees the world in a completely different light than everyone else and understands the shades of its beauty from a unique angle."

Janis nodded in understanding, well aware that I

didn't like labels and also wasn't willing to share details about my patients' medical diagnoses. "I bet he's a fun kid."

"The best. He loves to sing and dance. I introduced him to The Temptations and every time I see him, we sing 'I Can't Get Next To You.'"

"Excellent song!"

A timer went off, and I saw Janis tense as she glanced toward the other end of the kitchen. I suddenly remembered that she must have a million things to do before the bakery opened this morning, but she was making time for me.

"I'm going to get out of your hair so you can get to work," I said as I took the box out of her hand. "Want to lock up after me?"

"No, it's almost time for us to open anyway," Janis said as she glanced at the ovens again. "Call me so we can catch up. I miss your face."

"I don't miss yours because you're U-G-L-Y and you ain't got no alibi. You're ugly. Yeah, yeah, you're ugly."

"Why are we friends?"

"Because no one else is willing to deal with your attitude." I started giggling as Janis walked away and wasn't surprised to see her flip me off over her shoulder. Still laughing, I yelled, "I know I'm number one! Thank you!"

Even though I was too tired for the caffeine to have any effect, my morning went by quickly. However, my afternoon went downhill when a patient of mine had to be admitted to the hospital and then another threw up all over me before he spewed all over the walls of the exam room, his mom, and True, the nurse who was unlucky enough to be standing next to me at the time. Luckily, we had a shower in the employee bathroom, and I always kept a spare set of scrubs in my office, so I was able to change. Even though I was clean, I still felt like I needed another shower.

I was dreaming of a long soak in the tub and a bottle of wine when I walked into the exam room to do a consultation for my cousin Wren, a nurse-midwife, who saw patients here in the office along with the other doctors on staff. When my uncles, Terran and Spruce, and my aunt - their sister Jewel opened Parker Medical Clinic, they intended for it to serve people of all ages and to be a place where entire families could find medical professionals that they could trust. When my cousin Roscoe started practicing, he wanted to open his own women's health clinic, but they convinced him to join them and changed the name to Parker Hamilton Medical Center. As soon as I was able to practice pediatric medicine, I joined them.

Wren had been one of the RNs that helped start the clinic while she continued her degree to become an APRN - an Advanced Practice Registered Nurse - who specialized in midwifery and women's health. I worked closely with her and Roscoe, the OB/GYN on staff, and helped their patients feel secure in knowing that their children would have me on their side from the minute they were born.

Once I introduced myself to the patient, a lovely young woman named Meredith, and her husband, Alex, I leaned against the counter next to the stool where Wren was sitting and got ready to answer all of the questions they might have.

I loved the magic of pregnancy and had considered going into the obstetrics field of study, but my love of infants and children had won out in the end and led me to pediatrics.

Now I got to help new parents navigate the choppy waters of having a newborn in their lives as I watched their little one grow up.

As always, watching the expectant mother rest her hand on her belly as she eagerly asked questions about the future gave me a pang in my chest. I wanted so badly to have a child of my own, and since I'd been single for so long, I had started considering in-vitro options. However, I still held out hope that someday I'd find a partner to be by my side through everything from morning sickness to a colicky infant and then on throughout the rest of our children's lives until we became empty nesters who couldn't wait for our grandchildren to come and visit.

The romantic in me wondered if I'd met that man already. As if he could sense my thoughts, my phone vibrated with a text from Tama'i that made me smile.

We'd been texting back and forth since our lunch a few days ago, and I was gradually getting to know him better. Everything I'd learned so far made me glad that I had agreed to our date on Saturday, and I could tell from the countdown he had going that he was just as eager to see me again too.

As I slipped my phone back into the pocket of my scrubs, I forced myself to focus on the patients in front of me. Tama'i could have all of my attention when I was finished here. Hopefully, this day would end just like the last few - with him on the phone as I enjoyed a long soak in the tub before I went to bed.

Maybe someday he'd be waiting for me in bed instead of sleeping across town.

Maybe.

EIGHT

What does a hot dog use for protection?

Condoments

Text from Tama'i to Amethyst

AMETHYST

"I've tried everything I can think of, and I'm not sure what else to do," the concerned mom said as she urged her toddler to take a sip from the cup in her hand. "He's been this way for a few hours now."

"He seems very lethargic," I mused as I used the stethoscope to listen to his breathing. "His heart rate is slower than normal, but his breathing is fine and his lungs sound clear. You said this has happened before?"

"Yes. He was slow like this Sunday evening and went right to sleep without eating dinner. When he woke up Monday morning, he was fine. I didn't notice anything unusual again until . . . well . . . until I picked him up this morning."

"Picked him up from the sitter or . . ."

"His father. He gets him every other weekend and Thursday nights on his off weeks."

"Did he mention anything about his lethargy?"

"He was already at work, so I didn't talk to him. His girlfriend said that he slept all evening yesterday and then all through the night, which is weird. He's usually up and running around until he drops from exhaustion. I've never known him to sleep all evening and then all night unless he was sick."

"And you brought him right in this morning?" I asked.

"Yes," she said as tears filled her eyes. "He's not acting like himself, and I just . . . I'm worried."

I could hear her phone buzzing in her purse but noticed that she didn't seem to care. Her focus was on her child and nothing else. I could feel her concern from the second I walked into the room, and after examining her son, I shared it. He was clean and well-kept. His nails were trimmed, and his hair was freshly cut. All in all, he looked like a healthy boy except for his glassy-eyed gaze and obvious lethargy.

"He doesn't seem hungry at all, but he's thirsty," she said as she lifted the cup to check the contents. "He's almost out, though. Do you have any ice? I have a bottle of water in my purse, but I'm sure it's warm."

"It looks like there's juice in there now. Let me take it to the breakroom and rinse it out. I'll send the nurse in to get some blood and have them rush it at the lab. It might take some time, so . . ."

"Do whatever you need to do," she said as tears streamed down her cheeks. "Something's wrong with him, Dr. Hamilton. This isn't my little boy."

I asked her a few more questions about his usual

eating habits and activity level. Even though she was still distracted, she was able to answer me with what I considered normal responses. I couldn't find a single thing wrong with the child other than the visible signs I observed during my exam.

"I will draw some blood and then reassess after I get the results back," I told her as I ran my hands over the boy's fine hair. "I'd like for you to stay here while I wait on his labs. Hopefully, I'll be able to come up with an answer as to why he is behaving this way."

"We can stay as long as we need to."

"We'll figure it out," I reassured her. I took the cup from her and handed her a box of tissues before I promised that someone would be in as soon as they were free.

As I was walking toward the breakroom, I opened the sippy cup and looked down at the contents mindlessly as I mulled over what could be wrong. I stopped in my tracks when I caught a whiff of something I shouldn't have smelled and was taken aback when someone bumped into me from behind.

"Move it or lose it, Hamilton," Jewel said as she nudged me with her shoulder. "I almost ran you . . ." She stopped mid-sentence as she sniffed the air and asked, "Do we need to have a talk, Amy?"

"No. Why do you ask?"

"Honey, come with me," Jewel said as she took my elbow and ushered me to her office. She pushed me inside and then shut the door behind her. She leaned against it and took a deep breath before she said, "I know our job is stressful, babe, but I can't have you drinking while . . ."

"You can smell it too."

"Of course I can smell it. It's faint but obvious."

I thrust the sippy cup at her and said, "This has alcohol in it."

"Okay."

"My patient's mother brought this in, and he's been drinking out of it." Jewel's eyebrows rose as her mouth dropped open, and I said, "She said she just picked him up from his father's girlfriend after he spent the night. He's not acting like himself, and he was the same way the last time she picked him up. He's lethargic, and his heart rate is slow."

"The child is drunk?"

"I think so," I answered. "Who would do such a thing?"

"You need to make the call. I'll stay with you and watch the cup, although, at this point, I'm not sure it can be used as evidence." Jewel ran her hand over her mouth and said, "I'll call my contact at DCFS and go from there."

As Jewel pulled her phone out, I nudged her aside and opened the door. Jovi, one of our RNs, was the only person in the hall, so I called out for her to come into the office. She had her hands full and was obviously on her way to help a patient but put everything down on the desk as I said, "I need an immediate blood draw in Exam Five. Order a BAC, sCr, and liver panel. When you've got the draw, give it to me and I'll walk it down to the lab myself."

"Exam Five is that little boy . . . you want a BAC on

your patient?"

"Immediately, Jovi. Drop what you're doing, and go take the draw."

"Yes, doctor," Jovi said as she glanced at the desk and then out into the hallway. "Will you let Terran know I was redirected?"

"Not a problem," I assured her. "Get what you need, and I'll find someone to go into the room with you for the draw."

"Okay," Jovi said as she walked toward the supply station.

I walked around Jewel's desk and logged in to her computer with my password and sent a message to the assignment board calling all available nursing staff and doctors to Jewel's office immediately. Within seconds, Wren appeared in the doorway followed by True, another of our RNs.

"True, please accompany Jovi into Exam Five and witness her draw and then I want you to stay in the exam room with the patient and his mother until one of us comes to relieve you."

"Okay," True said without question before she turned around and walked back out into the hall.

"What's going on?"

"I've got a patient who ingested an unknown amount of alcohol. He's lethargic and . . ."

"DCFS has been notified, and they have someone on

the way. I'm calling 911," Jewel interrupted.

"Oh, no. It's a baby?"

"Toddler. He's almost three."

Wren put her hand over her mouth and sighed as she slowly shook her head. "Who would do such a thing?"

"She said she picked him up from Dad's girlfriend, and he had the sippy cup with him at the time. She brought him directly here because she knew something was wrong with him. I can't believe that Dad and his girlfriend would be so . . . so . . . I just . . ."

"That's what she says happened, but it's not up to us to investigate or place blame," Jewel reminded us. "Our job is to protect our patient."

"When will your contact be here?" I asked.

"She's on her way, and so are the cops."

"Gamma is right," Wren said sadly.

"What do you mean?" Jewel asked.

"Some people just need killin'."

It had been one thing after another all day, but I saw a light at the end of the tunnel when I realized that I was about to see my last patient on the schedule. Of course, I was supposed to be off by lunch today as each doctor rotated through a half-day Friday schedule, but it rarely happened.

I was so close to being done that I could hear the bubble bath calling my name.

I signed a few papers for one of the nurses, called and spoke to an ENT about a consult, and then made my way into the exam room and found one of my favorite patients crying softly on his mom's lap.

"What's going on, Zachary?" I asked as I sat down on the stool and rolled closer to my patient. I reached out and took his hand and then laughed when he launched himself toward me. I caught him easily and smiled as he wrapped his arms and legs around me like a koala before I looked at his mother and raised my eyebrows in question.

"We were eating lunch at a restaurant downtown, and he shoved something up his nose."

"Food or . . ."

"It was a piece of gum he pulled off the bottom of the table," the mom admitted with a grimace. "The restaurant was busy, and they had run out of high chairs, so he was sitting next to me in the booth. I saw him looking under the table and distracted him a few times when he started to touch something under there, but I looked away for just a second and then . . ." The mom gagged silently and then swallowed hard before she continued, "I looked back just in time to see him shove something pink up his nose. I tried to stop him . . ."

"He shoved it all the way up there," Dawn, the mother's best friend, who had been here several times with Zachary and his mom, said with an exaggerated shudder. "I tried to see if I could get it out but realized I was probably making things worse."

"I even tried the trick my granny taught me after the bean incident, but it didn't work," Alison admitted.

"What trick is that?" I asked as I rolled over to the exam table and lifted Zachary to sit in front of me. Luckily, he was just high enough that I could see up his nose. Using my pen light, I easily spotted the pink blob his mom had described.

"I plugged the free side of his nose and blew air into his mouth," Alison said with a shrug. "It did bring the gum down a little bit, but I don't think I could have gotten it all the way out that way."

"It probably wasn't very pliable when he stuck it up there, but now it's warm and moist, so it's gonna be very stretchy," I said as I smiled at the little boy. His eyes filled with tears and I said, "Your mom is going to have a funny story to tell people, and she'll probably even use it to embarrass you when you're older."

"Do you think you can get it out, or should I take him to the emergency room?"

"They'd just try the same tactics I'm going to use before they refer you to an ear, nose, and throat doctor," I told her. "He seems pretty worked up, so I'll give him something to help him relax before we start."

"Can I have a double shot of whatever it is you're giving him?" Alison asked.

"That would make things easier, wouldn't it?"

133

I took my shoes off and put them in their place by the doorway as the garage door came down behind me. As I walked through the doorway into the laundry room, I stripped off my clothes, letting out an audible sigh as I unhooked my bra before taking it off and adding it to the washer along with my scrubs, socks, and underwear. I put the detergent in the machine but didn't turn it on. Instead, I stepped into the shower I'd had installed in the corner of the room and did a quick but thorough wash and then turned the washing machine on as I was drying off.

Since this was my daily routine, I had a basket of comfortable clothes on the shelf nearby and pulled out a pair of leggings and a T-shirt to wear before I applied my lotion and face cream. As soon as I was dressed, I walked into the kitchen and pondered what to do first: nap or start dinner.

Since dinner included a trip to the grocery store, that meant the agenda for this afternoon was a nap because dinner would be takeout or pizza. I knew that after the day I had, there wasn't a chance I'd make it out of the grocery store without an assault charge and a viral video labeled 'crazy woman loses it in the produce section' blasting my face all over the internet.

I could probably handle the assault charge and didn't care a whistle about what people on the internet thought about me, so the grocery store *might* be an option if I didn't want a nap so badly.

When I walked into my living room, I realized that my nap wasn't going to happen because there were already two women sleeping on my couch and another sleeping in my recliner. Since those someones just happened to be my best friends, that took the sting out of it but not by much considering they were sleeping and I was not. Today was Zoey's normal day off, but it wasn't usual for Cydney or

Bella to take the day off since they were as driven and structured as me. However, the empty bottle of wine sitting next to a half-full one let me know that it wasn't just *any* day off. Obviously, it had been crappy for everyone, and I was a bottle of wine behind.

I picked the half-empty bottle up from the coffee table and walked towards the stairs. It wouldn't hurt to kill two birds with one stone - get my buzz on and enjoy the bubble bath I'd been dreaming about all day while I waited for my friends to rouse themselves and get started on round two.

NINE

I've never been held hostage, but I was added to a group text that includes at least half of your family, and I think that's almost the same thing.

Text from Tama'i to Amethyst

TAMA'I

"You look well-rested." I was able to tell the lie with a straight face but couldn't help but laugh when my sister reached up and scratched the side of her nose with her middle finger. She was in the common room of their barracks, and because of her rank, she needed to practice at least a little decorum, so she couldn't reply to me the way she would if she was alone. Knowing that, I felt the urge to push it just a little more and teased, "You know, I was thinking the other day that I might need to buy a new mattress when y'all come back. Your bed is so freaking comfortable that I . . ."

"Ou te faamoemoe e te ula ma toe pau i ai."

"Is that really the kind of language one would expect from an upstanding US Marine, Kiki?"

"What did she say?" Tutu asked as she walked into the room.

"Don't you dare . . ."

I interrupted my sister with a grin as I tattled, "She

136

said she hopes I shit and then fall back in it."

Tutu went on a tangent about disrespect and vulgar language, and I watched my sister's face transform from tense and stressed to calm and happy just from hearing Tutu's familiar rant. We'd heard the same thing our entire lives, yet we still hadn't learned how to behave . . . or at least that's what Tutu seemed to believe.

However, the lessons our grandmother and parents had taught us over the years were very much a part of our everyday lives, and I hoped that my nephews and niece were learning the same thing from Tutu and my sister along with a little help from myself and my brother-in-law, Bart.

Tutu kept talking as she walked out of the room, flitting around and tidying up the house in preparation for the guests she had coming over this afternoon.

"How are my children?" Kiki asked. I knew she spoke to each of them as often as possible, and if possible, they had a family video chat including Bart once a week. It amazed me that even from half a world away, Kiki knew that something was wrong at home, but it wasn't shocking that she was worried about it. "Meka said everything was fine, but Aleki mentioned you were having problems with Kai."

"I'm pretty sure he hates me."

"He's a teenager. He hates everyone. That gets better . . . or so I'm told."

"Do you really want to know what happened while you're too far away to do anything about it? I handled it. Probably the wrong way, but I handled it all the same."

"Tell me everything," Kiki ordered. I told her about

the phone call and then what I'd heard when I walked into the school office and watched her face turn red with anger as her eyes narrowed and her lips pressed together so hard they were almost white. When I finished, she said, "He's lucky you're the one who got your hands on the phone because if I'd have been there, he'd have probably needed to have it surgically removed. Bart is going to shit himself when he finds out Kai was yelling at a teacher."

"Like I said, I think I handled it, but he's still pissed about the phone thing. Tutu sided with me and agreed that he won't be getting a new one until one of you comes home to deal with it."

"Tutu is doing okay with you in charge?"

"She's living her best life, Keeks. I think she might even have a boyfriend."

"No!" My sister's face lit up, and she whispered, "Do you know who it is? Find out a name, and I'll give you the scoop if I hear anything."

"I might have a source for information if I'm able to drag a name out of her."

"Did you meet some new friends through work?" Before I had a chance to answer her question, she said, "Good. I was worried about you becoming more reclusive than usual."

"Actually, I *have* made some new friends and even reconnected with an old one." Kiki stared at me as if she was trying to look into my soul, but I didn't get offended. She was looking out for not just me, but her children too. She just wanted to make sure I was surrounding them with good people. "You might know him or at least some people in his family. His name is Hawk Forrester."

"I know some Forresters." Kiki laughed for a second before she said, "If you're friends with Hawk, then you understand that when I say 'some,' I mean a few, considering there are at least a hundred or so."

"How do you know Hawk's family?"

"The Forrester family is well-known around town, not just because of the MC their patriarch started but because of the work they do to help the community. I'm acquainted with a woman named Jamie Forrester. We served on a planning committee for a fundraiser to help build the veterans center downtown." She looked thoughtful for a second before she said, "I remember her mentioning that she had children, some of them around our age, but I don't think any of them were named Hawk. That's a unique name, so surely it would have stuck with me."

"Do you know anyone in town named Hamilton?"

"Actually, yes. There was an Emerald Hamilton on the committee with us. I believe she's a doctor."

"I have a date with her sister Amethyst who is also a doctor. I'm taking her out for dinner tomorrow."

"Look at you, Tama'i! Hold on . . . her last name is Hamilton too? I wonder if she's related to my doctor. His first name is Roscoe. He works at . . ."

"Parker & Hamilton Medical Center?"

"That's the one. There's information in the folder about the kids' doctor. He's at the same office."

"It's not Amethyst? She's a pediatrician."

"No. By the time we moved to Rojo, the kids were all old enough for a GP, so they see Spruce Parker. Amethyst works with them?"

"She does."

"I'm impressed. Your tastes don't usually run to the dating-type."

"I'm older and wiser."

"Sure. We'll go with that. My guess is that she's a knockout who made you laugh. Am I right?"

"Actually, she's a knockout who talked me out of running away like a scared rabbit when I had to get a shot."

"Did you let her give you the shot?"

"Yes," I said petulantly before I shuddered at the thought of having to get another in a few months.

"I've seen how you behave around needles, so she deserves a reward."

"I'll let her know you think so."

"Where are you taking her to dinner?"

"Actually, I'm glad you called because I was just wondering about that myself."

"Well, as your big sister, I believe that it's my duty to tell you where to go and what to do, especially since you're new in town."

"You've been doing that our whole life."

"And I'm never going to stop."

"I need some help," I said when I was finally alone with Pearl. Stone had just run to the store to get drinks to restock the breakroom, and Fain was gone for the day, so we had a few minutes to chat . I was hoping to get some ideas about where to take her sister on our date.

"What can I do for you, big guy?" Pearl asked as she laid her sleeping daughter down in the wagon stroller that she used as a bed while she was at the shop. Once she was settled, she rolled it to the side and covered her with a blanket before she turned back to me. "Please tell me this is about your date because if I don't go back to the girls with some information, they're probably going to kick me out of the cool kids club."

"What does your sister like to do for fun?"

"Make our lives as miserable as possible." When I gave her a droll look, she laughed and said, "She really likes to shop." I grimaced, and she put her hand up and said, "You look like you might throw up, so let me explain."

"Please do."

"She loves to go to thrift stores and find things she can upcycle. Our friend Lotus owns a shop where she sells things that she has created, and she has workshops and classes where she helps people with their own projects."

"Hmm. How does that work? Is she going to have a

class tomorrow, by chance? That might be something fun to do on a date."

"Let me check," Pearl said as she picked up her phone and started scrolling. I thought she might be looking at a website, but when the phone started ringing, I realized she was calling someone instead. I listened as a woman answered by saying, "Buried Treasures, this is Lotus. How can I help you today?" As Pearl greeted her and they spent a few minutes catching up, I used my phone to look up the business.

By the time Pearl got around to the reason for her call, I'd already discovered that there wasn't a class tomorrow but found a link to another local business that I thought might be fun to check out.

"Does Amethyst like to break things?" I interrupted.

"I'm not sure, but she's got enough repressed rage inside her that I think it would be a great idea." The woman on the phone laughed as Pearl asked, "Are you talking about that new feature at The Gauntlet?"

I nodded and said, "That's it. Have you ever been there?"

"I have, but I haven't had a chance to do the Wreck Room yet. Amethyst hasn't either."

"I wonder if they have any openings or if they're . . ."

"Believe me, if I call, they'll make an opening."

"You think you're that important, huh?"

"I *know* I am," Pearl said cockily.

"Well, I plan to pick her up at seven and take her to dinner, so if you can make reservations for us at the Wreck Room for eight-thirty, that would be perfect."

The bell over the door signaled that my morning appointment had arrived just as Pearl assured me, "I'll take care of everything."

The next few hours passed quickly, and I was happy to get out of there when I did because Pearl and Stone were dealing with two of the most annoying type of clients - a loud and boisterous young guy who was accompanied by a couple of his equally obnoxious friends and a crier who acted like Pearl was torturing her for information and had brought three of her twittering friends with her to watch the show. I'd done my fair share of work on both types and would most likely do plenty more. Today, however, I had plans with my niece that would beat the hell out of listening to the chaos of those clients.

When I pulled up in front of Tameka's school, I was able to find a place to park near the door and backed my motorcycle into it so I could watch for my niece when the bell rang. Since I had a few minutes, I pulled my phone out while I got comfortable and basked in the sun.

I called my friend who owned the shop I'd worked at in Vegas and couldn't help but smile when, instead of a normal greeting, he answered the phone by saying, "I would give my left nut for you to tell me you're coming back because if this fucking idiot who took your place doesn't shut his mouth, I'm going to end up back in prison."

"Aww. You miss me already, huh?"

"If you hadn't left for a good reason, I'd still be pissed at you, but yeah, the shop's not the same without your grumpy ass."

I chuckled, knowing that my gruff and outspoken friend wouldn't ever come right out and say he missed me. "Either way, are you still planning to bring me my shit?"

"Do you have a place to put it yet?" Dice asked.

"Got a lead on one this morning, as a matter of fact. Just so happens that a guy I was locked up with lives here, and his cousins are some sort of real estate moguls. They own a whole fucking neighborhood and aren't opposed to renting to a guy like me. If I like living there, I'll even have the option to buy later."

"Absolutely not! Your ass is coming back to Vegas, and you're bringing Tutu with you. I haven't eaten anything worth a shit since the last time she visited because she's ruined me for anything other than her cooking."

"I'll let her know you're coming so she can prepare for your gluttony, my friend."

"Do that. And you might go ahead and tell her to wear something picture-worthy so one of you can video it when I propose to her."

"Again?"

"I'm a determined man, Tiny, and I've decided she's the woman for me."

The school bell rang, and I knew I had just a minute or two until I was surrounded by kids. Dice was not the kind of guy you had on speakerphone around sensitive ears, so I wrapped up the call. We confirmed his arrival date, and I assured him I'd have a place for him to stay. After a little more whining about how much he wanted me to come back to the shop, we said our goodbyes.

Tameka started running as soon as she caught sight of me. I lifted my phone to video her joy, knowing that my sister and her husband would appreciate it. The second she got close to my bike, she yelled, "I get to ride today?"

"No, I thought I'd make you walk beside me while I ride," I answered sarcastically. "Of course I'm taking you for a ride. You aced your history exam *and* got an A+ on your essay in English. You deserve a treat."

"You're so awesome, Uncle."

"I know, right?" I asked as I unstrapped the helmet I'd brought for her from the seat behind me and handed it over. "I've got another surprise for you too."

"What is it?" Tameka asked excitedly as she tried to latch the helmet beneath her chin.

I reached out to help her as I teased, "I'm not telling. You'll find out when we get there."

"I love you so much, Uncle. I'm glad you came to stay with us."

"I'm glad I did, too, Itiiti."

"I'm not little anymore, Uncle."

"You'll always be my little one, Meka, no matter how big you get."

The ride to our surprise location didn't take long, and I felt Tameka tense when she realized how close we were to the tattoo shop.

I shut the bike off and heard her sigh before she asked, "Is my surprise in there?"

"Your surprise is a few doors down, but this is my parking spot, so I'm gonna use it."

"A few doors down?" Tameka asked as she climbed off the bike and started removing her helmet. Her excitement was back in full force when she looked at the other storefronts on the street. "Where are we going?"

"I thought that you might like some salon time and a bit of shopping. When I was leaving the gym this morning, I noticed a T-shirt in the window of that boutique nearby that would be perfect for you."

Tameka was almost vibrating in anticipation as she handed me her helmet. She took off ahead of me, so I started after her. Apparently, I wasn't quite fast enough, so she ran back and grabbed my hand. I let her try to tug me along, working hard to get me there faster even though she was less than half my size.

When we got to the boutique, I pushed the door open for her to go in ahead of me and watched as she looked around in awe. Her expression reminded me so much of my sister that I felt my heart lurch, and when she smiled at me, I couldn't resist pulling her to my side for a quick hug.

"You can get one outfit, Itiiti."

"What about shoes?"

"That's negotiable."

"I'm good at negotiation."

"I guess we'll see, won't we?"

It didn't take her long to find a few choices that she liked as I amused myself listening to her chatter. Just then, a saleswoman walked around the counter and asked if there was anything she could help us find.

On a whim, I asked, "Do you have a shirt I could wear on a date?"

The woman bit her lip as she studied my chest and arms and slowly shook her head. "I'm sorry, sir, but I'm positive we don't have a single thing in your size."

"That's not a problem. Most places don't have anything that will fit me other than T-shirts, so I'll make do with what I have."

"There's a big and tall men's shop across town. Let me look up their address for you."

"Thank you."

"Uncle, what do you think?" Tameka asked as she held a black T-shirt and jeans in front of her. "Life would be easier if I just dressed like you."

"Be nice to me, little one, or that's all I'll buy you."

Tameka hurriedly put the T-shirt back and picked up another one she'd been carrying around for a few minutes. "I think I'm ready."

"I'm not going to argue because I am positive this is the shortest shopping trip on record."

"There's a reason for that, you know."

"What's that, Itiiti?"

"If I don't make you stay long, you might do this again soon."

"Ah. A sort of bribery situation. I like it."

"I *am* the smart one in the family."

"The smartest."

After we paid for her purchases, Tameka took my hand again and tried to drag me to the salon next door, but I shuffled my feet and took small steps just to spite her. As we walked in, she was grumbling at me, and I heard a woman laugh before she said, "Tiny! What brings you here?"

I looked up and found Opal, one of the Hamilton women that I'd shared dinner with the other night, standing at one of the stations in the salon brushing a woman's hair. I looked around and saw Willow was also here at a station across the room.

"We're having a spa day," Tameka announced.

"We have an appointment," I told Opal.

"You're our next appointment?" Opal asked incredulously.

"Yes, ma'am. Tameka did very well in school this week, so I thought she should be rewarded with some relaxation and pampering."

"And you're going to get pampered, too, right?" Tameka asked.

"As if I'd miss hanging out with you," I scoffed. "I'm getting the works, too, but I don't need color."

"But we should match, Uncle."

"You want me to paint my toenails?"

"And your fingernails."

"Not negotiable."

"I did *really* well in school this week," Tameka reminded me.

"Toes only," I insisted.

"Woohoo!" Tameka cheered. As she walked toward the wall of polish, she said, "You're the best, Uncle!"

"Tiny, I think you just became one of my favorite men," Willow said as she walked across the room toward us. She wrapped her arms around my waist and gave me a tight hug, and I uncomfortably patted her on the back before she pulled away. "Not many men would spend hours in a salon."

"I want Tameka to feel special."

"I think she probably can't feel any other way with you in her corner."

TEN

*What's the difference between the Black Eyed Peas
and chickpeas?*

*One of them can sing you a tune, and the other can
only hummus one.*

Text from Tama'i to Amethyst

AMETHYST

"Now that we're all sober, should we rationally
discuss the decisions we made last night?"

"I was perfectly rational," Bella insisted.

"That's why you made a phone call that required you
to go off alone into a bedroom so you could channel your
inner skank and have phone sex?" Cydney asked.

"Or better yet, is that why you booked an impromptu
flight to Vegas that leaves in less than four hours?"

"Shit!" Bella yelled as she sat straight up in bed.
Since she was between us, her sudden movement yanked the
covers off of Cydney's face, and she whimpered as if the
sunlight streaming through my window was painful. "I've
only got three hours?"

Bella jumped out of bed and took the covers with her.
I tried to move as little as possible as I reached down to grab

the blanket and pull it back up.

"She's nuts," Cydney said as she rolled over and put her face in the pillow.

"Why aren't you freaking out?" Zoey asked without opening her eyes.

"Why should I be?"

"You're on the same flight, Squid," I reminded her.

The bed shook as Cydney tensed, and I felt her gaze on me as she asked, "What did you say?"

"You don't remember that part?"

"Remind me."

Zoey's voice was barely more than a whisper when she said, "You made her a pinky promise that you'd go along to make sure she wasn't wowed by the bright lights of Sin City and the hot man with the dimples and more money than God."

"I did?" When I nodded, Cydney's face dropped back onto the pillow, and luckily, it muffled her scream. When she ran out of breath, she lifted her head again and stared at me before she asked, "Y'all are going, too, right?"

"I can't. I start the day shift tomorrow," Zoey explained.

"Nope. I have a date tonight."

"Oh, yeah," Cydney mumbled as she rolled to her

side so she could look at me. "What the fuck?"

"The heart wants what it wants."

"I'm not sure it's her heart that's making the decisions right now," Zoey mumbled.

"All the more reason for her to have supervision so she doesn't do something stupid."

"Bella isn't exactly the type to do irrational things."

Zoey agreed, "She's right. Bella's got her head on straight. She's not the irrational type."

"The impromptu Vegas trip doesn't seem irrational to you?"

"I can hear you talking about me, hags!" Bella yelled from the bathroom. "It's not irrational, it's impulsive. We made a pact to try new things!"

"When I said I wanted to do that, I was talking about changing my hairstyle and maybe . . . just *maybe* . . . considering a new color."

"What did I agree to?" I asked in confusion.

"You agreed that you wouldn't let your family run this guy off and you'd give him a chance to impress you with his personality and sense of humor before you wrote him off and never called him again," Zoey reminded me.

"Oh. That."

"I also believe that you sent him a text telling him your intentions," Cydney said happily. "I, on the other hand, didn't do anything but agree to a trip to Vegas where I can eat crab legs that are as big as my forearm, visit the Neon Museum, and then lay by the pool and get waited on hand and foot by a hot cabana guy."

"You're only going to be there for a day, Squid," Zoey reminded her.

"Then I guess I'll have a full belly while I work on my tan."

"You're not going to do any of that if you don't get your ass in gear and go home to pack!" Bella said as she hopped into the bedroom while trying to pull on her shoe. "You're dropping us off, right, Amy?"

"Sure. It's the least I can do." I laughed as both women stared daggers at me, and then what they had said struck me. In a horrified voice, I yelled, "What do you mean I sent him a text?"

"What'cha doin'?"

"The girls are on the plane."

"That sounds like code for something illegal."

"Trying to get two grown women packed and ready for a weekend trip in less than two hours should be an Olympic event."

"It's Saturday afternoon, and they're only going for the weekend?"

"I'm supposed to pick them up tomorrow evening around nine."

"For a thirty-six hour trip, I would need one set of clothes, deodorant, and my toothbrush."

"I should have let you help them pack."

"Absolutely not."

I blew out a breath and then steeled myself to start the conversation about the text I had sent last night. I'd been avoiding the subject throughout the messages we'd exchanged today in the hopes that he'd forget.

I realized in the next few seconds that he had not forgotten and was not going to just let it slide.

The subject of packing reminds me of a question I have. Should I bring enough clothes for one night or two?

"Amethyst Hamilton, you're a grown woman who makes life and death decisions every day. It shouldn't be this difficult to tell the man what you want," I said out loud as I bumped my head against the headrest of my seat. "Of course, you had to be drunk to open your mouth the first time, so that's the problem, isn't it?"

Suddenly, my phone rang in my hand, and it scared me so badly that I screamed and tossed it onto the passenger floorboard. It kept ringing, and I luckily had the presence of mind to hit the button on the dashboard display to answer the call as I crawled over the console to retrieve my phone.

"Hello!" I said in a rush right before my hand slipped and my shoulder slammed into the passenger seat, coming alarmingly close to dropping me on top of my head.

"Explain that injury to the ER nurse, why don't you?"

"What injury? Are you okay?"

I realized it was Tama'i calling, probably wondering why I hadn't answered his question yet, so I lied and said, "I'm fine."

"What are you doing?"

"Oh, just a quick upper . . ." I couldn't help the grunt that escaped when I tried to push myself up with one arm, gravity and my substantial boobs fighting me every inch of the way. "Upper body workout."

"Is that so?"

"It's a . . . Yeah. . . There's a little mix of . . . labradoodle trucking . . . Holy guacamole!"

"Amethyst? Are you there? I think you're cutting out."

"Tama'i, I'm going to have to call you back."

"Why?"

"My day has gone completely upside down. Yeah. That's it. Let me get this . . . thing I've got going on . . . Ugh. Let me take care of this, and I'll . . ."

"As much as I love the view, sweetheart, I'm going to have to ask you to reach up and open the passenger door before all the blood rushes to your head and you pass out."

"How did you . . ." I stopped talking when I realized

that the laughter I could hear in the background of the call was outside my vehicle and couldn't bite back the groan of mortification I felt when I realized I had an audience.

"Open the door, Amethyst."

I quit trying to pull myself up and sighed before I let go of the small amount of leverage I'd worked so hard for and blindly felt around the door until I found the lever. The second I had the door unlatched, it flew open. In the next instant, strong arms slid under my shoulders and hooked beneath my arms. I let out a yelp when I was lifted up so my body was parallel with the seat before I was pulled out of the passenger door. The front of my body hit a hard surface just as my eyes focused, and I saw Tama'i's smiling face even with mine.

I realized that I wasn't touching the ground, and he was holding me up by my arms like an adult would a child. Without thinking, I lifted my legs and wrapped them around his waist as I put my hands on his shoulders.

"Fancy meeting you here," I quipped as Tama'i's hands slid down my sides and around my waist.

"Hi."

"He plucked your ass out of there like you were a toddler," I heard my cousin say through his laughter.

"Oh, shit," another cousin said before a third asked, "Did you get that on video?"

"Why are you with the birdbrains?" I asked.

"The birdbrains?"

"My aunt named all of her children after birds, and as far as her male offspring goes, that seems to have been very fortuitous because their brains are the size of walnuts, maybe even pecans." I turned and glared at Hawk, Crow, and Phoenix and then realized that even more of the men I grudgingly considered family were nearby, also watching the impromptu show. I didn't say anything to my cousins before I looked back at Tama'i, whose face was just inches from mine and asked, "Why are you hanging out with the riffraff?"

"Hawk invited me over to play a pick-up game and introduce Tameka to his cousin. Cousins. Hold on. I'm confused about the . . ."

"Technically, they're both our cousins because . . . Wow. Our cousins are getting married and having a baby. That kid's gonna be . . . What would you call that?"

Without looking at him, I ordered, "Phoenix, go ask one of the children to draw a diagram to help you figure out the connection."

"You little shit," Phoenix muttered.

"I know things about all of you that would make your mother cry. Go away. Now."

"We know things about you too," Crow argued. "How's life in that glass house, Amy?"

"How is that rash, Crow?"

Phoenix and Hawk, who had been standing next to their brother, both took a step away as Crow's mouth dropped open in shock. "That's doctor-patient confidentiality!"

"I'm not your doctor, birdbrain."

"That was low even for you, Amy," Hawk chided. When I tilted my head in question and smiled, his eyes got wide and he shook his head as he put his hands up in defeat. "Don't aim that mouth at me, woman. I didn't do shit."

"Go. Away."

"I'm not poking the bear. Nope. You know how the gems get when they're cornered."

As my cousins walked off, I looked back at Tama'i and smiled. "You can put me down now."

"I kind of like having you here. Besides, if I put you down, I'll just get embarrassed, so let's hang out like this for a while." I could feel the length of his "embarrassment" against me and wiggled a little bit to test it. Tama'i groaned and said, "Stop moving around and talk to me to take my mind off of it."

"Most people don't realize that ejaculation has nothing to do with the brain. It's actually controlled through the spine, although thinking of something else to focus your mind can often hinder the spine's commands to ejaculate and . . ."

Tama'i groaned again and interrupted, "Your cousin referred to you as a gem. Is that because your name is Amethyst?"

"My aunt named her children after birds, but my mom and dad went with gemstones for their children. My sisters are named Emerald and Diamond. The only one of us that doesn't follow the theme is my brother Lazlo who was named after my father."

"And that was when you realized your dad's name wasn't Lout?"

"Exactly. It's Lazarus. Apparently, the first time they talked about having children, my mom said she'd name their first son after Dad and call him Lazlo, so that's what they did."

"I've met Opal and Pearl. Oh, and Jett. What's the other one called?"

"Two others. Onyx and Flint."

"Okay," Tama'i said as he slid his hands back to my sides and gripped my hips. He held them tight and pulled me away from his body, so I let my legs slide down as he set me on the ground. He cleared his throat and said, "I think I'm decent now."

I still had my hands on his shoulders and threw caution to the wind as I molded myself against him and said, "That's unfortunate."

"I convinced myself that I should wait to do this, but you're making it very hard."

"I am? *That* is fortunate," I said with a grin.

"Fuck it," Tama'i grumbled before he squatted down, wrapped his arms around my hips, and picked me up. Suddenly, we were eye to eye again, and I realized why he'd picked me up when his mouth touched mine.

I felt him turning a split-second before he pressed my back against the window of my SUV. I wrapped my arms around his neck and deepened the kiss as my legs went back around his waist. He held me with one hand as his other roamed up my side before he hooked his thumb under my jaw and tilted my head the way he wanted it, holding me still as his mouth devoured mine.

I was lost in everything Tama'i - his scent, his heat, his large hand gripping my ass, and the growling coming from deep in his chest. Time seemed to stand still as the tentative kiss turned into a whirlwind of passion, and I lost the ability to think of anything but how he was making me feel until I heard a sweet voice ask, "How can they breathe like that?"

Tama'i pulled his lips from mine and sucked in a long breath through his nose as he rested his forehead against mine.

"Dad said we should interrupt them," my cousin's cheerful voice announced. "Uncle Crow said we need a water hose, but I'm not sure why."

"Are they sleeping now?" the first voice asked.

"They're kissing like Mom and Dad do. It's icky." I recognized another voice and sighed when I realized we had even more of an audience than I'd first thought.

"Lyric, sweetheart, take Juni and your friend over to your dad and ask him to explain why he doesn't drink water."

"Huh?"

"Just go ask him."

"Okay!" my young cousin said cheerfully before she urged the girls, "Come on. I want to know because he makes me drink water."

The girl's voices got further away, and I finally opened my eyes to see Tama'i staring at me, just inches away.

"Why doesn't your cousin drink water?"

"Because fish fornicate in it."

Tama'i sputtered out a laugh as he looked over his shoulder at my cousins. "And you sent that little girl to ask him about that?"

"He sent them over here to interrupt us, so I thought it was the least I could do."

"You've got me all worked up again, Amethyst."

"I can feel it," I said as I squeezed my legs tighter to get him even closer to me. "You picked me up like I don't weigh anything. You know that's weird, right?"

"You're short. I don't want to get a crick in my neck."

"I'm five-foot-ten, Tama'i. According to the CDC, that's almost seven inches taller than the average American woman."

"I'm six-foot-seven, sweetheart. That's still nine inches shorter than me, so that makes you short in my book."

"You lifted me up like I was light as a feather. I'm

not going to tell you how much I weigh, but let's just say that's impressive."

"Once I get you alone and naked, I'm going to lift you up for an entirely different reason and then let you work those strong thighs I appreciate so much to . . . Nope. Nope. Not gonna go there yet."

"We're within walking distance of my bedroom. It would take about ten seconds for you to carry me into my house where we could make use of my kitchen table. Go there," I urged without thinking. Suddenly, I realized what I'd just said. "Shiitake mushrooms. I don't know what's wrong with me. I don't usually invite men I barely know into my house to . . . do things."

"I wonder if you keep your vocabulary G-rated while you orgasm."

"It's been so long since I had one with anyone else involved that I wouldn't know."

"And now I have a new mission in life."

"Are we playing ball or what?" Crow yelled from somewhere behind Tama'i.

"The Darwin in those boys is strong," I said with a sigh. "I need you to do something."

"What's that?"

"Go play football with your little friends, and every time one of them is carrying the ball, I want you to remember that they're the reason we're not naked and screaming inside my house right now. I'll give you a kiss for every time you flatten them like a pancake."

"I might hurt them."

"That would bring me great joy."

Tama'i started laughing as he reached back to unhook my legs from around his waist. "I can't hurt your family, Amethyst. I want them to like me."

"That's too bad," I said as my feet touched the ground again. As Tama'i took a step back, I said, "Go play your game. I'm going to go upstairs and finish what you started before I get ready for my date tonight."

"You're . . . Are you really going to . . ."

"Absolutely. I can't think when I'm this worked up, so I need to take the edge off."

I smiled as I hooked my arm around his neck to pull him down for a kiss. "Go out there and trample my big mouth, orgasm-blocking, irritating cousins while you imagine me upstairs moaning your name while I use my waterproof toy in the tub. I'll see you this evening when you pick me up for our date."

"But . . . I just . . ."

As I walked through my open garage door, I said, "Oh! I almost forgot to answer your question."

"I don't even know my own name right now, let alone what question I asked you," Tama'i said in a choked voice.

"I've decided you should pack for two nights, not just one."

ELEVEN

If you send me one more stupid dad joke meme, I will fold your clothes with you still in them.

Text from Amethyst to Tama'i

TAMA'I

I parked my motorcycle and then took a deep breath and blew it out slowly before I threw my leg over to stand up. I hadn't asked Amethyst if she was willing to ride tonight, but since she'd already informed me that I should pack an overnight bag, I had to assume she trusted me.

I sincerely hoped that was the case because I couldn't imagine anything better than having her pressed against me with her arms holding tight while I felt the wind on my face and the freedom of the open road ahead.

Okay, that was a complete lie. I could imagine quite a few things that would be better, but riding with her ranked somewhere in the top ten.

"Focus, dumbass," I muttered as I shook my head. I stepped onto the curb in front of Amethyst's home, a very nice house on the main street of the neighborhood just down from the entrance gates. If I did decide to rent the house from Hawk's cousin, who I'd since found out was actually Amethyst's brother-in-law, I'd live just a few blocks away.

Earlier today when I brought Tameka with me to visit

Hawk and his family, I'd gotten a quick tour of the neighborhood from Adam Forrester. He'd shown me the options of available rental homes and even let me tour two that were vacant so I could see the different floor plans. The funniest thing about that scenario was that when he mentioned square footage and what I would need to be comfortable, all I could think of was how many years I had lived in a concrete cell whose walls weren't even far enough apart for me to extend my arms out all the way.

I did appreciate the spacious rentals he had available and assured him I'd make my choice and get back to him early next week. Now, looking at the neighborhood again, I noticed even more things to appreciate about it, including how well-kept the properties were while they still maintained the unique characteristics of the people living in them.

For instance, Amethyst's front yard looked gorgeous with well-maintained grass and flower beds that showcased bright colors and different textures that reminded me of all the facets of her personality - or at least the few I'd had the pleasure of witnessing so far. I knew that there was much more to the woman and planned on taking my sweet time enjoying getting to know every last bit.

I made my way to the porch and pushed the button to ring the bell. I laughed out loud when I saw the doormat. It was black with a simple font that read, "Welcome-ish. It depends on who you are." I made a mental note to ask her where she got it because I knew my sister would get a kick out of the sentiment, and it would be funny to put it on her porch before she returned.

Suddenly, the front door opened, and the sight of Amethyst took my breath away. She had her braids pulled up into an intricate swirl on the top of her head and a dark purple bandana folded and tied so that the ends were in the front. Light purple gems dangled from her ears, and I followed their direction down to see her ample and absolutely fantastic chest covered in a long-sleeved button-up shirt that was tied in a knot at her waist above faded jeans that fit her like a glove.

They molded to her hips and thick thighs perfectly. I had to swallow hard and take a deep breath as I lost the war with my cock and felt it start to rise at the sight before me.

Black leather boots were laced up almost to her knee, and the chunky sole made her at least an inch or two taller so that when my gaze finally traveled up to her face again, I found that her kissable lips were *almost* high enough for me to consume without getting a crick in my neck.

Those lips I'd dreamed about tipped into a smile before she drawled, "You don't look so bad yourself, big guy."

I cleared my throat and found my voice so I could say, "You look beautiful, Amethyst."

"Thank you. I thought you might be riding tonight . . . Actually, I hoped you would be, so I dressed accordingly."

"Yeah, I took a chance that you already knew I wasn't a serial killer and brought my bike."

"Oh, I know nothing of the sort, but as far as I can tell, you're at least a manageable one."

"A manageable serial killer?"

"Manageable might not be the right word, but you

get what I'm saying."

"Actually, I don't," I admitted.

"Do you want to stand in my doorway and discuss word choices, or are you going to kiss me and then sweep me away on your fine metal steed?"

I didn't say a word, just closed the distance between us and swept her into my arms. When her head tilted back at just the right angle for my lips to meet hers, I felt every nerve in my body go off like fireworks at the touch.

Our kiss was more than just a greeting, but a promise of things to come. I knew she was feeling the same way when she tilted her head back to look up into my eyes and say, "We have about three seconds to get out to your motorcycle before I lose my mind, yank you into my house, and ravish your body until you're begging for mercy."

"Am I supposed to argue that because I don't see a single problem with that scenario," I admitted as I nudged her backwards. She shook her head and pushed back with our bodies still molded together. I understood she wasn't quite ready, so I loosened my hold on her and took a step back to put some distance between us as I said, "Dinner first, and then we'll play out that idea you mentioned if you haven't changed your mind by then."

"Let's do it."

Amethyst used the keypad on the door to lock it behind her and then put her hand in mine as we walked toward my motorcycle.

"Oh, that's a beauty," Amethyst said in awe as we

walked down the sidewalk. "Custom stretch? That looks longer than a factory Road Glide."

"You know your bikes."

"I may have been around one or two in my life," Amethyst teased.

"It is custom," I answered. "I had to have some specialty work done on it to make it a little more comfortable for my height."

"And your arm span. I'd imagine that you feel like a grown man riding a kid's bicycle on a regular motorcycle."

"Exactly."

"I love the paint job. The flat black suits the style, especially since you've blacked out all the chrome."

"I'm glad you approve."

Amethyst slowly walked around the bike and then bent down to look near the forks at the front. "Even your guardian bell is blacked out!"

"It was a gift from my friend Chef's old lady. She said I needed one, but it had to be as dark and twisted as the bike itself."

"It's perfect," Amethyst said as she stood up again. "I'm ready for a long ride. Maybe after dinner, we can take one around the lake and . . ."

"Can we do that on our second date? I've already made reservations for dinner and our entertainment for this evening."

"Entertainment?"

"I got some input from your sister."

"You have to be more specific," Amethyst said with a laugh as she adjusted her bandana.

As I threw my leg over the bike and got settled, I said, "Pearl helped me out."

"That's not quite as terrifying as the idea of Diamond giving you input, so I'll take it."

"What would Diamond have told me to do?"

Amethyst threw her leg over the back of the bike, settled her boots on the foot pegs, and situated herself on the seat behind me before she wrapped her arms around my waist. "Knowing Di, she'd have you take me to some movie marathon that would be a total snoozefest."

"She likes movies more than you do?"

"She enjoys the fact that people don't talk in the theater. Actually, she enjoys almost anything that includes people not talking to her, which is funny because she's a great conversationalist when she wants to be."

"She seemed pretty funny the other night over dinner."

"Until she bailed because she had plans - which I was right about, by the way. She went home to watch the next episode of one of her favorite shows."

"Are you ready?" I asked as I pushed up the

kickstand.

"Words can't even begin to describe how ready I am."

I started the bike and let it idle for a second as I scrolled through the app on my phone and selected a playlist. Once I had the phone secure in the holder I'd attached to the handlebars, I revved the engine just a touch and heard Amethyst laugh out loud.

Before I had a chance to put the bike in gear, Amethyst asked, "Does your bike have a name, Tama'i?"

"No," I said as I shook my head.

"I'm gonna name her."

I looked over my shoulder as I leaned back against Amethyst's chest. We were eye to eye and almost lip to lip when I asked, "What's her name, then?"

"Bubbles."

"What?"

"She's better than a bubble bath."

I was still laughing when I put the bike in gear and pulled away from the curb. I realized that riding my bike alone would never be quite the same again because every time I took a curve or came to a stop, I'd always remember the feeling of Amethyst nestled against my back with her legs bracketing my hips and her arms wrapped around me.

She could call my motorcycle whatever she wanted as long as she was willing to ride with me.

"I've lived here my entire life and never heard of this restaurant," Amethyst admitted as she perused the menu. "To be quite honest, I'm not sure I'd have come if I had."

"Why's that?"

"I don't know the first thing about Polynesian food. I have no idea what to order."

"It's our custom to try a little of everything, so I think you should do that."

"I wouldn't have the first clue where to start, though," Amethyst admitted as she frowned at the menu. "I trust you. Order the things you like most, and I'll try them."

"What if you don't like them?"

"I didn't get this thin, svelte figure by skipping meals, Tama'i. I'll always find something I like no matter where we are."

"And you're willing to try something new?"

"Absolutely. This evening will be a night of firsts."

"Our first date, and our first ride together."

"And the first time I've ever asked a man to order my food for me," Amethyst added.

"Thank you for letting me wow you with the culinary deliciousness of my people."

"Your entire face transforms when you do that."

"What?"

"When you smile. You don't do it often enough."

"You make me smile all the time."

"You should find things other than me that bring you enough joy to wipe the frown off your face."

"Like what?"

"Anything. Everything."

"You'll have to be more specific," I teased as I looked over the menu and chose a few appetizers and four entrees to share. She'd already seen me eat and even helped me finish off my lunch the day we met, so I wasn't worried about her thinking it odd that I would order this much food. "Off the top of your head, name ten things that make you smile."

"That's easy," Amethyst said as the server approached the table. I gave him our order, and as soon as he walked away, Amethyst put up a finger as she listed, "The feel of the wind on my face when I'm on the back of a motorcycle, the smell of warm, freshly laundered clothes as you pull them out of the dryer, how good clean sheets feel that first night after they've been washed, the excitement you feel when your phone rings and you see it's someone you haven't talked to in way too long, fat baby feet, a bee covered in pollen from the flower it just visited, a juicy peach, a handful of peanut M&M's, a big yawn accompanied by a full body stretch while I wait on the coffee pot to work its magic, and a marshmallow that's from a bonfire that's burned black, ready for me to eat the crispy outside before I make a mess enjoying the gooey center."

"I love how I feel when I'm on my bike, I hate doing laundry, but you're right about how good it smells, clean sheets are freaking awesome especially if you've just showered the day away. I like to hear from my friends as often as possible, but I don't wait for them to call me - I call them when I think of something I want to talk about or sometimes just because I can. Everything about babies is a miracle, and I get what you mean about their fat little feet. I remember the first time I got to sit down and really look at Kai - he was just a little over a year old. I remember thinking that his toes looked like little jelly beans."

"Puppy feet."

"What do you mean?"

"The pads of a puppy's feet look like little jelly beans to me."

"And I bet they make you smile, too, don't they?"

"Of course."

"I don't think I've ever seen a bee covered in pollen."

"Well, let's add it to your bucket list because it's just . . . beautiful and awesome and magical all at the same time."

The server appeared with our appetizers, and I watched Amethyst study the food in front of us with an eager expression. I had to admit that I wasn't nearly as open-minded about food as she seemed to be. I wasn't one to try new dishes and always seemed to choose the same food no matter where I ate. I had a specific Italian dish I liked to order and rarely, if ever, strayed from it. I always ordered the same pizza, I never varied my order at Mexican restaurants, and I liked my burgers a certain way.

Amethyst, on the other hand, was excited to try new things and had even trusted me to order for her. It was refreshing. Most of the women I had dated over the years were too busy counting calories or following the newest diet trend. That made it hard to find a common ground as far as food went - and I was a big man with a big appetite.

And after our kisses at her house and the bike ride, watching Amethyst smiling eagerly at me and ready to enjoy our evening together gave me another appetite altogether.

As we turned into the parking lot, I realized the place we were going to was next to a few other businesses I'd seen advertised around town. The Gauntlet, one I'd planned on visiting soon, was an extension of the gym up the street where I did my workouts almost every day, and an armory and gun range called Protect the Queen shared the same parking lot. Obviously, with my felony conviction and ongoing parole, I would not be visiting *that* establishment any time soon, if ever.

"I think you must be psychic," Amethyst said as soon as I shut off the engine. I leaned to the side and looked at her, but she was smiling at the side of the building, admiring a mural that depicted a wrecking ball decimating a quaint little town. "After the week I've had, I think this will be really good for me."

"You mentioned that it was horrible, but you didn't give me details."

"I can't," she said with a shrug. "What I can say is that some people aren't fit to care for a cactus let alone a small, trusting child, and those people need to experience long-lasting pain with permanent scarring."

"I completely agree."

"Since I can't do that, I think breaking stuff is the next best option, don't you?"

"Is the child you're talking about safe now?"

"I suppose, but how long will that last?"

"If that ends, I want you to let me know."

"And what will you do about it?"

"Deliver long-lasting pain with *extensive* permanent scarring."

Amethyst leaned forward and gave me a kiss on the cheek. "I believe you, and I appreciate the offer, Tama'i."

"Just give me a name, sweetheart."

"Someday, I might just do that."

TWELVE

I'm not saying you're dumb, but conversations with you do not inspire intellectual discussion.

Text from Amethyst to Phoenix

AMETHYST

"Well, look who finally decided to come see me," Lazlo drawled as he leaned his arms on the counter and looked Tama'i up and down. "And you even brought a friend."

"I haven't come to try out your new venture yet because anytime you're near me and I have a bat in my hand, intrusive thoughts start to creep in," I said as I stepped in front of Tama'i and glared at my brother. "Be nice, Lazarus."

"Oh, no!" Lazlo said as he put his hands up in the air. "How scary! She's using my whole name! Whatever shall I do?"

"If you're not careful, the next search and retrieval expedition you're involved in will be to get my boot out of your patootie!"

Lazlo looked at Tama'i and asked, "How can I take

her seriously when she can't even say 'ass'?"

Tama'i stuck his hand out as he said, "Tiny Fuamatu."

My brother shook Tama'i's hand and introduced himself. When Lazlo winced, I looked up at Tama'i and saw him raise his eyebrows in question. When Lazlo finally let go of his hand, I saw him flex his fingers a few times and realized he'd tried the 'strong grip' intimidation handshake, but it had backfired spectacularly.

I was grinning when I asked, "I assume we have an appointment?"

Lazlo nodded as he said, "Pearl made the arrangements earlier, but then I guess she talked to you a little later and called to make some changes."

"Changes?" Tama'i asked.

"We've got different set-ups, and Pearl said that Amy probably needed the extreme room after the week she'd had."

"It must have been really bad," Tama'i said as he studied my face.

I felt myself starting to shut down as I thought about today's events, but my brother got Tama'i's attention when he said, "Do you think that fucker is going to give you any more grief?"

"What fucker?"

I sighed and answered, "One of my patient's parents

disagreed with something I did Friday and came to the office to express his displeasure."

Lazlo scoffed. "His *displeasure*, Amy? Seriously?"

"Did he put his hands on you?" Tama'i asked in a deadly calm voice.

"Uncle Terran intercepted him and then got the cops involved, but she needs to be careful because they won't keep him locked up forever," Lazlo explained.

Without thinking, I blurted, "He was angry because they took his son, Lazlo. Of course he shouldn't have . . ."

"I don't give a fuck what happened. No man is allowed to threaten you other than me and the boys."

"The boys?" Tama'i asked, his expression so angry that it took everything I had not to take a step back.

Somehow, I knew he would never hurt me, so I stayed in place as I said, "Lazlo and my brothers have been forcing me to whoop them on the regular since they were small children. Just because they're adults doesn't mean I have to stop."

"Oh, really?"

"I love hard, but I hit harder," I boasted.

Tama'i burst out laughing as Lazlo grumbled, "Damn right, she does."

"Speaking of, show me where we go to hit things before I start with you."

"You do realize that you're a doctor now, and you're supposed to be a rational adult who is an upstanding citizen and all that shit, right?" Lazlo asked as he pulled a key off the rack behind him. He turned around and glared at me before he said, "You'll get to pick your weapon, but you better not come after me with it."

"We'll see. And just so you know, Tama'i, I'm a perfectly rational adult and very professional doctor who loves my patients and wants what's best for them. That doesn't mean I can't also be a big sister whose little brothers occasionally need a physical reminder of who is in charge."

"When was the last time you gave one of them that reminder?" Tama'i asked.

"She dislocated my finger at Thanksgiving last year."

"And then I put it back where it was supposed to be," I reminded him. I looked at Tama'i and said, "Can you believe he's *still* whining about that?"

"And why did you dislocate his finger?"

"He stuck it in the middle of the pumpkin pie so I wouldn't want a slice."

"Your family has a thing about food, don't they?" Tama'i asked.

"We're very territorial about it," I confirmed.

"I watched you eat off of everyone's plate but your own at dinner the other night!"

"It's irritating, isn't it?" Lazlo asked. "Word of advice: When you're eating in the presence of my sisters, hunch over your plate and be prepared to stab whoever comes after your food."

"I'll keep that in mind," Tama'i agreed.

"We're in the middle of a date, Lazlo." I snapped my fingers a few times because I knew how irritated that made him and then motioned toward the key in his hand. "Get to work."

"One of these days, you're gonna do that and I'm going to dislocate *your* finger," Lazlo threatened. When Tama'i growled low in his throat, Lazlo said, "Dude, I think it's great that you're protective and all because I am, too, but you can't really think you'll be able to stop a war that's been going on our entire lives."

"He'll learn to sit back and enjoy watching me whoop on you just like Dad does," I assured my brother.

"You're going to keep me around that long?"

"We'll see," I said with a grin.

"If you're smart, you'll drop her at her house this evening, make sure she gets inside safely, and then run for the hills."

"Not gonna happen," Tama'i said as he smiled at me, instead of looking at my brother.

"You're gonna regret that," Lazlo promised.

"I guess we'll see."

Tama'i and I followed Lazlo down a long hallway past several closed doors until we finally came to one that he used the key to unlock. As he waved us past him into the room, he said, "For safety, you've got to put on the Tyvek suit including the booties. Make sure the hood covers your hair and put the goggles on so that the strap secures it over your head." Lazlo picked up one of the suits and held it up in front of him before he winced and said, "Pearl said you'd need the biggest size we have, but I'm still not sure it's going to fit." He looked down at Tama'i's boots and said, "I can guarantee the booties won't."

"I'll wear the suit, and my feet will be fine without any covering."

"They're leather, so you're probably right," Lazlo agreed as he handed Tama'i the suit in his hand. He picked the other one up and held it out towards me, but when I tried to take it, he held on and said, "Take as long as you need in here, Amy, and if this isn't enough, let me know and I'll put you in another room."

"Thanks, Lazzy," I said with a smile as he finally released the suit.

"Love you. Call me if you need anything, alright?"

"Just open the door and . . ."

"I mean anytime."

"Of course," I assured him. When he nodded, I smiled and said, "Love you, little brother."

Lazlo rolled his eyes as he walked back out. "Whatever."

As soon as he shut the door, Tama'i said, "Your family dynamic is hard to understand."

"Not really. It's like I said earlier - we love hard, but we hit harder."

"Then I guess I brought you to the right place."

"That was better than therapy," I said as I walked out ahead of Tama'i. I flexed my bicep and said, "And now I won't need to lift weights next week because that definitely worked my shoulders and my arms.

"I don't know who came up with the concept of having people pay to break worthless shit, but I have to say, it's genius."

"When you hit that television, it *exploded!*" I cheered.

"I have a feeling I'm going to keep your brother in business . . . at least until I tell my club brothers about this place. They'll come in like a plague of locusts and take out his entire stock."

"That won't ever happen. He's got every person in our family stopping at garage sales and thrift stores, haggling to buy any breakables they can find."

Tama'i threw his leg over his bike and sat down before he held his hand out to help steady me as I got on behind him. "Do you feel better now?"

"I do."

"I understand you had a bad day, and I want you to know there's no pressure about what we discussed earlier," Tama'i assured me.

"First of all, I don't cave to pressure. It's not in my nature. Secondly, I'm relaxed and energized after the best date in history. If you are even half as skilled with those long fingers as I hope you are, I'll sleep better after an orgasm."

"Just one?"

"Are you passing out multiples?" I asked saucily. When Tama'i grinned, I shivered and took his hand.

"You only mentioned my fingers, sweetheart. You didn't even consider what my tongue can do." Tama'i laughed when I gasped and then said, "I'm not tooting my horn or anything but . . ."

"Take me home, and I'll do that for you," I blurted.

Tama'i burst out laughing and then revved the engine before he leaned to the side and looked back at me. "I want you to know that I'm not saying this because I hope I'm about to get laid, but you're a pretty awesome woman, Amethyst Hamilton."

"Thank you for the compliment, Tama'i. However, I think you should know that hope is a wonderful thing, but certainty is even better."

The ride across town only took a few minutes, but by the time we pulled up in front of my house, I knew that my hands and mouth had pushed Tama'i to the edge. I used the fact that I was up against him with my arms around his body to my advantage and ran my hands over his chest and abdomen while occasionally reaching further down and cupping his thick erection through his jeans. Of course, while I was exploring him with my hands, I kept my lips and teeth busy against the back of his neck and felt him shiver when I hit a sensitive spot.

I'd known since the evening he shared dinner with my family that I'd end up inviting Tama'i to spend the night sooner or later. The day we got together for lunch clinched it. Since then, we'd been texting back and forth almost constantly, talking on the phone every night before bed and even a few times during the day when we happened to be free at the same time.

I wasn't usually one to invite a man back to my house after spending just one evening together, but I *was* the type to always follow my instincts. Right now, they were screaming that the decision I had made was right. However, there was still a part of my brain that kept nagging me. *"What happens after one night? Is that all you're worth? Is that all* he's *worth?"*

The second he turned the bike off, Tama'i pushed down the kickstand and stood up. I barely had a chance to let go of his waist before he lifted his leg over the bike to stand next to the curb. Before I knew what was happening, I was in the air and Tama'is mouth was on mine. He turned us away from the curb and started walking purposefully toward the front door. He was a man on a mission, and I was all in.

I pulled away so I could turn my upper body toward the keypad but punched the wrong buttons when Tama'i started jostling me. By the time I'd punched the code in wrong three times, he stopped so I was able to get us inside on the fourth try. The door swung open, and he walked through it and kicked it closed behind him before he looked around and found the stairs. Without a word, he took them two at a time, and when we got to the top, he wasn't even winded. I wanted to hate him a little bit, but I was too busy trying to untuck his shirt so I could rip it off the second he found my bedroom.

"End of the hall," I murmured with my lips against his neck.

For once in my life, my fear of the dark came in handy. The night lights I had strategically placed all over the house lit the way for Tama'i to easily find his way down the hall, and within just a few seconds, we were in my room.

As Tama'i bent forward to lay me down on the bed, I held on to his neck and kept him with me. I finally did what I'd imagined so often and ran my fingers through his hair, pulling out the band he used to hold it back and letting it fall like a curtain on either side of my face. Suddenly, Tama'i stood up, and I had to force myself to let my hands drop.

I finally got what I'd been waiting so impatiently for and watched as he pulled his shirt off and tossed it aside. The muscles of his chest rippled, and I watched the play of the dim lighting highlight the dark tattoos on his chest and abdomen.

Without thinking, I said, "Damn, you're pretty."

Tama'i laughed as he picked up my left leg. As he unzipped my boot, he said, "Isn't that supposed to be my line?"

"You're welcome to tell me that, but I just thought

you should know it applies to you too."

Tama'i tossed my boot aside and started on the other one as he said, "You're not pretty."

"Oh. Well . . ."

He threw my other boot aside and leaned forward. I thought he was about to come close enough for me to touch, but instead, he unbuttoned my jeans and pulled down the zipper before he grabbed my ankles and started tugging at the hem.

"Help me out here, sweetheart," Tama'i ordered. I shimmied, and my jeans slid down my legs and landed with a thump on the floor. As Tama'i reached for my panties and slowly pulled them down, he said, "You're not pretty, Amethyst. You're beautiful. Funny. Gorgeous. Smart. Stunning." As he tossed my panties aside, he dropped down between my knees and said, "And I bet you're delicious."

I barely had time to react before his hands pressed against my thighs to spread them wide and his tongue touched my clit. I clutched the sheets at my side, trying to find purchase to hold me down on the earth because with the magic he was creating between my legs I felt like I was going to float off into the ether. I *felt* him chuckle - the vibrations doing miraculous things as he sucked my clit into his mouth, and then realized he was laughing at me.

Without even thinking about it, the grip I had on the sheets was transferred to his hair, and I was pulling him closer than humanly possible. I wasn't sure how in the hell the man had managed to breathe so far, but since he hadn't stopped, I assumed he was managing. He was a big man and could take care of himself. Right now, I could only seem to focus on how well he was taking care of me.

Those fingers I'd admired more than a few times moved up my thighs and explored my entrance before he slowly pushed two inside. I felt his other hand slowly move around my leg to rest on my abdomen right above my pubic bone and then suddenly push down with firm pressure. I wondered what he was doing for a second, but then his fingers spun around and pressed upward as if he was trying to feel the movement with his hand on my stomach. He pushed down a little more firmly at the same time he made a come hither motion with his fingers right before I saw fireworks.

When I heard a woman screaming his name, it took me a second to realize that the hoarse shout was coming from me. I was the one screaming as my body writhed beneath him with the most intense orgasm I'd ever experienced. Just when I thought I was about to come down and be able to catch my breath, he moved his fingers a fraction and it started all over again.

I was a breathless, panting mess when he pulled his mouth away from my clit, and I whimpered as his fingers slowly slid out of my pussy and tugged my hands from his hair. I couldn't focus, couldn't think, couldn't do anything but stare as he rose up like a bronzed god and locked eyes with me as he unbuttoned his pants and let them slide down over his thighs. He pushed his boxer briefs down and his cock sprang free, bobbing as he stepped out of the pile of clothing at his feet.

I had a moment of panic when I thought of how big he was in comparison to what had entered my body before, either with previous sexual partners or the toys that I had collected over the years. The scientist and medical professional in me knew that it would fit, but the woman who would be sore tomorrow cowered at the thought of the damage a cock like his could do.

I was still pondering that thought as he finished rolling a condom on and then laid down on the bed beside me and slid his arm under my back. With an ease I could barely comprehend, he lifted me up and rolled me toward him at the same time until I was laying over his body, sprawled out like a starfish, still unable to move my limbs.

My legs naturally fell to the side until I was straddling his hips. I felt his hand move over my thigh right before his cock bobbed beneath me and slid up and down against my sex. He swirled it around my clit a few times before he slowly pushed inside me, and without conscious thought, I pushed my hands against the bed to lift my upper body so I could slowly slide down his length.

Just like I knew it would, my body stretched around him, but I held myself still for a few seconds while I looked down into his handsome face.

Without thinking, I said, "You know that shouldn't fit, but it does anyway, but now I'm not sure if I should start moving or run away."

Tama'i burst out laughing while he used a hand to push against my shoulder, forcing me to sit up straighter and naturally helping me to take him even deeper. Once I was fully settled on top of him, I rested my hands on his chest.

His skin was so soft that I couldn't help but run my hands over it and only stopped when he tugged my shirt up. Once I'd thrown it aside, I leaned forward to brace myself, and the second I lifted up, he moved his hips and followed me. Before I could lower myself any further, he started moving, his grip on my hips holding me still as he flexed beneath me.

The rhythm he set worked perfectly with the way I moved my hips, and within just a few minutes, I could feel myself on the brink of another orgasm. The second I let go, so did Tama'i, and he flipped us over so that he was above me, his strong hips powering into me so deep that I knew I'd never feel this way with any man but him. As I mindlessly moved beneath him, caught in the throes of the way he was making me feel, he let out a string of words I didn't understand. The second I felt myself relax after my orgasm, he moaned loudly and collapsed on top of me, holding himself up by his forearms so that he didn't crush me with his weight.

As his lips met mine in a languid kiss, I felt his cock twitching deep inside me, and I knew that he was feeling the same bliss I'd felt multiple times already. As he slowly moved back and forth, his cock started to soften, but when I felt him start to pull out, I wrapped my arms around his neck and murmured against his lips, "Not yet. Stay with me."

Tama'i pushed all the way in again and held himself above me, his nibbling kisses against my neck the perfect end to the wave of bliss I'd felt.

"I've gotta clean up, sweetheart."

"I know, but I like this part."

"Give me two minutes."

Grudgingly, I let him go. When he stood up beside the bed, I turned onto my side and curled up into my favorite position. I was more relaxed than I'd been in months. My entire body felt like it was humming with the afterglow of the attention Tama'i had paid it. It didn't take long for him to finish in the bathroom, and when I heard him washing his hands at the sink, I opened my eyes, hoping to get a show as he walked back to bed.

I was not disappointed.

THIRTEEN

I wouldn't exactly describe Tutu as mean, but she's got this magical ability to turn a flip-flop into a sedative.

Text from Tama'i to Amethyst

AMETHYST

Tama'i's broad shoulders and thick biceps fit him perfectly. He did have muscles, an abundance of them, but he wasn't thin and muscular. No, he was thick with an astoundingly solid frame. His stomach was firm with a hint of the abs that were so prominent on romance novel covers and advertisements. He wasn't overweight by any means, but instead, the very definition of *thick*. He had a massive neck, broad shoulders, huge biceps, a strong chest, and thighs like tree trunks. And that wonderfully thick cock that was now content and happy, hung there like it was just waiting to thicken again.

"You keep looking at me like I'm dinner," Tama'i warned.

"I was just admiring your body, and let me reiterate that there is nothing tiny about you. I don't know where you got that nickname, but I'm not ever going to use it because I have personal experience that proves you aren't any kind of tiny."

"You're good for my ego, but I have to tell you that you've been calling me Tiny since we first met."

"Not even once," I argued.

"My name is Tama'i Koa Fuamuatu. I was so premature that the doctors warned my parents that I would most likely be a sickly child and adult if I survived. Since they weren't sure how long I'd live and because I'd already beaten so many odds just by staying alive my first few days, they gave me the name 'tiny warrior' - Tama'i Koa."

"Malarky!"

"I know that's a word, but I've actually never heard it used in real life," Tama'i remarked as he crawled into bed. He slipped his arm under my pillow and then threw his other over my waist. "You never cuss, do you?"

"Never."

"I don't think that's a bad thing, but I am curious about it."

"Everyone in my family cusses. My youngest brother's first word was the f-bomb and his first complete sentence was instructions on exactly where to kiss him. Most people think I don't cuss because I work with children, and while that's a good reason, that's not really why."

"Tell me why."

"I'm the only member of my entire family, most of the children included, that doesn't curse."

"So the fact that you don't makes you unique."

"Exactly, and in a family as large as mine, it's hard to find something that can do that. We're all more alike than we'd probably care to admit, so each of us has found a thing that makes us special."

"There are many things besides your vocabulary that make you special."

"Name five."

"Brains, sense of humor, the way the left side of your lip lifts just a little higher when you smile . . ." Tama'i's voice trailed off when my phone started ringing.

"That's Squid," I said, recognizing the ringtone. Before I could move, Tama'i rolled to his back and picked my pants up from the floor. As soon as he handed them to me, I pulled my phone out and hit the button to answer the video call. The second I saw Cydney's face, I asked, "What's wrong?"

"I knew you'd think something terrible happened, but I really needed to talk to you, so I called anyway."

"You're okay?"

"I'm fine."

"How's Bella?"

Cydney laughed wickedly and said, "Last time I saw her, she was on her way to being better than fine."

"What does that mean?"

"Are you naked?"

"Where is Bella?"

"Oh! I guess the date went better than I imagined it would."

"Have you been drinking?"

"I'm in Vegas, Amy. Of course I've been drinking. Is he still there?"

"Yes."

"Is he naked? Is he asleep? Show me if he lives up to his name. Okay, I guess that wouldn't . . ."

"He's not asleep, Squid. He can hear everything you're saying."

"Hi!" Cydney said cheerfully. "You probably don't remember me, but I met you at the wedding."

Tama'i got closer so Cydney could see him on the screen and said, "I remember. Are you okay?"

"I'm fine. I won't keep Amy long, I just need to get some information to her."

"Do you need me to get out of here so you can talk?" Tama'i asked.

"Just don't hold anything you hear against me, okay?"

"I won't."

"Okay, here's the scoop, Amy. I'm going to do something I've never done before and probably never will again. I didn't call so you'd talk me out of it, just so that you wouldn't kill me later when you found out I did a 'what happens in Vegas stays in Vegas thing.'"

"Don't you dare get married, Cydney Mason!"

"Girl, really?"

"What are you going to do?"

"I'm going to spend the night with a man I just met. Don't judge me."

"Not judging, just concerned."

"I'm going to send you a picture of his ID and then share my location with you so you know where I end up, okay?"

"Are you serious right now?"

"He's smart, funny, tattooed, and sexy. He doesn't know anything about me, and that's kind of refreshing, so, yes. I'm completely serious right now."

"You're gonna do this even if I give you ten reasons why this is a bad idea, aren't you?"

"Can I make a suggestion?" Tama'i asked.

"Sure," Cydney agreed.

"Where are you?"

"I'm at Caesars."

"Don't leave the hotel," Tama'i said simply. "If you want to bump uglies with a stranger, make him pay for a room and don't leave the property. Send Amethyst the picture of his ID, walk with him to the front desk to get the room key, and tell the desk clerk that you're going up to his room with him."

"Just throw my business right out there, huh?"

"They have facial recognition software all over that place. If something happens, you'll be on their radar from that point on, so make sure you have your hair out of your face so it can pick up your features. They'll also have him on record too."

"Good idea."

"I don't know that it will help in the event you're in danger, but it will at least give us some idea of where to start looking if something happens," Tama'i admitted grudgingly. "I've got some good friends there, so if you need anything, call Amethyst and I'll get you their contact information. If Amethyst hasn't heard from you by ten tomorrow morning, I'll call and have them track you down."

"I like him," Cydney said cheerfully.

"Girl, you're crazy. Send me a pic of his license."

"It's on its way. Love your face, hag! I hope I have as much fun as you obviously have with that whole afterglow vibe you've got going on. High five, big guy! You're doing something right!" Tama'i was still laughing when Cydney waved and then ended the call.

A few seconds later, I got the text with the picture of a man's driver's license. I saved it to my phone just in case something happened to the message and then put my phone down as I considered what was going on, not just in Vegas, but here in Rojo too.

"What are you thinking about?"

"I'm worried about Squid. This isn't like her at all."

"People do crazy things in Vegas. One night stands and hook-ups aren't uncommon. People are wild and free for a limited time, away from their home, and for some reason, want to do things they'd never do otherwise. I lived there for years, and believe me, I've seen some things."

"When you lived in Vegas, did you . . ."

"Did I what?"

"Were you the local hot guy that tourists tried to hook up with?"

"I wasn't a monk, if that's what you're asking."

"I've never had a one-night stand before."

Tama'i looked pensive before he asked, "Is that what you think this is?"

"Do you?"

"I'll tell you what I'd like to think this is," Tama'i said as he wrapped his arms around my waist and pulled me close again. "This is that time between wake and sleep where your mind starts to wander and think of all the good things about your day and the good things that are going to happen tomorrow."

"I guess I never really thought of it that way," I

admitted.

"So, right now, I am thinking about how much I loved holding you close in the sunshine, how your smiles and laughter somehow made dinner taste better, and how much aggression you had stored inside you before you finally let it all out tonight."

"I'm sorry I cried."

"Never apologize for showing true emotion, Lalelei," Tama'i said sternly. "I think you believe that you should hide your pain behind laughter and smiles, and while that may be true when you're working, that shouldn't be the case when you're with your family or me."

"I love my patients, and it hurts my heart to see them neglected or abused," I admitted. "Parents know that me and the other staff at the clinic are mandatory reporters. It's crazy how many parents come in with a running list of how their child got each bump, bruise, and scrape, but others come in with a child who is in obvious pain and don't seem to have any idea why or see the problem with that."

"Is that what happened today?"

"I can't give you exact details, but no, that's not what happened. A mom brought her son in because he wasn't acting like himself. It's obvious that she sincerely loves him and wants what's best for him, but I still had to make the call to take him away until they can find the root of the problem and make sure he's safe."

"Did they find out what's going on?"

"From the reaction of the boy's father, I'd say that they've narrowed it down."

"And he came in yelling at you about it?"

"His girlfriend watches his son while he's working, and from what I gather, the police believe she's been giving him alcohol to make him sleep while he's alone with her."

"What did the mother say?"

"She was beside herself, worried about long-term damage to his little body and furious that someone would do such a thing."

"And the father?"

"He insisted that his girlfriend would never do such a thing and it's just his ex making a play for full custody."

"And what do you think?"

"All I know is that when I opened that sippy cup, I smelled alcohol, and it's my job to make sure he's okay. Unfortunately, I'll probably never see him again to make sure of that because even though his mother *hopefully* didn't have anything to do with it, she'll never trust me again because I'm the person that set the wheels in motion to take her child away, at least temporarily."

"I'm sure she'll thank you for that one day, or at least be able to admit that it was the right thing for you to do."

"I hope so."

"Now, back to what we were talking about," Tama'i redirected. "I listed a few of the good things that happened today, and I'm now focusing on tomorrow."

"What are your plans?"

"I'm wondering if I'll be able to sneak into the kitchen and cook breakfast in bed for you before I explore your smooth skin with my tongue."

"Oh." I swallowed hard at that image and felt my entire body wake up at the thought of what that would entail. I finally said, "That sounds pleasant."

"Pleasant?" Tama'i asked. "Obviously, I've got some work to do because pleasant is not anything like I'd describe it."

"How would you describe it?"

"Hot. Wild. Loud. Fantastic."

"Those words work too."

"Tell me what you think this is between us, Lalelei."

"Does that mean Amethyst in . . . what language? Samoan?"

"It means beauty in Samoan."

"Thank you," I whispered shyly.

"Talk to me."

"I do want breakfast in the morning, but I'd rather cook it together after we wake up and have more of that excellence we just experienced."

"Excellence?"

"I've been trying to find another word to explain it, but for the first time in my life, I'm speechless."

"We're very different, you and I."

"You're never speechless? I guess that gives me a goal."

"I think what I'm trying to say is that you and I are on opposite ends of the spectrum as far as backgrounds and careers."

"I haven't ever been to prison."

"And you still haven't asked me why I was there."

I snuggled closer to him and rested my hand on his chest before I yawned. I asked, "Are you ever going back?"

Tama'i thought about it longer than I expected him to before he finally answered, "I can't say never because I'd go back again for the exact same reason if it came down to it."

I drifted off to sleep wondering what reason he could possibly think of that would validate him committing another crime that cost him months or even years of his life but didn't have a chance to ask about it before sleep pulled me under.

FOURTEEN

Somewhere out there, someone is thinking about you and the tremendous impact you had on their life.

It's not me. I think you're an idiot.

Text from Amethyst to Hawk

TAMA'I

"Have you lost your mind?" I heard my friend Hawk call out from somewhere to my right, but I didn't look over until I was done with my set. When I finished my count, I unhooked my legs from the parallel bar and then flipped backward and landed on my feet. "What the fuck are you doing?"

I looked toward the sound of Hawk's voice and found him walking across the grass with three men. I recognized Adam Forrester, Hawk's cousin who had given me a tour of the available houses here at Lonestar Terrace. One of the other men looked familiar for some reason. I was sure I'd met him somewhere before but couldn't remember his name. The other man had a baby strapped to his chest in one of those sling carrier things.

"I'm knitting a scarf. What does it look like I'm doing?" I asked when they were close enough so that I didn't have to yell.

"Causing a wrinkle in the space-time continuum by setting the phone lines on fire with gossip and waking up every damn woman in a three-mile radius."

"Well, I'm not knitting, but I'm not doing that either," I said with a bark of laughter.

"Oh, but you are," the man with the baby said as he shook his head sadly. "I was planning on having a nice, relaxing morning. I thought I'd get the baby back to sleep and then snuggle up with my old lady, but then her phone started going off before she got dressed and left for God knows where."

"I had plans, too, but Rain got a call and took off too," the familiar-looking man said as he stopped at the end of the monkey bars and reached up to test their stability. "I don't even know if I can do what you were doing."

"Try it," Hawk encouraged.

"You try it," the man argued.

"Fuck it. I'll try it," Adam said as he stepped up next to the first man.

Hawk scoffed. "Neither of you can handle it. Let me show you how it's done."

"I'm just gonna stand here and look pretty with Star."

"Pussy. You know you can't do it," Adam challenged.

"I sure the hell can!" the man with the baby argued.

"Prove it. I've got ten that says you can't do twenty reps," Hawk goaded.

"You better jump up there, fucker," the man growled as he started undoing the straps of the sling. Suddenly, he thrust the baby toward me and said, "Hold her while I school these assholes."

I didn't have a chance but to take the baby who was staring at me with wide eyes. I smiled at her while the men around me argued good-naturedly and then held her against my chest while I watched the competition that was forming.

"You're gonna have to be an impartial judge," the man who'd given me his baby to hold said as he stretched his arms above his head in preparation for the competition that was brewing. "Star can help."

"Is that your bike in front of Amy's place?" the man with the white streak in his hair, asked.

"Tiny, I guess I should introduce you to these rude asses," Hawk said as he started twisting at the waist to stretch his core. "The guy with the baby is my cousin, Ruf. That's his daughter, Star, you're holding. The guy with the skunk hair is Lucky, and you know Adam, of course."

"It's nice to meet y'all," I said as I settled myself down on one of the swings not far from the monkey bars and used my toe to gently sway back and forth to soothe the baby who wasn't nearly as comfortable in my arms as her father's. "What are the parameters of the competition? Are you just trying to get to twenty reps or see who can do the most?"

"And you can't forget the dismount," Hawk added. "Been an age since I did that shit, and I'm probably gonna bust my head open, but it looked cool."

"We're all gonna end up in traction," Adam said sadly as he put his hands on the bars and leaned forward, probably to stretch out his abs.

"What are you assholes doing out here at the crack of fucking dawn?" Phoenix, Hawk's brother, asked as he jogged toward us. "I was just in my house, minding my own fucking business, when I was invaded by *your* women who took over *my* coffee pot and are huddled in front of the picture window watching you fools out here measuring your dicks."

I saw Hawk wave at someone behind me and turned to find an audience of women, all holding coffee mugs, filing out onto the front porch of a house across the street from the park.

Hawk motioned for the women to join us and yelled, "Come on over, ladies. We need you to help keep score."

"I've got twenty on you, babe!" one of the women called out as she walked toward us. "You've got this!"

Lucky, the man with the stripe in his hair, preened from the attention and then elbowed Adam and said, "You're going down, old man."

"Fuck you," Adam scoffed. "Lazy ass."

"I didn't get this pretty being lazy," Lucky argued.

"If you try and hang with the young folks, you're gonna end up in traction," Hawk teased.

"You keep talking shit, and *you're* gonna end up in traction," Adam threatened. He yelled, "Em, come whip your cousin. He's talking shit."

"When is he not talking shit?" the woman retorted as she got closer.

"Are y'all gonna stand around or do some work?" the blonde woman I'd met at Dub's wedding and recognized as Hawk's old lady asked. She clapped her hands and said, "Get to it, babe. I've got twenty on you."

"What are all of you doing awake at this ungodly hour?"

Suddenly, I realized that Amethyst was walking my way, and it took everything I had not to laugh at her appearance. She was still wearing her sleep bonnet and had on a tank top and a pair of men's boxers with slippers that looked like bear paws. In her hand, she held a large aluminum mug that I hoped was filled with coffee because she still looked half-asleep and probably needed the pick-me-up.

Without any other greeting, Amethyst dropped a quick kiss on my lips and then sat down in front of me on the rubber mulch that covered the ground and promptly started talking shit to the men in front of us.

"You're too puny to play with the big dogs, birdbrain. Go sit down, and be quiet!"

"Do you hear her talking trash, Brighten?" Hawk asked the blonde woman. "Are you gonna let that slide?"

"Are you gonna whoop all their asses and leave them crying on the ground at our feet?" she asked.

"Of course," he boasted.

"Then there's no need to interact with the riffraff

since they'll see you're the best when it's all said and done."

"Riffraff?" Adam's pregnant girlfriend asked incredulously. She scoffed and then looked over at Amethyst and said, "Take care of my lightweight, little sister."

Suddenly, I put two and two together and realized the woman must be Emerald, Amethyst's oldest sister who was engaged to Hawk's cousin. Or she was his cousin . . . but so was he and . . . I shook my head, knowing that mapping out the family tree wasn't something I'd likely ever be able to do. I looked down at the sweet little girl in my arms. She was still blinking at me even though she'd stopped squirming, so I kept the steady rhythm of the swing going in the hopes of keeping her calm.

"I see why Mom gets all mushy and teary-eyed about it now," Emerald said as she studied me. "I'm feeling a little misty-eyed myself."

"That's not what I'm feeling," Amethyst muttered as she looked at the baby in my arms.

A woman I hadn't met yet sat down next to Amethyst and reached out to touch the baby's foot before she said, "When Ruf stretches out in the recliner, shirtless with the baby on his chest, my ovaries start doing somersaults." She smiled at me and said, "Hi. I'm Jovi."

"It's a pleasure to meet you," I said as I stuck my hand out to shake hers. "Is this your little girl?"

"She is."

"Do you want to take her?" I asked.

"I'll kill you where you stand," Amethyst threatened in a menacing voice.

"And that's a no," Jovi said with a grin before she turned to watch the men preen and stretch, getting ready for their competition. "Are your ovaries doing backflips, Amy?"

"Pickle you, cootie queen," Amethyst retorted.

"I got puked on by *two* of your patients this week, and now you're telling me to pickle off? Rude."

"I found a pile of human shit in the master bedroom closet of a house I was showing yesterday," Hawk's woman blurted.

"Puke is still worse," Jovi said nonchalantly.

"I love my job," Rain, Lucky's girlfriend, said as she laid down on the grass and propped herself up on one elbow so she could see the men bickering. "And the more I listen to all of you talk about your jobs, the more I realize that the best part of mine is that I don't have to talk to people."

"What do you do for a living?" I asked.

"I'm an accountant."

"I'm a tattoo artist."

"I know, honey," Rain said with an odd smile.

"That was rude," Amethyst snapped.

Rain asked, "Am I supposed to pretend that the hot new tattoo artist hasn't been the subject of *multiple* conversations lately?"

Her explanation made me feel better since I'd thought she was looking down on me for my profession.

"We all know he was on that television show because Fain and Wrath were arguing at the wedding about who got to keep him."

"I remember that," Emerald said. "They played rochambeau, right?"

"Technically, I had already made the choice to move to Rojo before I even met the Tempest family." Emerald shrugged as if she was dismissing my decision and thought I'd have ended up in Colorado Springs if the brother who owned that location of Tempest Tattoos had won the game. "I moved here to watch over my niece and nephews while their parents are deployed."

Emerald leaned closer and asked, "How is that going?"

"She's a shrink," Amethyst said with an eye roll. "You'll have to get used to that."

Without thinking, I asked, "Does that mean you're keeping me around?"

"How does that make you feel?" Emerald asked, her gaze intense.

"Back off, Cujo," Amethyst warned. She looked at me and smiled before she said, "You don't have to answer her. Sometimes she forgets that we're not her test subjects."

"Have you ever looked at our family? There are so many cases to study," Emerald said dreamily.

"Do you own a mirror?" Amethyst asked.

"Here you go, Amy," Brighten said as she thrust her coffee mug toward Amethyst. "Let's avoid bloodshed so early in the morning. I've already got a load in the washer *and* the dryer, so there's no way I'll be able to get rid of bloodstains before they set."

Amethyst ignored her friend's comment but took the mug. After she'd had a sip, she moaned and then asked, "Speaking of mirrors, why did you put a towel over the one in the bathroom?"

I shrugged and said, "That's what we do."

"We, as in a collective of . . ." Emerald let her voice trail off, leading me to give an explanation.

"In my culture, you cover the mirrors with something so that the dark spirits won't come to you at night if you accidentally look at your reflection."

Amethyst blinked a few times and then asked, "You cover all the mirrors in your home every night?"

"In my sister's house, all the mirrors tilt so that you can't see your reflection," I explained without exactly answering her question.

"Hmm," Amethyst said, her expression thoughtful.

"Are we talking about dark spirits like ghosts or something more sinister?" Rain asked.

"It depends on who you ask."

"Have you ever seen one?" Rain asked.

"No, but I've never tried. I'm not going to either."

"Big guy like you shouldn't be afraid," Emerald teased.

"Size is relative. Evil can seep in through the smallest cracks, and before you know it, everything you thought you knew is wrong."

"Are you speaking from personal experience?" Emerald asked.

"And we're out," Amethyst said as she suddenly stood up. She reached out and tugged on my hand so I would stand. "He promised me breakfast."

"Lucky dog," Jovi said enviously. "We're gonna be stuck here for an hour watching them try to one up each other."

"Come on," Amethyst said as she pulled me toward her house. I didn't even have a chance to say goodbye because she was moving at a fast clip like a woman on a mission.

We were already inside her house when I realized I was still carrying the baby. I looked down at her in shock and then toward the door, expecting an angry mob, or at least her parents to come barrelling in any second.

"What's wrong?"

"I've still got their kid," I said in shock.

"Oh," Amethyst said with a shrug as she set the two mugs down on the side table. As she walked over to the closet, she asked, "At least she's not screaming, right?"

"But . . ." I stopped talking as Amethyst pulled out an infant bouncy seat and a basket of toys and supplies.

"They'll come get her when they're ready."

"But I . . . They just . . ."

"It's not like you kidnapped her."

"I kind of did, didn't I?"

"Nah. They know where she is, and I'm clearly qualified to care for infants." Amethyst took the baby from my arms and held her close as she leaned down and took a deep breath. In a voice full of awe, she said, "She's got the smell."

"What do we do with her?"

"Knowing who her father is, I'd have to say the most important thing we can do for the next twenty years or so is make sure she doesn't get her hands on any weapons or matches. Basically anything sharp or flammable. The Forrester spawn are all unpredictable except for anything that has to do with engines, explosives, or fire."

"What happens then?"

"They race it, blow it up, or torch it," Amethyst said as if that was a given. "They're generally harmless as long as you know what to watch for."

"You make them all sound like they're certifiable."

Amethyst balanced the baby against her chest and reached out to pat my arm. "Honey, you have no idea."

"Can I borrow these?" Aspen asked as she walked like a supermodel across the kitchen, the heels on her feet tapping on the tile.

"You need to practice walking in them before you . . ."

"Absolutely not!"

"Those are fantastic!"

The young woman didn't seem phased that there were three people talking to her at once and answered, "I know they are, aren't they? I'll practice before I go anywhere . . ."

"You are not going anywhere in hooker heels like that, Aspen," Emerald informed her daughter. "You are fourteen, and there's no reason to . . ."

"I like these!" Loralei, the other young woman - I thought she might be Adam's daughter - said as she pranced out into the kitchen and did a pirouette. "What do y'all think?"

"Oh, hell no!" Adam called out from the living room. "Go take those off before you give me a coronary!"

"Where are you finding these shoes?" Emerald asked. She looked at Amethyst and said, "Why in the hell do you have shoes like this? I can't even remember the last time I saw you dress up, and I've *never* seen you wear either of those."

"She can't because she staggers around like a giraffe with vertigo if she puts on anything with a heel," Diamond, Amethyst's other sister who had joined the impromptu get together half an hour ago, chimed in. "Oh! That reminds me! Can I borrow your black platform boots?"

Amethyst ignored her sister and leaned closer to me as she squeezed my thigh. "I'm not sure if you're trying to punish yourself for some unimaginable sin or if you're honestly interested in all of this chaos, but I have to say that at any point you are welcome, and probably even expected, to run off and join the boys so you can burp and scratch and do all the things."

"I am out of my element here," I admitted.

"I'm sorry our breakfast together got hijacked by my family."

"I'm not. It gives me a lot of insight into you just by your interactions with them," I admitted.

"I hope you don't take anything you've seen in the last hour to heart. There are members of my family who make me want to go full Godzilla and raze the entire town every time I have to interact with them for more than five seconds."

"The birdbrains?"

Amethyst rolled her eyes and said, "I've been

arguing with them my entire life, and they still haven't realized that they lost the fight twenty years ago."

"History like that is priceless."

"So are dinosaur turds, but you don't see them stinking up my living room."

I burst out laughing and Amethyst squeezed my leg again before she leaned in and gave me a quick kiss. "I'm glad you packed for two nights because I don't think we're going to get any alone time until well after dark."

"They're all going to stay until bedtime?"

"No, but I have to go pick up Squid and Bella this evening and then deliver them home. You don't have to go on that adventure if you don't want to."

"If you're there, then I want to."

"That's sweet."

"Remember how we never quite finished our conversation about where this is going?"

"I remember," Amethyst admitted, recalling that she'd tried her best not to answer my question last night and not willing to get into it right now.

"I'm not going anywhere unless it's by your side, Lalelei."

"You think you want to stick around, huh?" Amethyst asked with a grin.

"I know I do."

"Keep that thought in mind, big guy, because this morning's invasion is just the tip of the iceberg."

"Do you have a shovel? If you don't, we've got one in our shed," one of the little boys who'd come over with Crow a few minutes ago asked when he stopped in front of Amethyst.

"Of course you do," Amethyst mumbled. "I know I'm going to regret asking this, but why do you need a shovel, Koda?"

"There are two ant colonies in your backyard," the other little boy explained. He looked at me and asked, "Did you know that if you take half the ants from one colony and add them to the other they'll go to war and kill each other?"

"I didn't know that," I admitted.

"You take half from colony A and put it in colony B and then repeat so that there are roughly half of each colony in each space. Both areas will have a war to the death, and you eradicate the pest problem naturally."

"Oh," I said in shock. "How old are you?"

"Is that true, Griff?" Hawk asked as he joined us in the kitchen.

"Absolutely," the little boy answered.

"That's freaking cool," Ruf said as he walked toward the back door. "Let's do it."

"Shovel?" Koda asked Amethyst.

"There are shovels in the shed," Amethyst answered.

"Are you coming to watch the show?" Crow asked me as he followed Ruf outside. Adam and Lucky were close behind along with a few others who had wandered in gradually.

"Go play mad scientist with the boys, Tama'i, but please don't let them corrupt you."

"You know I've spent time with men who are much wilder and crazier than these guys, right?"

"You think that now, but I'm doubtful. You'll see."

I gave her a quick kiss and then hopped up to go outside and join the guys. Just before I pulled the door shut behind me, I heard one of the women say, "Thank God they're finally gone. Amy, tell us *everything!*"

In a way, I wished I could be a fly on the wall for that conversation, but then Koda and Griffin appeared at the shed door with their shovels. I realized I was eager for this adventure, even if it was led by a mini-maniacal genius and his partner in crime.

That wasn't why I was so happy to be here, though. No, I was happy because Amethyst wasn't far away, and I had the promise of more time with her - as soon as we finished watching the ant invasion and the human invasion finally left her house.

For once in my life, I felt like I was right where I was meant to be.

FIFTEEN

You forget that I love hard, but I hit harder. It's either unconditional or unconscious. Take your pick.

Text from Amethyst to Lazlo

TAMA'I

"I'm glad everything went smoothly while I was away," I said as I rinsed out my coffee mug. I put it in the top rack of the dishwasher and then closed the door and started the machine. "How was Kai?"

"You act like I'm new at this," Tutu said sassily.

"I know you're not, but I'm the one that took this on for Kiki and . . ." One of Tutu's eyebrows rose menacingly - it was the angry one on the left, not the questioning one on the right. The woman had raised me, and I could identify each of her micro-expressions because I'd tap danced on every single one of her nerves at least once over the years. Most of them twice, and when I was feeling really stupid, I might hit them all in one day. Today, she'd skipped all of her progressions and gone directly to the angry eyebrow, so I knew I was in trouble. "You've done a wonderful job raising all of us, but it's time for you to relax and enjoy yourself. That's why I feel bad for leaving you to go to Amethyst's. This was the third weekend in a row I've spent with her, and I was even at her house for dinner one night last week."

"The relationship is new, so it only makes sense that you are trying to find your rhythm together. I would hope that at some point when the new wears off, you might bring her home to meet the family, but if you're ashamed of me, I understand." I gave Tutu a scowl, and she snickered. "When do I get to meet this woman, Tama'i? I've never known you to be this serious about a girl before."

"We talked yesterday and decided to make this official," I explained.

"It wasn't official after the first weekend you spent alone with her?"

"To me it was, but things are different now than they were when you were young."

"Do you think your great-grandfather traded me for two mules and a dairy cow? No. Your grandfather courted me the way a man should court a woman, and then he introduced me to his family."

"I've been hesitant to do that because things aren't completely in the open between me and Amethyst."

"She's been lying to you?"

"No!"

"Then you've been lying to her."

"Absolutely not. She doesn't know why I went to prison, and she doesn't seem to care."

"Do you love this woman, Tama'i?"

"I think so." I felt my breath catch when I realized that was true and then admitted, "That's the first time I've said that out loud."

"If you love her, then you should tell her so. Our time on earth is fleeting, Tama'i Koa. I lost your grandfather when your mother was just a young girl, and I've missed him every day since. When something happens in my life, it makes me sad that he isn't here to share it - the births of our grandchildren and great-grandchildren, watching all of you grow up . . . those are things that your grandfather and I dreamed about together, but he didn't live long enough to see them happen. Tell your woman that you love her before it's too late."

"I want to tell her why I did what I did and make sure she understands the circumstances before I say the words to her."

"You should do it soon, Tama'i. Kai is restless again."

"What did he do?" I asked.

"What did who do? Why would you think something happened?"

I leaned against the counter and crossed my arms over my chest. "You'd think that since you can spot even the smallest lie from any of us that you'd be better at it yourself."

Tutu's smile disappeared, and she seemed to deflate as she rested her arms on the table and sighed. "He's so bitter, Tama'i. I don't know if it's because his parents are gone or what, but it seems that he's directing all of his anger at you. I don't understand it."

"I think I understand."

"You do?"

"How did he find out?" Tutu's eyes darted away, and I knew there was more she wasn't telling me, so I asked, "What happened, Tutu?"

"Six months ago, he started acting differently toward Bart - he seemed angry at him for no reason. I noticed his disrespect, but Bart blew it off and said it was a surge of testosterone and he was trying to find his place in the pecking order at home and at school. Some days it was fine, but then he was suddenly angry again. Your sister was very worried, so she looked on his computer to see if there were any clues there."

"What did she find?"

"She found that he'd been talking to some members of his father's family."

"Bart's family is awesome. How are they affecting his . . ."

"No, Tama'i. His birth father's family."

"Oh."

"Kiki had a long talk with him, and she thought things were settled. He told her that he didn't have any questions for her, so she left it alone, but she asked that he not talk to them any more."

"But when he did, they poisoned his mind against me," I said simply.

"I think so. Unfortunately, your sister got her orders, and there wasn't any other choice but for her to leave the children with us."

"Is he still talking to them? Has he had any contact with Leaga?"

"From what Kiki could gather, he didn't ever speak to his father. Leaga is in prison, you know."

"He is?"

"He must have forgotten the lesson you gave him."

I shook my head and not for the first time thought I should have just ended that man's life rather than leave him half-dead, but at the time, I wasn't thinking about the future, just the vengeance that was owed to him.

"Now Kai thinks I'm a monster."

"Deep in his heart, he knows that you love him more than life itself. You gave up so much for him, Tama'i. He shouldn't. . ."

"He doesn't know that, Tutu, and as far as I'm concerned, he never will. He should love me because I'm family, not because it's expected."

"He does love you, Tama'i, he just has a lot of emotions running through him right now. I remember how you were at his age - full of energy and uncertain about the world around you."

I laughed as I walked over and sat down in the chair next to Tutu. "I don't remember anything about those years other than my urgent need to get laid as often as possible."

Tutu frowned and slapped my arm, but there was no heat in it. I'd experienced her anger before, and this was half-hearted.

Suddenly sober at the thought, I said, "My actions back then are affecting him now, and that's exactly what I didn't want to happen."

"You did what you felt was right and just, Tama'i, and none of us fault you for that. You paid the price with years of your life, but you're back among your family now, and I can tell by the light in your eyes that you've found something good here in Rojo."

"I think I may have."

"I haven't seen you smile this much in . . ." Tutu burst out laughing and said, "Well, ever! You've always been my rain cloud, Tama'i, but it seems like the sun is starting to peek through."

"That's a good description of Amethyst. She's the sunshine, and everyone around her can feel her warmth."

"This is new, but I have a feeling that you'd like for it to stand the test of time."

"I think you're right," I admitted, ignoring the fact that it had only been a few weeks, and in the grand scheme of things, I had barely scratched the surface of everything Amethyst Hamilton. We'd been talking for a little less than a month, but I couldn't imagine how dark my life would be if I didn't get to see or hear from her every day. I finally admitted, "I'd like that."

"Does she understand how important family is to

us?"

I laughed again as I relaxed against the back of the chair. "Tutu, I'm not sure that anyone could understand the importance of family more than Amethyst."

"What makes you say that? Does she come from a large family?"

"I've met dozens of people she considers family."

Tutu looked skeptical when she asked, "Dozens?"

"Let me tell you about the neighborhood she lives in . . ."

The heat coming off the asphalt paired with the heat coming from the engine of my motorcycle was almost oppressive, but the wind in my face made up for it as I took the gradual curve around the loop that skirted Rojo. Living in Vegas had been difficult for me, surrounded by buildings and throngs of people, but I'd found routes that took me out into the desert. Even though it was hot as hell, those trips helped me find my center and sanity. A few days after I arrived in Rojo, I mentioned to Fain that I wanted to take a long ride but wasn't sure where to go. He told me that when he needed some wind therapy, he rode the loop around Rojo, sometimes over and over.

Since I'd been riding for almost an hour now, taking the route Fain had suggested, I'd had time to gather my thoughts and think about the situation with my nephew, Kai, and my budding relationship with Amethyst. It worried me that she didn't seem to care about my background, but not in the way most people would expect. I'd never tried to hide the fact that I'd spent years in prison, so that wasn't something she could find fault with in the future.

However, I was concerned that she felt fine about my criminal history but would later find out that I'd almost killed someone - and had tortured him mercilessly - and change her mind about me. I'd met people before who seemed like they didn't have a problem with my background at first, but then something would happen and that was the first thing that came up.

Even though I'd never stolen anything in my life and that had nothing to do with my incarceration, the tattoo shop I worked at the year after I was released had been burglarized in the middle of the night. I found out about the crime when the police showed up at my door to question me because the owner had suggested I might have been involved since I was an ex-con. The man I thought was a friend had instantly gone from jovial and trusting to suspicious and hesitant.

I quit working there within the week and moved on, this time to another shop where I was sure I'd be accepted. I was, until there was a rash of muggings downtown that left one man beaten unconscious and I was rounded up as a suspect for the lineup. I knew that I hadn't done that and would *never* commit a crime like that, but standing in the lineup waiting for a stranger behind the glass to decide my fate was terrifying. What if they identified the wrong man? What if I was charged with something I had nothing to do with? My parole would have been yanked away, and I'd have found myself back behind bars - all because my history put me in the path of suspicion.

I didn't know if I'd be able to handle watching Amethyst's face change when she found out that I was considered a violent felon. Even this early in our relationship, the thought of letting her down filled me with anxiety. I didn't want to ever experience that reality.

Out of the corner of my eye, I saw a vehicle speeding closer in the left lane, cresting the hill I'd just come down. A speeder wasn't really a problem as long as I watched myself and they had their eyes on the road. However, the police car with lights and sirens that appeared soon after the speeding car was a big problem. I hit the brakes and hugged the yellow line, avoiding the emergency lane where there was gravel and debris that could make the tires lose traction, until both cars passed me. I watched them climb the next hill and disappear and made a mental note to tread carefully when I got that far, just in case the officer had pulled the speeder over on the other side that I couldn't see quite yet.

Because I knew that was likely the case, I moved over into the left lane now so I could avoid any problems and resumed my ride. As I crested the next hill, I wasn't shocked to find both cars at the bottom. The driver's door of the speeding car suddenly burst open, and a man jumped out and sprinted toward the officer who was walking toward the car. The officer had enough time to brace himself for impact before the man hit and they slammed into the ground and rolled out into the right lane of the highway. I hit the brakes, not just because I wanted to avoid them if they rolled further but because I couldn't pass by when an officer, or anyone else for that matter, was in distress.

By the time I stopped my bike in the center emergency lane a few hundred feet ahead of the stopped cars, another man had exited the vehicle and joined the first next to the patrol car. I jumped off my bike and sprinted toward them, making note of just how hard the officer was fighting back even though he was outnumbered and much smaller than the two men.

Without any warning, I barreled into the man who was kicking the officer and crushed him against the patrol car. I heard the glass shatter behind him and saw the light leave his eyes when his head snapped back and slammed into the roof of the car. Without even considering what that might mean for my future, I spun around in time to see the other man wrap his hands around the officer's neck and lift him . . . Holy shit! The officer was a woman!

He yanked her off the ground and slammed her into the asphalt before I could get to him. As he lifted her a second time, I did a roundhouse kick like I'd practiced on the heavy bag at the gym during my workouts and hit the man in the side of the head. He fell, but since his hands were still around her neck, he yanked her down with him.

I could see that she was still breathing as was her assailant. Without a second thought, I kicked him in the head again just to make sure he stayed out and if he happened to wake up, he wouldn't be able to do any more damage.

I dropped to my knees next to the officer and pulled off her mic that was clipped on her shoulder. I took a deep breath and engaged the mic before I said, "Officer down. I need help. Send an ambulance and . . and . . . Send everybody. She's down and needs help."

AMETHYST

I looked over the chart as I listened to the mother and daughter having an argument behind me. The girl's mother was convinced she was on drugs, but the preliminary tests that I'd had the lab rush showed nothing of the sort. According to her blood work, she was a healthy fifteen-year-old girl with no illegal drugs in her system.

"Just tell me what you're on."

"I'm not *on* anything, Mom!"

"There's no reason for you to be behaving this way. You fell asleep while you were in driver's training, Emily!"

"I didn't mean to."

"You were the one driving!"

"But I'm just so tired!"

"You slept through dinner last night, and I had to drag you out of bed to get you to school on time. I want you to remember that honesty goes a long way during the punishment phase. You know how I work, Em. Tell me the truth."

"Okay! I've been taking vitamins!"

I slowly turned around and asked, "What kind of vitamins?"

"Who gave them to you?" her mother asked.

"I bought them at the pharmacy."

"What kind of vitamins?" I asked again. The young woman looked at me and then at her mom before she bit her lip and hung her head. Finally, she mumbled something, and I was positive I'd misheard her. "Say that again, honey. I didn't hear you."

"Melanin."

I saw the girl's mother tilt her head in question and then she looked at me with her eyebrows raised. "Is there a vitamin for that?"

"You're taking *melanin?*" I shook my head and asked, "What exactly is the purpose of this vitamin?"

"It's supposed to help me tan without the harsh rays of the sun. I don't want to look old before my time, but my skin is so pale that I need something to help me."

"And you bought this at the pharmacy? Straight off the shelf?"

"Yeah! Me and Tracy each bought three bottles."

"What do the pills look like? Do you remember the brand name?"

"They're gummies. I think mine are supposed to be wild berry or something like . . ."

"I need the brand, not the flavor," her mother snapped.

"Nature something. Nature Worth? Nature Gold? I can't remember. They're all natural, though! They're even vegan!"

I shook my head and closed my eyes as I tried to think of something . . . anything . . . other than the idea I'd come up with, but I found nothing. I asked, "You think these vitamins are going to help you tan?"

"Yes! They're called melanin!"

"Could they be called *melatonin*?"

"You are fucking kidding me!" Emily's mom shouted.

I pulled my phone out and used the search engine to look up melatonin sleep aid gummies with a brand name that started with "nature" and found a few different choices, one of which was wild berry flavor. I held the phone out toward her and showed her the screen as I asked, "Is this what you're taking?"

"Yes! That's it! See, Mom! I'm not on drugs."

"Is it bad that, at this point, I'd be relieved if she was?" Emily's mom asked me.

I cleared my throat, and when that didn't completely suppress my laughter, I coughed. Once I had control of myself, I took a deep breath and schooled my features before I said, "Emily, the color of your skin comes from genetics and DNA, not a bottle that you buy at the pharmacy."

"Just weed. I could handle weed!" Emily's mom said in exasperation.

I cleared my throat again and then explained, "Melanin is made by special cells in your body called melanocytes. Everyone is born with the same number of melanocytes, but some people's bodies make more melanin than others. Your melanocytes make less melanin than mine do, that's why my skin is dark and yours is pale. There is melanin in every part of your body, and it works uniquely according to your DNA - your hair and eyes are light and so is your skin. That's because your melanocytes don't work like mine. My body makes more melanin than yours, and that's why my skin is dark and so is my hair and my eyes."

"I want to get a tan, but I don't want skin cancer."

"You have *got* to be kidding me right now, Emily."

"The gummies you've been taking are called melatonin. That's a hormone that your brain produces to help you go to sleep. It kicks into high gear as the light outside wanes and makes you start to yawn around dusk. You've been taking a synthetic version of that hormone, and rather than darken your skin, it's made you very tired."

"Am I being punked right now?" Emily's mom asked as she looked around the room. "Please tell me someone with a camera is about to pop out and yell, 'surprise!.'"

"Mom, let's just look at this as a learning experience for Emily that taught her she shouldn't take any type of medicine or pills *or gummies* that she doesn't completely understand."

"Do you want a Tic Tac?" her mother asked sarcastically. "They brighten your teeth."

I sniffed and looked at the floor as I squinted my eyes and bit my lip so hard I was sure I broke the skin. Emily's mom was on a roll, and I knew that if I laughed, she'd get even more irritated and Emily's feelings would be hurt.

"If I tell you to eat an apple, are you going to eat a Jolly Rancher?"

I snorted and then cleared my throat as I turned back to my computer. When I was sure that I was going to be able to handle myself professionally, I turned back to Emily's mom and said, "We'll bill this as a well visit, and I'm sure your insurance will take care of it. If not, I'll waive the office fee, and you'll only be charged for the labs."

"Me? I'm not paying for shit. She can use her melanin money to pay today's bill!"

"That's between the two of you," I said before I put my hand on Emily's shoulder. "Sweetheart, someday, you and your mom are going to laugh about this until you're both crying. Today is not that day, but this is the kind of story that's going to become legendary in your family. Right now, your mom is understandably upset"

"I just want to be tan."

"You're right to avoid too much sun, but I'd suggest that you save your money. If it's really something you want to do, *make sure you get permission from your mother* and consider a spray tan." I started to turn back to my computer and then remembered a fiasco with Bella, Cydney, and Gracy so I put my hands up and said, "From a professional! Not from something you get in a bottle at the pharmacy."

"I have the irresistible urge to call your grandmother and apologize to her."

"For what?" Emily asked.

Emily's mother shook her head. "I have no idea, but I'm sure she deserves one."

"And I believe that I should call my mom and do the same thing. Emily, you understand me when I say that you shouldn't take anything unless you clear it with your mom first, right?"

"I understand."

"I'm sorry we wasted your time," Emily's mom apologized.

"This is in the top three wildest consultations I've ever experienced," I told her. "It wasn't a waste at all. Believe me."

"How long before that stuff gets out of her system?" Emily's mom asked over the sound of her loud yawn.

"I took one earlier when I was in the bathroom," Emily admitted.

"You have got to be kidding me right now!"

"Don't take any more, okay?" When Emily nodded, I smiled at her mother and said, "Let her sleep it off, drink lots of water to flush out her system, and get back to me if there are any problems or changes in her behavior."

"Like . . . oh, I don't know . . . *smart* decisions?"

"Whenever that happens, we'll just call it a win." I logged back into the computer program and listed the patient as complete and checked my messages as they gathered their things to leave.

I said goodbye to them and started prepping the room for the next patient as my messages loaded. I had just finished replacing the paper on the exam table when Terran rushed into the room with Spruce not far behind.

"We've cleared your patients for the afternoon," Terran said gruffly.

"I only have one, and it's a . . ." When I turned around and looked at him, I gasped at the pain I saw on his face. "What's wrong? Who's hurt?"

"It's Zoey. They're flying her in from a traffic stop she did in the country somewhere," Spruce explained. "I'll take your last patient. You go to the hospital with Terran, and I'll come up when I'm finished."

"Was she shot?"

"Esme said that the good samaritan who saved her explained it was a head injury, but that's all we know," Terran said as he took my hand and dragged me into the hallway. "Obviously, I can't be her doctor, but I can supervise."

I went into my office and used my key to unlock my desk where I kept my purse before I joined Terran in the hall again. "Let's go. Have they called Sam and Carlie?"

"I'm sure Esme's taking care of that," Terran called out from behind us.

"I'm driving," I said as we walked out into the parking lot.

"I don't think so. I choose life," Terran said as he walked toward his truck. He sounded so much like his father that even in my terror at the thought of Zoey being injured, I almost laughed when he said, "Get in or get left."

The ride to the hospital was short and brought back memories of how crazy Griffin Forrester, my cousin Hawk's son, was when he raced on the track behind Uncle Bird and Aunt Summer's house. We parked in the doctors' lot, and I hopped out of the truck and jogged alongside Terran toward the service elevator. Just before the metal doors closed, I heard the whump-whump-whump of the helicopter rotors that signaled Zoey's arrival at the hospital. As the car took us up to the landing pad, I closed my eyes and said a silent prayer for one of my oldest friends. I knew that Terran was feeling the same fear and emotion when he gripped my hand tightly and held it until we arrived on the roof of the building and saw the Life Flight nurses jogging next to the gurney as they told the ER nurses Zoey's stats and listed her injuries.

I tried to remain detached as I watched the elevator doors close behind Terran who had squeezed into the car with the team, but it proved impossible since snippets of memories that all included Zoey flashed through my mind. I couldn't remember a time when she wasn't part of my life, and I couldn't imagine a future without her in it. The sight of her on that gurney, immobilized for her safety during the flight, would be ingrained in my memory forever now.

Even though there was nothing I could do for her medically, I took the elevator down to the ER so that I could listen at the door of her exam room and then report details back to our families and friends that were surely gathering downstairs right now. There was one other thing I could do - hope and pray for my friend to not just survive, but to fully recover from whatever injuries she'd gotten on duty today and become even stronger than she was before.

Just before the elevator doors opened, I wiped my tears away so I could put on a brave front - a facade that was only for show because right now, I was more afraid than I'd been in a very long time.

SIXTEEN

Jail is temporary, but memories are forever, so go ahead and throw that punch so we can all look back and smile.

Text from Emerald to Amethyst

TAMA'I

I looked down at my socks and wondered how in the hell this day had gone so awry. My relaxing ride had turned into a nightmare for me and for that poor officer who had been so gravely injured.

In a way, considering my appearance and history, I could understand why they assumed I was involved. But then again, as far as I was concerned, the evidence spoke for itself. One would think that everything would work itself out, and they would release me from the cell where they had locked me up in the false hope of getting retribution for the fallen officer.

However, before I got out of prison, I read my release agreement repeatedly, and it specifically listed "arrest for any crime" or "commission of a violent act" as two reasons to revoke my parole and send me back to prison for the remainder of my sentence. As I rubbed my wrists, sore from the tight handcuffs, I tried to imagine how I could get out of this. I knew how the contract was worded, and it very specifically said that even if I was not convicted of a crime, I could still be sent back if I was arrested. I knew my parole officer wouldn't hesitate to take this to a judge just to ship me off again.

There was no crime for me to be convicted of today, and I knew it was all a misunderstanding. But in reality, I *had* been arrested. They'd read me my rights twice to make sure I understood them and then took my mugshot before they made me remove my cut, my clothes, and my boots for evidence since they were covered in blood.

Unfortunately, I hadn't been allowed to wash up, so my hands still had blood on them from the officer who I had tried my best to save. I had no idea if I was even successful because when I asked the jailer how she was doing, he'd only growled at me. I hoped that the medics were able to stabilize her on the flight and that she was getting the best care.

And almost as fervently, I hoped that the two men who had attacked her were either rotting in hell or on their way. I didn't even care that I was the one who introduced them to their fate. I knew that someday I'd appreciate the irony that I served time in prison for *almost* killing a man on purpose, but killing one or two men in the act of helping someone else was what was going to send me back.

I knew the second the first man's body dropped that he was dead - his eyes open and staring at nothing as he slid down the side of that car. I wasn't sure if the man I kicked was alive or not since the last thing I saw before the angry police officer slammed me face down onto the hood of his car was medics feeling for his pulse.

The booking officer sneered at me as he watched me take off my cut and gently fold it before I handed it to him. It took everything I had to keep my mouth shut when he tossed it toward a chair and let it fall to the floor. My cut was the least of my worries, though.

I didn't want to think of what this would do to Tutu and the rest of my family. Bart would be home soon, and not long after, Kiki would be here, but Tutu would be alone with the kids until then - and they'd all be dealing with the shame I'd brought to our family. Again.

But the kicker of it all was that I wasn't ashamed of whatever crime they were trying to throw at me just like I wasn't ashamed of the one that sent me to prison in the first place. Any man who put his hands on a woman or child didn't deserve to live. If I happened to be the one to dole out their punishment, I was more than willing to do so and pay the consequences.

But my family would have to pay, too, because this would cause ripples in the town until the truth came out that I wasn't in league with those thugs and that I didn't attack the officer - I helped her.

"Get up," the officer who appeared outside the cell ordered as he glared at me. "You get a phone call. Make it count."

As he cuffed me to take me out of the cell, I scrambled to think of who I could call. Unfortunately, I didn't have any phone numbers memorized other than my own, so I was shit out of luck unless they let me look at my contacts. I could tell by the jailer's demeanor that wasn't going to happen, so I hoped that he'd let me access a phone book to call a place where I knew they'd answer. Grudgingly, he looked up the number for me and dialed the phone before he thrust the receiver my way. Since my hands were cuffed behind my back, I almost lost the phone when he let it go but managed to squeeze it against my shoulder with my head.

"Tempest Tattoos," I heard Pearl say when she

picked up.

"Pearl, it's Tiny. I've been arrested, and I need you to get in touch with Tutu and tell her she's on her own until I get out." I ignored the snort of the cop who was still glaring at me and continued. "My bike is out on the loop near where an officer was attacked. If you could find someone to go pick it up, I'll be forever grateful."

"What happened?" Pearl asked.

"Two men overpowered a police officer during a traffic stop. I stopped to help but . . . Well, they think I was involved."

"Oh, fuck no!" Pearl snapped. "You're at RPD?"

"Yeah. Just call Tutu, and let her know. She's got access to my accounts, so she can get me a lawyer. If she doesn't know a good one, do you think someone in your family can . . . Hawk's a lawyer! Will you call Hawk?"

"Sit tight and keep your mouth shut, Tiny. I'll have someone there within the hour."

"Call Tutu and . . ."

"There's no sense in calling her and worrying her about nothing. I'll take care of this."

"And my bike?"

"I'll take care of that too. Sit tight, Tiny. I've got you, buddy."

"Thanks, Pearl."

Without warning, the officer reached out and took the phone away before he slammed it down to hang up. He sneered at me and said, "Get up."

I stood up and looked down at him. He took a step back, and I wasn't shocked. My size had always been a factor - either in my favor for intimidation or against me when a smaller man felt less than and tried to prove he was more powerful. This guy was obviously one of the latter. I'd heard my sister refer to it as "little man syndrome," and I completely agreed. He puffed up like a rooster as he jerked me by my arm and led me back down the long hall to my holding cell.

All I could think was that I hoped Pearl didn't tell Amethyst what was going on until I could see her face while I explained exactly what happened. Just like Tutu and the kids, I didn't want Amethyst to think badly of me, but right now, it looked like that was more than likely to happen.

I wasn't sure how long I'd been sitting there staring at my feet and worrying about what was going on outside before I heard a woman's voice say my name. I looked up and saw a gorgeous Hispanic woman standing just outside my cell smiling at me.

"Hello, Tama'i. I'm Esme Cardenas."

"Hello."

"I just wanted you to know that you handled yourself very well on the radio this afternoon and thank you for your help."

"You know I helped her? Can you tell the cops that?"

She gave me a mysterious smile before she said, "I've already put the bug in the chief's ear, and you're about to witness some heads roll. You've got visitors on their way back. They're signing in right now, but I wanted to reassure you that you won't be here for much longer."

"That's all well and good, but the fact that I'm in here right now is a violation of my parole."

"I know a guy who can pull some strings," she said with a wink. "Amethyst is a lucky woman because you're a good man, Tama'i."

"Call me Tiny."

"I'll call you anything you want as long as I can also call you my friend."

"I'd like that."

"I'm about to get off duty and . . ."

"How's the officer? Is she doing okay? I had no idea what I could do to help her, so I just blocked the sun and let her know I was there for her in case she could hear me."

"Last I heard, Zoey was on her way to surgery. You can go see for yourself when you leave here."

"I'll have to find my bike and talk to my family and my . . . my girlfriend," I stammered. This was the first time I'd ever referred to Amethyst that way, and I wondered if that would still apply after today.

"Your motorcycle is on its way here, so it will be waiting for you when you're released."

"You're awfully sure that's gonna happen."

"Like I said, I know people."

"Is Hawk one of the people coming to see me?" I asked.

"No. Hawk wasn't available, so Pearl upgraded."

"What does that mean?"

Esme actually giggled like a kid before she said, "You'll find out."

She turned to look down the hall right before I heard a woman say, "If there's a mark on him, I'll have you flying a cargo plane full of rubber dog shit out of Tokyo by tomorrow!"

"I think it's supposed to be Hong Kong, Petra, but I get where you're coming from, and I completely agree," a man said cheerfully. "Although, I doubt the little man has his pilot's license."

"Probably not. I'm sure there's a height restriction for things like that," she replied.

"Here comes the cavalry," Esme said with a grin. "I'll talk to you soon, Tiny. Thanks again for helping Zoey. We'll forever be in your debt."

"No debt. It was the right thing to do."

As my new friend walked off, I heard the people in

the hall greet her and then a beautiful white woman appeared next to an older Black man who looked familiar somehow even though I knew I'd never seen him before. Out of respect, I stood and nodded at the newcomers and got a smile from the woman in return.

The man's face was blank, but I could see his eyes glittering with anger as he stared menacingly at the jailer. "Open the fucking door, and let him out."

"I can't do that."

"Then let us in," the woman ordered.

"I'll have to process him through and get you a conference room."

The powerful looking man leaned a fraction closer to the jailer and said, "You realize you're skating on ice so thin I can see the words of your termination letter through it. I can also read the words on the paperwork I'm going to file for the lawsuit on my client's behalf. Unlock. The fucking. Door."

The jailer swallowed hard and then hurriedly unlocked the cell door. As he slid it aside, the man pushed his way past him, and the woman followed close behind. I was shocked when she veered around the man and barreled into me, wrapping her arms around me tightly as the jailer slammed the cell door shut.

"Thank you," she whispered, and I could hear the tears in her voice.

"You're scaring him, Petra," the man said as he broke into a smile. "Tiny, this is your lawyer, Petra Parker, and I'm your other lawyer, Marcus Hamilton."

"Hamilton?" I asked, unable to extend my hand to shake his because the woman still had my arms pinned to my sides with her tight hug.

"Amethyst is my niece."

"You're her dad's brother. I see the resemblance."

"We've already got everything in the works to get you out of here, and I can assure you that there will be no charges filed," Marcus said firmly. He pulled Petra a few steps back so she was standing beside him and then put his arm over her shoulder to comfort her as tears streamed down her cheeks. "I know you're upset, sweetheart, but you need to put your game face on."

"I'm trying, but he's covered in Zoey's blood, Marcus."

"Is the officer a friend of yours?"

"Yes, and she's one of Amy's best friends. They grew up together. My brother and I have been close friends with her parents since before she was born and consider them part of our family."

"How is she doing? That other woman, Esme, said she's going into surgery."

"She's stable, but she has a severe head injury along with other injuries from the beating she took before you rescued her."

"And those other men?"

"One is dead and the other one insists on trying to live, although I don't know why because once he recovers, I'm going to make sure that he wishes he was dead with every breath he takes."

"Okay, here's the deal, we're waiting on Nick to get here and start swinging. Then we'll spring you so you can go get cleaned up. Amy is at the hospital with the rest of the family, and I'm sure she'd like to talk to you as soon as possible," Petra explained.

"Who is Nick?"

"That's Esme's father. He's. . ."

Footsteps in the hall interrupted Petra's explanation, and an older Hispanic man appeared with a furious scowl. He used his key to open the cell door and then motioned for Marcus and Petra to come forward. They walked out into the hallway, and he stared at me with raised eyebrows before he said, "You're free to go, Mr. Fuamautu."

"I am?" I asked in shock.

"Your belongings have been delivered to my office, and my wife is on her way with another pair of boots for you."

I looked down at my feet and then back up at the man before I said, "I'm not sure how she knows my size but . . ."

"She went to your house and explained the situation to your grandmother who gave her a pair of your boots. I'll need the ones you were wearing today as evidence, but I'll return them to you as soon as they're processed."

"Evidence against me?" I sighed before I said, "I guess I should call my parole officer and let her know . . ."

"She's waiting for us in my office. I'm sure they've already processed your hands. You'll be able to wash up once we get there."

"Is she going to revoke me?" I asked.

"Only if she wants to start a war," the man in charge said angrily.

Petra gave me a blinding smile before she said, "Come on, Tiny. Let's get you out of here."

I didn't realize who I was walking with until we arrived at the door of his office and I saw the etching on the window that said he was the RPD chief. I knew he must be beside himself at the thought of his officer in trouble and hoped he understood how much I wanted to help her even though I had no idea how to do that.

Before I could figure out how to say that, he opened another door and motioned for me to go inside.

"Take your time - there are clean washcloths and towels in the cabinet above the toilet. I don't have a scrub brush for your nails, but I can find one."

"I'm sure it will be okay," I said as I walked into the simple but clean bathroom. Once again, I thought of how much I needed to pee, so I asked, "Do you mind if I shut the door for a second?"

"You're not under arrest, Mr. Fuamatu. You're here as my honored guest. Take as long as you need."

"Thank you." I shut the door before I turned to look at my reflection in the mirror. There were specks of blood on my face. I had no idea where they'd come from, but the streaks of blood across my shirt were from wiping my own hands after I checked her pulse before I kneeled next to the police officer to shield her injured face from the harsh sun.

I wondered if there was a dark spirit over my shoulder watching me, laughing about the shitstorm he'd stirred up in my life, and then shook the thought off. For once, my luck seemed to be holding if the fact that I was in the chief's office as a guest rather than a prisoner meant anything at all.

Now I'd have to see what my visit to the police station had done to my family. I could imagine the kids were in an uproar and Tutu was beside herself. As much as I wanted to go check on Amethyst and make sure she was holding up okay while her friend was fighting for her life, I needed to take care of my family first. At least I could be sure that Amethyst's family was taking care of her.

SEVENTEEN

You look like something that came out of a slow cooker.

Text from Phoenix to Amethyst

AMETHYST

I knew that it would be a few more hours before we got any more information about Zoey's condition, so I decided to walk with Wren and Roscoe down to the maternity ward so I could detour into the nursery and get a baby fix to help soothe my soul and ease my mind.

Even though I didn't have any patients in the nursery right now, there was always at least one or two babies who could use a little attention. The nurses always welcomed an extra set of hands.

We had just stepped off the elevator when my phone buzzed with an incoming text, so I shooed Wren and Roscoe off to do their rounds since they both had patients recovering from birth and Roscoe had another in the early stages of labor. I was shocked as I read the details of the message from the answering service and hoped it was a mistake.

I turned around and pushed the button to call the elevator back so I could go to the pediatric floor. Once the doors opened, I rushed out toward the nurses' station. A nurse I'd worked with when I first graduated from medical school before I started at the clinic with my family greeted me with a grim smile before she said, "I heard about your friend, and I want you to know that we're praying for her every chance we get."

"Thank you."

"Your patient was rushed to the emergency room by ambulance after suffering from heat stroke," Cheryl said as she handed me a tablet with all of the pertinent information on the case. "A woman loading her groceries into her car spotted him alone in the car next to hers, but he was already unconscious. He's stable now but under constant supervision by a patient care specialist that Child Protective Services sent over."

"And his mother asked you to call me?"

"Yes. She was very firm when she requested that you be his primary doctor. The father argued against it, but it was really up to the specialist, and she agreed since you have history with the patient and the mother obviously trusts you."

I asked, "Did the dad mention that I was the one to call CPS in the first place?"

"He was very vocal about that."

"Good. I'm glad I made an impression. Unfortunately, it doesn't look like it stuck."

"I'll come with you," Cheryl offered.

"I'd appreciate that," I said with a sigh. I looked down the hall toward the room my patient had been assigned to and said, "I guess there's no time like the present."

"That's usually what I say about having an ice cold beer."

"I'm not much of a beer drinker, but I could put a couple back right about now."

"Have faith, Dr. Hamilton. Your friend will be just fine."

"She's a fighter, so I know you're right, but it's hard not to worry," I said as I walked down the hall beside Cheryl. We stopped at the closed door, and I took one more look at the tablet to re-familiarize myself with the parents' names and the patient's latest stats before I knocked lightly and then walked inside. I nodded at Susan, Archer's mother, and then glanced over at Archer's father, John. I was happy to see that John's girlfriend wasn't in the room and hoped I wouldn't have to meet her today. Or ever. The limits of my patience and tolerance were stretched thin right now, and I was sure that interacting with her might get me a prison sentence. "Ms. Hayes. Mr. Massey."

"You've got a lot of balls showing your face after what you did."

I slowly turned to face my patient's father and took a deep breath while I counted to ten before I replied. Ms. Hayes took the words right out of my mouth when she said, "You've got *no* balls considering you let that fucking bitch around our son again."

"It was an accident, Susan. Tell me you've never done something you regret and . . ."

"That's easy. Marrying you ranks at the top of the list. However, that didn't almost kill my son *twice,* so there's that."

"If you're going to argue, then you should do it somewhere else. He might be sleeping, but the tension in this room will do absolutely nothing to help his recovery," I snapped. With them now silent, I walked over and rested my hand on Archer's soft hair and studied his face. There were dark circles under his puffy eyes, but his breathing was steady. I looked up at the IV bag and checked the fluid rate before I gave instructions to the nurse on how to proceed with his care. Once I was finished assessing him, I hugged the tablet against my chest and faced his parents. "I'm going to keep him in the hospital for at least forty-eight hours for observation."

"I want a second opinion."

"Technically, I am the second opinion since the attending in the ER already wrote the orders."

"Well, I want another one."

Suddenly, I snapped, and all of the professionalism that I'd trained so hard for and worked to cultivate disappeared. "It was 104 degrees today, and the woman you chose to let take care of your child less than a month after she insisted she didn't realize that giving a toddler alcohol to make him sleepy would be dangerous to his health *accidentally* left him in the car when she went into the grocery store. Making sound decisions clearly isn't your forte, Mr. Massey, because the odds are against her, and I firmly believe that she is trying to get rid of your son because he takes your attention away from her."

"You can't talk to me like that!" When I didn't respond, he said, "It was an accident, and Jill is beside herself with guilt. She'll never let anything happen to Archer again."

"I'm sad to hear that you're willing to take that risk because I'm not. The odds are that the next time your girlfriend has an *accident* involving your son, it's probably going to kill him." I looked over at the CPS worker and said, "Let your supervisor know that I'll be calling the judge from the previous case to explain what happened today and ask if he'd like to change his opinion on the matter. I'll also be contacting the judge assigned to this case to give him my thoughts on what's safe for my patient. I'm going to put in his medical record that the father's girlfriend is to have no contact with him, supervised or otherwise. As far as I'm concerned, that should be a permanent resolution, however it may come about."

"What the hell? She's my fiancée and soon to be his stepmother. There's no way in hell I'm going to keep him away from her."

"And obviously, you care more about her than you do for your son, so that's enough of an answer, Mr. Massey. I'll make sure and express your opinion to the judge when I speak to him."

For the first time since I'd walked into the room, I saw relief on my patient's mother's face. I decided to make it my mission in life to keep it there. It wasn't often in my line of work that I drew a line in the sand and dared someone to cross it, but this case was definitely one I felt justified in fighting for.

I walked over to the notepad that was on the table by the phone and wrote my personal cell number on it along with my uncle's office number. I handed it across the bed to Archer's mother and said, "Call me anytime, night or day, about concerns for Archer, and call the number to that law office first thing in the morning and ask for Marcus Hamilton. I'll let him know what's happened so far and that you'll be in touch."

"Thank you, Dr. Hamilton."

"As for you, Mr. Massey, it seems that you have a choice to make, and it shouldn't be a hard one. Choose wisely because the decisions you make during the course of this investigation will affect you for the rest of your life."

"That sounds like a threat."

"No, sir. That wasn't a threat, but I'll give you one. Tell your girlfriend that I'll do whatever it takes to make sure she sees jail time for neglect, and if that's not possible, I'll figure out another way to show her that abuse doesn't always just happen to innocent children. Occasionally, it happens to adults, too, and when it does, it's much, *much* more painful." I handed Cheryl the tablet and smiled at her when I said, "I'll be back to check on him before I leave and then again in the morning. Make a note that the father's girlfriend isn't allowed to visit the room for any reason."

"Yes, doctor."

I nodded at the CPS worker who had been watching the drama with wide eyes and then at Ms. Hayes before I said, "Make the call."

"I'll do it first thing in the morning."

"Good." I looked over at Mr. Massey and smiled before I said, "Congratulations on your engagement, Mr. Massey. I'm sure you and your *wife* will have a wonderful life alone together."

Since I'd been upstairs for so long, I got on the

elevator to go back down to join my family and hopefully get an update on Zoey's condition. When the elevator doors opened, I saw that even more family and friends had arrived, some of whom had traveled from Colorado Springs.

I greeted them all with hugs and hesitant smiles, considering the situation, and then went into the packed waiting room to find my parents. Dad was off in the corner with some of his club brothers - men I'd known as my uncles for my entire life, while Mom was sitting next to Gamma, Aunt Summer, and almost all of the women I loved as if they were blood family.

"Any news?" I asked before I leaned down and kissed Gamma on the cheek.

"What happened?" Mom asked in concern.

"I just went upstairs for a few minutes. One of my patients was admitted."

"Are they okay?" Gamma asked. "You've got a strained look on your face, Amy. Talk to me, sweetheart."

"An odd look?"

"She's being nice. What she means is that you have that crease between your eyebrows that means you're either about to lose your temper or you've already blown up. What's going on?"

I gave them the short version of my patient's history with his future stepmother and watched Gamma's eyes narrow in anger as my mother's face showed that she was plotting a slow and painful death. Their reactions weren't a surprise to me because I knew how the women in my family felt about protecting not just their own children but any child.

"Have you talked to Tiny in the last few hours?"

"I should call him and let him know I won't be able to see him this evening since I plan to stay here," I said as I pulled my phone out.

"You don't know?"

"Know what? I can't take any more bad news right now, Mom."

"Pearl called your Uncle Marcus to go down to the police station because Tiny needed a lawyer. He was arrested at the scene because the officers thought he might have been involved in Zoey's attack," Mom explained.

"How could he have been involved in that? The last I heard, he was going for a ride."

"He was the man who pulled over and saved Zoey's life," Mom explained. "The good samaritan was Tiny."

"Oh my goodness," I whispered. "And they arrested him?" I stood up suddenly and said, "I've gotta go to the station. They can't do that! He'd never hurt her. I know he wouldn't."

"Marcus is on the case, sweetheart. He sent word that Tiny is out and going home to check on his family. I'm sure he'll be here soon," Mom assured me.

"I can't wait to meet him," Gamma said with tears in her eyes. "I owe him my everlasting gratitude. So does everyone else here."

"You haven't met him yet?" Willow asked. She looked at me in question, and I shrugged.

"We've only been seeing each other a few weeks, and he's already met so many of the cousins that I'm already worried he might bolt."

"I'll meet him today, whether he comes here or you take me to him," Gamma said in a tone of voice I knew better than to argue with. "Sam, Carlie, and the rest of the family will want to thank him in their own ways, but I want to get my hands on him and give him a hug."

"I'll text and ask him to come up as soon as he can."

"Do that right now."

By the time I got out of the shower, Tutu had already left to pick up Tameka from school and deliver her to dance class. The boys were together at school for their own sports practice, and Tutu had assured me that she'd explain what had happened over dinner tonight.

In return for her taking care of what was supposed to be *my* job, especially since this was my day off, I had made a promise that I'd bring Amethyst to meet her in the next few days. Even though I was closer to forty than thirty, I'd even asked if Tutu would mind Amethyst staying over now and then. Tutu was much more progressive than a lot of people her age and said she'd love to have Amethyst around, especially since she knew that she was the reason I'd been smiling a lot more lately.

I hoped Amethyst would agree - not that I worried at

all about how she'd handle being around the kids, but because I felt bad that I abandoned Tutu to take care of them from Saturday when I got off work until Monday morning when Amethyst had to go into the clinic. If Amethyst would agree to stay over with me, I could be more present with the kids on my day off *and* have her get to know my family like I'd already gotten to know so many members of hers.

Once I was dressed, I pulled my hair back and then went outside to fire up my bike. It was hard to explain how relieved I was when I walked out of the police station and found it parked on the sidewalk, shiny and whole with a young man named Duke Conner standing guard. He thanked me for helping his friend Zoey and explained that his boss was her twin before he assured me that there would be no charge for picking up my motorcycle at the crime scene and bringing it over.

I was about to pull away from the curb when I got a text from Amethyst asking me to come to the hospital and letting me know which floor they were on and how to get to the waiting room where she was sitting vigil with her family. The drive didn't take long at all, and within just a few minutes, I was parked and walking toward the building. I was anxious to hear how the officer was doing and knew that Amethyst would have the latest news, but even more than that, I wanted to see her and get things out in the open about why the cops were so eager to arrest me today.

It seemed like all roads led back to the day I almost killed my brother-in-law. No matter how much I'd changed since then, I knew that at my core, I was the same man who so easily beat and tortured another human, even though he was close to the bottom of the rung as far as humanity was concerned. When I asked the woman at the front desk where to find the stairs, she directed me toward the bank of elevators, so I had to ask again. She looked at me like I was crazy and reminded me that I would be climbing four flights of stairs but shrugged and showed the path I needed to take to get to the stairwell. By the time I got up there, I was almost winded, so I decided to consider that my workout for today since it was unlikely that I'd make it to the gym. I walked out into the hallway and knew exactly where Amethyst was waiting with her family because the crowd was overflowing - some men and women sat in chairs alone, others had a man seated with a woman or child perched on his lap, and even more people standing in small groups talking in hushed voices.

I had just reached for my phone to send Amethyst a text asking her to meet me in the hallway when Emerald appeared in the doorway. Her face lit up with a smile, and she hurried my way. I walked toward her, not quite matching her speed, and was surprised when she threw her arms around me and gave me a tight hug.

"I'm so glad you came," Emerald said as she let me go. "Let me take you to Amethyst. I'll let her introduce you to Sam and Carlie, and I'm sure Gamma wants to get her hands on you too."

"I've heard about your gamma. She reminds me of my tutu."

"She's the best. You're gonna love her. Papa Smokey too."

"Amethyst has mentioned him many times. I'm not sure I've got the stamina to keep up with the man. He sounds like a wildcard."

"All of them are, and don't discount the women," Emerald said as she hooked her arm in mine and led me toward the waiting room. "I'll call you a liar if you tell anyone I said this, but the women are much more terrifying than the men give them credit for."

"I believe that, but I'm sure Amethyst isn't nearly as crazy as you think. She's the calmest woman I've ever met."

"Still waters run deep, my friend, and just because Amethyst is better at hiding her crazy than the rest of us doesn't mean it's any less."

"I'll keep that in mind."

I walked into the large waiting area with Emerald on my arm and realized that I recognized more than half the people here. I'd met several of them at the tattoo shop when they came in to see one of my co-workers, my favorite smartass barista was sitting next to the woman who helped me and my niece at the bookstore the other day, the waitress who had served me the best chopped beef I'd ever tasted was sitting with the woman who owned the garage where I rented a bay to work on my truck, and the woman from the bakery who I accidentally proposed to after she served me the most amazing croissant I'd ever had was slumped in her chair, napping with her head resting on Amethyst's shoulder.

Even though I knew that Amethyst had a huge family - some of her blood and some of her heart, I had no idea that they were like threads that connected her to almost every corner of Rojo. The people in the room varied from business professionals to obvious working class and everything in between, and the colors of their skin were just as diverse. Black, white, Asian, and Hispanic people were all represented and intermingled seamlessly just like I wished could happen all over the rest of the world.

"Special delivery for Amethyst Hamilton," Emerald announced cheerfully when we stopped in front of Amethyst's chair.

She smiled at me and then looked at her friend who was sleeping peacefully against her shoulder and whispered, "I want to get up and give you a kiss but . . ."

I leaned forward and rested my hands on the arms of her chair before I gave her a chaste kiss on the lips and stood up again. "Hi, sweetheart. How are you holding up? I understand the officer is one of your closest friends."

"She is. Our fathers grew up together, and I've known her since we were just babies."

"Let me help you," a woman who was sitting on the other side of the sleeping woman said. "Em, swap out with Amy."

As if they'd done it a million times before, the woman lifted the sleeping lady's head so that Amethyst could get up, and Emerald slid into her spot before the other woman gently let their friend's head rest against her shoulder.

"That's Janis. She starts working at the bakery in the wee hours of the morning, so she's learned to sleep anywhere," Amethyst explained.

"And we've learned not to wake her up because she's cranky even when she's happy, but when she's tired, she's like a rabid grizzly with its foot stuck in a trap," the other woman explained. She stuck her hand out and said, "I'm Holly, by the way."

I shook her hand and said, "It's a pleasure to meet

you."

"Holly is my cousin," Amethyst explained. "I heard what you did for Zoey, Tama'i, and words can't even express how grateful we are."

"I did what anyone else would have done in that situation," I hedged.

"No. Too many people would have just passed by and thought a call to 911 was enough, but by the time help arrived, Zoey would have probably been dead," Emerald argued. She looked at Amethyst and said, "Take him to meet Gamma, and let her go with you when you introduce him to Sam and Carlie."

"That's a good idea," Amethyst agreed as she squeezed my hand. "Come with me."

I walked with Amethyst to the other side of the room, and halfway there, I noticed that the majority of the people were watching our progress. A few of them looked confused and were whispering to each other, but most of them looked happy to see me, their smiles belying their puffy eyes and tear-stained faces. When Amethyst stopped walking, I looked ahead and saw an older woman sitting on the knee of a silver-haired man. Her eyes got wide and began to well with tears as she hopped off her perch and took a few steps toward us. Without a word, she threw her arms around us both. Over her small frame, I watched as the man she'd been sitting with stood along with the couple who were seated next to them.

Suddenly, the woman let us go and grabbed Amethyst's hand as she put her other hand up to touch my face. "Thank you so much, young man. If you hadn't helped our Zoey, we'd be gathered for an entirely different reason."

"It was the least I could do. I'm just sorry I didn't get there sooner."

"I understand that one of the men died instantly and the other is downstairs lingering . . . for now."

"I hadn't thought to check on him," I admitted.

"No sense in it," the woman said dismissively. She sighed as she let her hand drop from my face and said, "It's too bad the other one went so quickly."

My mouth dropped open in shock as the man standing behind her coughed to hide his laughter. He pulled her up beside him as he stuck his hand out to shake mine. "I'm Smokey Forrester, and this lovely woman is my wife Martha."

"You'll call me Gamma like everyone else in my family."

"Yes, ma'am."

"I thought I'd take him to meet Sam and Carlie. They're in the surgical waiting room with Aunt Sandy and Uncle Tink."

"I'll go with you," the woman insisted.

Amethyst squeezed my hand again before she smiled at me and said, "I'm really glad you came, Tama'i."

"I am too."

EIGHTEEN

People who grew up with siblings close to their age make great Marines. They know how to handle combat situations, psychological warfare, and are good at sensing suspicious and nefarious activity.

Text from Kiki to Tama'i

TAMA'I

"I'm not sure I'm ready to meet Tutu, Tama'i," Amethyst argued as I settled down in front of her on my motorcycle.

"I've got your mom and your dad in my corner on this, sweetheart, and none of us think you should be alone tonight."

"But I'm not looking my best, and I'm not really sure I'll be good company."

"You've had a very stressful day, and she understands that. Believe me. She even had quite a shock or two herself."

"If I'd have known they took you into the station, I'd have put a stop to that much quicker."

"What would you have done about it?" I asked.

"I'd have found Uncle Nick and given him a piece of my mind and then busted you out myself if he didn't act quickly enough."

"Uncle Nick as in Chief Cardenas?"

"Yes. He's my niece's father and . . ."

"How? Hold on. Esme said she was his daughter and . . ."

"Emerald is Esme's birth mother, but she was very young when she was born, so Uncle Nick and Aunt Cindy adopted her."

"Oh. That's good," I said, trying to do the math in my head. Amethyst had said that her older sister was about ten years older than her, and Esme looked to be about Amethyst's age which meant that . . .

"I can hear the abacus in your brain clicking while you try to figure out how that is possible, so I'll just say that Emerald was not quite thirteen when Esme was born."

"Holy shit."

"Our families are very close, and I was raised with Esme as if she were my sister, and Emerald got to watch her grow up."

"That sounds like the perfect situation for a scenario like that."

"It really was," Amethyst agreed. Finally, she said, "Take me to your house, Tama'i. I don't have the strength or the energy to argue with you about it especially since I think you're right. I don't need to be alone right now."

As soon as I fired my bike up, Amethyst's arms went around my waist and I felt her lay her head on my back. I was happy that she was comfortable enough to let her guard down with me and promised myself that I'd make this evening as relaxing as possible for her now that we had gotten word her friend was going to be okay.

I pulled into the drive and parked next to Tutu's SUV. I had called ahead and asked her to set an extra plate at the table and listened to her excitedly exclaim that I should have warned her I was bringing a guest so she could have made a special meal. She calmed down when I told her that everything she cooked was special, and Amethyst was a definite foodie who loved to eat. She made me promise to bring her back soon after she'd had time to make something a little more sophisticated.

As soon as I shut the bike off, Amethyst hopped off and stood beside me, looking up and down the street as if trying to get her bearings about where exactly I'd brought her. Suddenly, she lifted her hand and waved, and I looked down the street and found a woman about my age - a neighbor I'd seen a few times before - waving back.

"You know her?"

"That's Rosie. She's an old friend of mine."

"Let me guess . . . you grew up with her?"

Amethyst laughed before she said, "As a matter of fact, I did. She's probably on her way back to the hospital. Her mom was good friends with Zoey's when she lived here as a teenager."

"Let's go in and eat and then we'll relax before bed. I've got an idea of something that might help you sleep."

"So do I, but I'm not sure that's a good idea in a house with your grandmother and the kids."

I burst out laughing and suggested, "If I fuck you from behind, you can scream into the pillow."

"I like how you're thinking. I'm going to hold you to that."

I held Amethyst's hand as we walked up the driveway to the mudroom entrance and then held the door open for her. As I bent over to unlace my boots, I said, "There's a basket of slippers over there if you'd like some, or you're welcome to go barefoot."

"Oh! That explains a lot. I just thought you liked running around in your socks!"

"We don't wear shoes in the house."

"Good to know," Amethyst said as she stepped out of her wildly colored sneakers that matched the cartoon character scrub top she was wearing. Suddenly, she said, "I don't have any clean clothes."

"Your mom said she'd send someone over with a bag for you," I informed her.

"Of course she did," she replied with a smile. "No matter how old we get, she still takes care of us."

"That's what a mom is supposed to do."

"When will I get to meet your mother? Have you told her about me yet?"

"I have," I assured her. "She'll be stateside next month, and she and my dad plan to come visit after they reconnect in Virginia."

"I can't wait to meet her. She sounds like a badass."

"All of the women in my family are. Kind of like the women in yours."

"They are pretty awesome."

"You're pretty awesome," I added. I put on the slides I liked to wear around the house and then took her shoes and set them next to mine beneath the bench against the wall. "Let's go talk to Tutu. She's been anxious to meet you."

"I'm nervous."

"There's no reason to be. She's going to love you as much as I do."

AMETHYST

I was still reeling from Tama'i's offhand remark when we sat down to dinner, but his nephews' reaction to today's events took my mind off of it. Aleki, the oldest, was cheerful and happy while Tamkea, Tama'i's niece sounded excited when she asked if he was going to get an award from the police department.

"I heard he beat a man to death, which makes sense because that's what he does, right?" Kai asked snidely.

The entire table went quiet before Tutu reached over and slapped Kai's arm as she hissed, "You mind yourself, Kai Rubin!"

"I'm not lying. Everyone knows it's the truth."

"I did not kill Leaga," Tama'i said in a tortured voice.

"But you tried."

"If I had wanted to kill him, he would be dead. I wanted retribution, and I got it."

"Whatever. He never did anything to you!"

"Kai!" Aleki yelled. "Shut your mouth before I put my fist in it."

"What? You don't like the truth either? What about you, Meka? He's not such a bright star now, is he?"

"Tameka, go to your room," Tutu said as she nudged Tameka's plate toward her. "I will come get you for dessert when it's ready."

"But I . . ."

"Now," Tama'i growled.

"If she doesn't go, are you going to beat her too?"

"Shut the hell up, Kai," Aleki yelled. "You don't know what you're talking about!"

"I know what he did to our father."

"That man is not our father!" Aleki responded.

Kai didn't let Aleki's outburst phase him and said, "You tortured him. What kind of monster does that?"

"Tama'i is not the bad guy in this story," Tutu said reasonably. "Kai, please stop. We don't talk about the past because there's no change to be had."

"No, we don't talk about the past because that might make big, bad Tama'i look like the monster that he is." Kai scoffed before he said, "You broke his arm, his leg, and all of his toes. What did you do? Sit on him with your fat ass, *Tiny?*"

"Shut your fucking mouth!" Aleki said a split second before his arm swung around and he punched his brother in the eye. Kai's chair flew back, and he sprawled on the floor for a few seconds before he hopped up like he was on a spring. By the time Kai was on his feet, Aleki was ready for him.

Kai slammed into Aleki hard enough to knock him back a step, and he bumped into the table and then into Tutu who wasn't braced for impact and started to fall from her chair. Tama'i knocked his drink off the table as he reached for her and then held her up while she grappled for a hold so she could sit up straight again. She was almost steady when Kai pushed Aleki again and Tutu went flying.

I let Tama'i take care of Tutu and jumped up to usher the boys outside. I used the skills I'd learned as an older sister to my advantage and came up on their blind side as I reached out to grab them by the hair at the nape of their necks. Once I had a good hold, I yanked them apart and then used all of my strength to slam them back together, knocking their heads hard enough to stun them. I did it a second time and then a third until both boys were limp and dizzy. While they were trying to get their bearings, I dragged them to the open sliding door and threw them out onto the patio.

"Take that malarkey outside and finish it, but you're

not hurting your grandmother and wrecking this house in the process!" I yelled right before I pulled the door shut and locked it. "Lucky I don't just whoop them like they deserve and . . ."

My voice trailed off when I realized that Tama'i and Tutu were sitting at the table with their eyes wide and their mouths hanging open in shock at what they'd just witnessed.

"Peas and rice! I'm so sorry! I overstepped. That wasn't my business and . . ."

Tutu put her hands up and started clapping slowly, and Tama'i grinned as he joined her. Within just a few seconds, they were both clapping as if their favorite music artist had taken the stage. When I heard a shrill whistle, I looked over to find Tameka standing in the mouth of the hall grinning.

I bent my head before I bowed deeply and stood up. Since the mood had lightened, in my best Elvis impersonation, I cracked, "Thank you. Thank you very much."

"Are we just going to let them beat each other up?" Tameka asked worriedly as she looked past me out into the yard.

I turned around to find the boys in the grass, whaling on each other like they were prizefighters going for the title.

"In my experience, sometimes you have to let them get it out of their system," I mused as I watched Aleki hit his brother with an impressive right hook. "Kai is angry about something and his words made Aleki just as angry. Let them fight it out until their bodies wear down enough for their ears to start working again. If nothing else, they'll be too out of breath to argue when you try and talk sense into them."

"Fa'aipoipo ia te ia, a leai o le a ou su'e lou faia'oga faasaienisi i le vasega valu ma fai o ia ma ou tama matua fou."

Tama'i looked horrified, and Tameka burst out laughing at whatever it was that Tutu had just said in Samoan. She said something else, and Tama'i answered her, but for some reason, none of them were willing to translate for me, so I had to make my own assumptions about what was said.

"You just told him that you think I'm barbaric, didn't you?" I asked sadly. "I'll go break 'em up."

"No, tamaitai lalelei atoatoa. Let them fight."

"What do those words mean?"

"That you're perfect just the way you are."

"But you didn't say I'm not barbaric."

"You're real, and that's what makes you wonderful. Sit down, and let the boys fight it out. I'll wade in when they start dragging ass and then let you doctor them up while they talk like rational humans instead of snarling like rabid animals."

Tameka, who had been standing next to Tama'i's chair, leaned over and kissed him on the temple before she said, "Someday, I'm going to marry a man just like you, Uncle."

"That's the sweetest thing anyone has ever said to me, Itiiti."

"When you and Amethyst have babies, make sure at least two of them are girls, okay?"

I was shocked when, without even thinking about it, Tama'i agreed, "I'll do my very best."

"This is going to sting a little, but it will numb the area so that you can't feel the stitches," I warned Kai as I prepared the syringe of lidocaine. Once Tama'i pulled the boys apart, they had injuries that were more than I could handle with a regular first aid kit, so we brought them up to the office. "I'll do a few small shots around your wound and then give it a few minutes to work its magic before I clean it up and start sewing."

"Is it going to leave a scar?"

"Only if you want it to."

"That could be kind of cool."

"But do you really want to have a permanent memory of the time you and your brother tried to kill each other in the yard?"

"Maybe."

"Why do you hate your uncle?"

"He tried to kill my biological father. My grandmother said she's never gotten over how she felt when she saw her son in a hospital bed with broken bones and burns all over his body."

I heard the door open, but no one came inside, so I asked, "I know I haven't known Tama'i for very long, but I can't imagine him doing that."

"He went to prison for it," Kai said forcefully. "They don't send innocent men to prison."

"Hmm. Sometimes they do, but I'd imagine that if your uncle was convicted of that, then he probably had a good reason for his actions."

"Why are you defending him?"

"How big is your father, Kai?"

"I don't know."

"Tama'i is a giant compared to most men. I always thought the men in my family were huge, but he's inches taller than them and more stout and muscular too. Don't you think that a man of his strength and size could easily kill a man if he really wanted to?"

"He killed a man today. Maybe two."

"That man was helping another one try to beat up, and maybe even kill, my very good friend who had the misfortune of catching him speeding. He injured her so badly that they might have to take out a piece of her skull to relieve the pressure on her brain from the swelling. She may never be the same, and even if she is, it will take her months - maybe even years - to get back to the woman she was when she woke up this morning. If your uncle hadn't stopped to help her, she'd be dead right now."

"That's different from what he did to my father."

"Have you ever asked him why he did what he did?"

"No."

"Why don't you?" I asked.

"I know why," I heard Aleki say from behind me. I glanced over my shoulder but quickly looked back at Kai's wound that I was working to clean. "If I tell you, will you believe me or are you going to keep being an asshole?"

"Where is your uncle, Aleki?" I asked, hoping that he'd come into the room before I heard something he might not want me to hear or the boys started throwing punches again.

"He got a call, but the reception was bad so he took it outside," Aleki explained as he walked further into the exam room. "Do you want to know?"

"Yeah, but how do you know and I don't?"

"Because you were too young. I remember watching it happen and then sitting in the hospital with Uncle while he cried."

"He cried over our father after he beat him?"

"That man is not our father. Dad is our father and has been since the day he met Mom. The man you're talking about deserved every punch and kick he got and then some, Kai."

"Why? What did Uncle do to him?"

"He broke his arm, his leg, and three of his fingers, busted up his face, burned him with cigarettes on his

274

stomach and legs, broke his toes, and knocked out two of his teeth. He was very specific about how he injured that man, Kai." Kai tried to turn his head to look at his brother, but I had a solid grip to hold him still. I was just inches from his face and saw his eyes widen in shock as his brother kept speaking. "Think about it, Kai. What are those scars on your belly from? What about the ones on your legs? Why does your hand hurt when it rains? And why don't the toes on your left foot look like the ones on your right?"

"He hurt me?"

"When I said I sat on Uncle's lap while he cried, it wasn't that man's bed we were beside, it was yours."

"Oh my God," I whispered as tears filled my eyes. Kai was having the same reaction, and I watched as tears spilled down his cheeks. I remember hearing Tama'i say that he noticed his nephew's toes while he was laying in the bed in front of him and thought that memory must be from the time Kai spent in the hospital after such horrible abuse.

"You were just a baby, Kai. I was four or so, I think, and you'd just started walking. Everything's sort of a blur, but I remember you screaming one day and I saw him hurting you. The next thing I remember is sitting on Uncle's lap while he told me it was all going to be okay, but it wasn't. He went away for a long time because of what he did, but he didn't do it because he's evil like those people are trying to tell you, he did it because that's exactly what that man did to you."

"They didn't tell me that."

"Of course they didn't," I heard Tama'i say. "His mother knew what was happening because you lived in her house with your father while your mother was deployed.

She testified at my trial that it was all a misunderstanding and you were just a clumsy little boy."

I sniffed back my tears when I said, "I've seen enough children just learning to walk to know that they're clumsy, but not clumsy enough to break their own bones."

"Or burn themselves," Aleki whispered.

"I believed their lies," Kai whispered. "I turned my back on my family because I believed what they told me."

I finished the last stitch and put my equipment on the tray before I pushed it aside so I could get closer to the young man in front of me. Without a word, I put my arms around him and pulled him closer to my chest to absorb his tears and let my own fall into his dark hair that looked so much like his uncle's. I felt a hand on my back and turned to find Tama'i standing beside me, rubbing Kai's back.

"I'm sorry, Uncle," Kai said as he let me go and turned to Tama'i. "I never should have doubted you."

"I'll try to be the kind of man you never doubt again, aloalii."

I moved away so Tama'i could wrap the young man in his arms and took a few steps back until I was standing with Aleki who was almost as emotional as the rest of us. I wiped my tears with one hand as I used the other to grab Aleki's hand. He squeezed it as tears ran down his face, and I marveled at the strength he showed today after all the things he'd witnessed at such a young age.

I already respected Tama'i as the man I'd come to love. However, after hearing why he went to prison, I didn't just love him, but also admired and respected him for what he had been willing to do - and continue to do - for his family.

Maybe, if I was lucky someday, I'd have children who would grow up admiring him too.

NINETEEN

Life is short, and so is my patience.

Text from Lout to Amethyst

TAMA'I

I woke up when Amethyst pressed against me and sighed when I realized that she was still sleeping. I could see the first hint of morning light creeping around the edge of the blinds and made a split-second decision to start this day out right.

"Wake up, Lalelei," I whispered as I gently shook her shoulder. "Rise and shine. We need to hurry."

"Hurry where?" Amethyst grumbled. "My alarm hasn't gone off, and I don't have to be at the clinic until nine."

"Come on, sweetheart. Wake up for me. This is important."

Amethyst's eyes fluttered open, and she asked, "What's wrong?"

"Nothing's wrong. Brush your teeth and put your boots on. Let's go."

"Go where? The sun's not even up yet," Amethyst argued.

"Please?"

"Is there coffee where we're going?"

"We'll see. Maybe later. Hup hup, baby. Let's go."

"I hope you know there's a field littered with the bodies of people who expected me to rush before I've had my first cup of coffee," Amethyst griped as she stumbled toward the bathroom. "We've been together for almost a month. How did I not see this side of you before?"

"What side of me?" I asked as I pulled on a pair of jeans.

"If you're a cheerful early riser, I'm going to have to reevaluate this entire relationship." I laughed at her declaration but then zipped my mouth shut when Amethyst walked to the bathroom door with toothpaste foam around her mouth and eyes glittering with anger as she pointed at me.

"Just this one time, Lalelei. I promise." I heard her spit and rinse and then the sink ran for a few seconds. I knew from the other times we'd woken up together that she was washing her face. When she reappeared in the doorway with a frown as she swept her silk bonnet off, I said, "After this morning, I promise I won't wake you up before dawn ever again."

"If you value your life, you'll keep that promise," Amethyst said with a pout as she dug through the bag her mom had sent over and found a pair of jeans. "It's a good thing we showered last night or this impromptu motorcycle ride wouldn't be happening."

"It was fate directing us to stay up late and shower

together."

"Hmm. I thought it was because we were horny."

I burst out laughing and walked into the bathroom to brush my teeth while Amethyst got dressed. By the time I walked back into the bedroom, she was sitting on the edge of the bed, fully dressed in jeans and a T-shirt with a bandana around her hair, nodding off while she sat upright.

"Come on, Lalelei. If we hurry, we might have time to get an omelet at Gamma's diner."

"Ew." Amethyst frowned as she stood up and walked toward the bedroom door. "I only eat butt nuggets if they're inside a cake."

"Butt nuggets?"

"Eggs. I know where they come from."

"So do I, and they're delicious."

"In a cake, yes. In their natural form, all icky on the plate, no." Amethyst shuddered. "You really need to get your priorities straight, Tama'i."

"I have. That's why we're going where we're going."

AMETHYST

The cool morning breeze woke me up and had me

shivering before we even got to the highway. I pressed closer to Tama'i's back and let him be my windbreak as I rested my head between his shoulder blades and thought about the events of last night and what that meant going forward.

Yesterday, he'd said that he loved me, and even though he hadn't said it directly to me, I knew that he meant it. The men in my family demonstrated their love for their wives and families in many different ways. My father was grumpy and gruff most of the time, but when he looked at Mom, his face softened and he got a light in his eyes that was unmistakable.

I saw that same light when Tama'i smiled at me and already knew that I wanted to see that light for the rest of my life.

Last night after we got back to his house, Tama'i sat on the patio with his nephews for over an hour and talked to them about what had happened all those years ago and why he went to prison. Originally, I had planned to let them have a private discussion, but Tama'i took me by the hand and led me outside as he explained, "I want you to hear this, too, so there are no secrets between us."

The revelation of what his brother-in-law had done made me so mad that I wanted to hunt him down and finish the job Tama'i started, but it also broke my heart. In my profession, I saw children from all walks of life - from happy families where they had fulfilling childhoods to stressed and tense families where the children became mired down by the ill effects of their home life.

I saw little ones covered in bumps and bruises that came from being a kid and remembered all the wild things I'd done as a child playing with the other kids in my family.

But I also saw children with suspicious bruises and shadows in their eyes that told a story of abuse without them having to say a word.

Tama'i explained that he had happily gone home to Hawaii to visit his sister's family and the friends he'd left there when he was young. When Tutu arrived for the planned visit, she and Tama'i picked the boys up from their father and found them living in horrible conditions - nothing like things had been when Kiki left for her deployment. Tama'i and Tutu took the kids to the hotel with them and cleaned them up before they spent time with them. Tutu cried when they had to take them back home.

Tama'i and Tutu extended their trip until they could get in touch with Kiki, but that took some time. When they were finally able to get in contact with her, they explained that the boys weren't safe or well in their home and needed to go somewhere else. Kiki was able to take emergency leave from her unit and fly home, but again, that took a few more days.

Tama'i had called Leaga, his brother-in-law, over and over again to get more time with Aleki and Kai, but he'd been rebuffed with one excuse after another. Finally, he decided to take matters in his own hands and left the main island to travel to the island where Leaga had the boys. What he found horrified him. Kai was barely conscious with visible bruises and burns on his body, and Aleki was locked in the closet of the bedroom while Leaga lay unconscious on the living room floor - either high or drunk. Tama'i wasn't sure and didn't care.

Tama'i called for Tutu, and when she arrived, she took the boys with her to the hospital while Tama'i stayed and tortured Leaga for hours, making sure to do everything to him that he'd done to his son in what was probably a drunken and drug-induced rage. He left Leaga in the same closet where he'd found Aleki and joined Tutu in the hospital to sit at Kai's bedside.

Before long, the police arrived to investigate what had happened to Kai and to arrest Tama'i for what he'd done to Leaga. Tama'i had gone willingly and pled guilty to the charges against him without any remorse whatsoever. By that time, Kiki had come back to the island and joined Tutu and the boys. Before Leaga had even left the hospital to recover from his injuries, all of their things had been packed up and moved to the mainland where they would live in Tama'i's parents' home.

Tama'i was transferred to a federal penitentiary on the mainland where he served his sentence, and with Tutu's help, Kiki raised the boys while still serving in the Marines where she met the man she married who loved and raised the boys as his own children and was happy to call them his sons.

Leaga had served a sentence too short for what he'd done to Kai, but he had also lost his rights as their father, which angered him and his family still to this day. Just as Kiki had feared, their poison had seeped into Kai when he got in touch with them. That all came to a grinding halt yesterday when everything came to light and Kai's eyes were opened to reality and he was reminded of why he loved his uncle, the man who had given up years of his life in his defense.

I'd known for quite some time now that I was in love with Tama'i, but yesterday's revelations clinched it. I had never cared what Tama'i had been to prison for because I knew the man he was today, but finding out that he'd been punished for seeking vengeance to pay for what was done to an innocent child was icing on the cake, as far as I was concerned. I knew that if my family ever found out, especially my father and uncles, they'd probably throw him a party and make him an honorary member of the brotherhood they shared.

But Tama'i was already part of a brotherhood and was eager to introduce me to the other men of his MC, including the man who was on his way to Texas with a moving truck full of Tama'i's possessions. With his brother-in-law, Bart, coming back soon, Tama'i would be moving into his own place - a modest house just a few blocks from mine.

Since he'd told me that, I had been at war with myself, trying to resist asking him to just move in with me. I'd gone back and forth, listing all the reasons moving in together this quickly was a bad idea, but always came back to my parents' love story, which was just as quick, if not quicker, than our own.

I realized where he was taking me when he turned off the highway onto a two-lane road that led to the back of Uncle Bear and Aunt Autumn's property. I wondered how he found this place but didn't even think about asking him to turn around. Bear might not want strangers on his property, but I was family, and if the future turned out the way I had been dreaming, Tama'i would be too.

When Tama'i pulled his bike over and shut it off, the sun was peeking over the horizon, painting the sky with a gorgeous show of pinks and oranges. I knew he was appreciating the beauty of the moment when Tama'i sat still and tilted his head back to soak it all in. He slowly turned to look at me and smiled.

I studied his handsome face for a few seconds before I laid my lips on his for a long, slow kiss. My arms were still around him when I felt his hand grab my wrist an instant before I was yanked off of my seat and pulled around his body. His lips met mine again, but this time, the kiss wasn't slow and sweet, it was full of passion and fire. His fingers tugged at my jeans, and when he lifted me up with the arm holding me around my back, I felt the cool breeze on my ass.

I laughed and asked, "A little eager there, huh, buddy? We don't exactly have a place to get comfortable or even a place to . . ."

"Right here," Tama'i growled as he slid his hand between my hip and his crotch just before I heard the zipper of his jeans, and then he lifted me again and slowly settled me on his thick cock. Just like it had every time we'd been together before, it took a few seconds for my body to adjust to his size. I gasped when I felt the burn and stretch that told me what was to come. "Fuck, you feel so good, Amethyst."

"That's so good," I whispered as I tried to figure out how I could find a way to move against him.

He leaned forward and pressed my body against the gas tank of the motorcycle as his arm held my legs up and pushed himself even deeper inside me. With his feet on the ground on either side of the bike, he started to move, and I reached up to grip the handlebars to hold me steady as I let him guide me to what I could already tell was going to be an explosive orgasm.

The cap of the gas tank pushed painfully into my back, but I didn't care. The fire that Tama'i was stoking in my body was quickly turning into an inferno that was sure to consume me, but I welcomed the feeling. As I got closer and closer to the pinnacle, I couldn't hold back the moans that I'd had to stifle in bed last night. By the time my orgasm crashed into me, I was screaming Tama'i's name.

He grunted as he slammed into me one last time and then let out a low moan as his cock twitched deep inside me. Tama'i shuddered as my body clutched at his, trying naturally to pull him deeper along with the seed that I secretly hoped might take root and create a child for us.

Tama'i slowly let my legs fall from where they were propped against his shoulder as he leaned over me. He gave me a lingering kiss and then whispered against my lips, "I love you, Amethyst Hamilton."

As he pulled back just far enough to look into my eyes, I smiled and answered, "I love you, too, Tama'i Fuama . . . Fua . . . Fuama . . . Goshdarnit! I was trying to be romantic!"

Tama'i laughed as he leaned back, his cock still deep inside my body. I felt his hand at my hip and then he leaned over me again and gave me a kiss as his hand trailed up my forearm to my hand. I felt something warm against my palm right before he slipped a ring on my finger.

"You're going to have to learn to pronounce our last name, Lalelei, unless you don't want to change it from Hamilton."

"You're . . . Is that a proposal?"

"It is," Tama'i said before he gave me another kiss that *almost* made me forget what had just happened. "Do you need the words?"

"I'd kind of like to hear the words."

"Amethyst Lalelei Hamilton, I love you more than the sun loves the sky and the earth loves the rain. Will you do me the honor of becoming my wife? Will you live with me, raise children with me, watch them grow with me as we get old together, and stay by my side until I leave this world?"

"Yes," I whispered breathlessly as I stared into his eyes. "I want to do all those things."

"I love you," Tama'i said before he gave me a soft kiss.

I heard a familiar whistle. To anyone else it might sound like the call of a bird, but I knew better.

"Shit!" I whispered as I started to shimmy up the tank, trying to sit up so I could get decent. "Put your dick up, sweetheart, we've got company!" I let out an answering whistle, and Tama'i looked at me like I was crazy. "Help me, Tama'i!"

"What's going on?"

"Get up! Get up! Hurry!"

Tama'i lifted me off his now soft member and deposited me beside the motorcycle. I hurriedly bent over and pulled up my underwear and pants, wincing at the thought that I wouldn't be able to clean up. I had just heard Tama'i's zipper when the brush not far away started to shake and Bear, one of my father's good friends, appeared.

"Amy, sweet girl, I've known you since you were just a baby, and the thought of having to tell you this makes me shudder deep inside my soul, but I've got rules out here, and one of them is that nobody fucks in this canyon besides me and my wife."

I held up my left hand and said, "I'm getting

married!"

Bear pursed his lips and slowly shook his head before he said, "Well, shit. Give me a minute to get out of hearing range and then get on with it."

"Thanks, Bear! Love you!"

Bear lifted his arm above his head and gave me a thumbs up as he walked back into the brush, and as was his way, he quickly blended into the scenery and disappeared.

After a few seconds of silence, Tama'i whispered, "What the fuck just happened?"

"That was Bear," I explained. "He's my . . ."

"Uncle, I'm sure," Tama'i interrupted with a grimace.

I realized exactly what that meant and called out, "Please don't tell anyone until I talk to my parents!"

All I got in answer was a whistle, but I knew that meant Bear would keep my secret. He was very good at that since he'd been keeping secrets with my dad and all of the other men for decades.

"I meant to speak to your father some time today and ask for your hand, but I got caught up in the moment."

"Do you want to keep this a secret until you do that? I think he'd appreciate getting to threaten your life before he agrees." Tama'i raised his eyebrows in question, and I shrugged before I looked down at my ring. "This is beautiful, Tama'i. I love it."

"It belonged to Tutu. My grandfather bought it for her on their anniversary before he died. I asked her for it last night, and she gave it to me when we came home from the clinic."

"Is that what you were talking about at the table when I couldn't understand you?" I asked.

"No. Sort of. No." When I stared at him in confusion, Tama'i laughed. "Tutu knows just where to hit a man to get her way."

"What did she say?"

"Before I tell you, I have to say that this was all my idea."

"Tell me," I insisted.

"She said I needed to marry you or she'd find my eighth grade science teacher and make him my new grandfather," Tama'i explained with a look of horror. He swallowed hard and then said, "And if I don't have a ring on your finger and a baby in your belly by Valentine's Day, she'll never cook for me again." I burst out laughing, and Tama'i smiled as he said, "I told you she was meaner than she looks."

I glanced down at my ring and then grinned at Tama'i before I said, "There's a very comfortable bench right up the trail, but I want to do one thing."

"What's that?" Tama'i grunted as I jumped into his arms and wrapped my legs around his waist. He held me there and then shifted to make me a little more comfortable, which was perfect because that lined my clit up with his zipper and rubbed just perfectly. "Well, okay then."

"I just wanted to see what that felt like." Tama'i tilted his head in question, and I gave him a kiss before I explained, "That's how my mom has greeted my dad since they met. She doesn't do it as often now that they're older, but it's not uncommon to come around the corner and find Mom and Dad making out with her in his arms just like this."

"That's kind of cool."

"I just wanted to see what it was like to jump and know that the man you love is going to catch you."

"This is what it feels like, and I'll always be there to catch you, Lalelei."

TWENTY

I hope your pH levels are thrown off-balance and you get a yeast infection.

Text from Amethyst to Diamond

AMETHYST

"I came up on my lunch break and talked to her for a few minutes. She's in good spirits," Cydney said as she walked around the back of her SUV and waited with me for Wren and Bella to park so we could walk in together.

"I thought she must be. She asked me to bring Tama'i, so he's meeting us in the lobby."

"You two have become quite the couple," Cydney commented.

"Haven't they?" Bella asked as she got out of her truck.

As Wren walked toward us, she said, "I think they're adorable."

"He's pretty awesome," Cydney admitted. "You've definitely got our vote."

"Good. I've got something I've wanted to tell you for a few days, and since we had dinner at my parents' house last night, I can," I said slyly. I smiled brightly at my friends and then lifted my left hand up and wiggled my fingers. "We're getting married!"

"Holy shit!" Bella squealed.

Cydney's mouth dropped open in shock, and she burst into tears - not the 'happy for my friend' tears I was expecting, but great big wracking sobs that shook her whole body. Bella and I were shocked at the emotion, but Wren just looked at the ground uncomfortably while we tried to soothe our friend.

"What's going on, Squid?"

"I'm just so happy for you! It's great news, Amy!" Cydney said through her tears. "This is wonderful, isn't it, girls?"

Bella was studying Cydney's face as if there would be an answer there to the questions we both had, but she finally smiled at me and agreed, "Congratulations, Amy."

Wren lit up when she looked up at me with a smile. "I'm happy for you, cousin. He's a great man, and I think he'll do whatever it takes to make you happy."

"Just like I'll do for him," I promised. As Cydney wiped the tears off her face and checked her makeup in the side mirror of the car we were next to, I said, "Should I wait to tell Zozo? She's got a lot on her mind right now and . . ."

"And good news will only help make her feel better," Wren assured me.

We were already on the sidewalk when I spotted Tama'i and picked up the pace to get to him faster. I was only about ten yards from him when he suddenly frowned and opened his mouth to yell. Suddenly, I was hit from the side. I lost my footing and went flying as I heard my friends and Tama'i screaming my name. I curled up to lessen the impact on my body like I'd learned to do in my wild childhood and hit the ground with a thump before my body naturally rolled.

~/~

My roll abruptly stopped when I hit the brick wall, and I heard a woman grunt right before someone tugged my hair as if to get me to stand. Not a stranger to a good brawl, I reached up and grabbed the wrist attached to the hand in my hair and used that leverage to spin around on my ass to face my attacker. I punched the strange woman as hard as I could dead center between her legs and heard her let out a squeak before her hand let go of my hair.

I was up on my feet in the next second and had my forearm on her throat when I slammed her into the brick wall. She started to squirm, and I yelled, "Who the fuck are you?"

"Let me go!"

"Answer me!"

"Please let me go."

"Answer me!" I screamed.

"He broke up with me because of you! I can't even go see him because you blocked me from visiting Archer!"

"You!" I growled when I realized that this was Mr. Massey's girlfriend - the woman who had almost killed my patient, an innocent little boy who trusted the adults around him to keep him safe and healthy.

"You're hurting me!"

"I just got started, bitch! You come at me like that and then don't expect me to go completely fucking sideways on your ass? That tells me you're even more fucking ignorant than I first thought. You're lucky we're in public because if we were alone, I wouldn't just kick your ass, I'd end your fucking life without even blinking twice, and then I'd make it a point to go back to your shallow grave every time I need to take a shit."

"Camera on your right, Amy," Wren called out as she walked over to block the view.

"Watchers behind us and to the left," Cydney warned. I saw her raise her hands as if to wave people by, and then she called out to strangers, "What are you looking at? Haven't you ever seen two women kissing before? Jeez!"

"Move along, people!" Bella yelled.

Wren got close to my back and said, "Figure out how you want to fix this because we've got maybe two minutes before people start to get antsy."

"Want me to get the truck?" Bella asked.

"I think I can carry her, but you'll have to knock her ass out."

"I could end you right now, bitch," I said as I pressed against her neck even harder, cutting off her air for a few seconds before I backed off enough for her to catch her breath.

"Fuck me," I heard Tama'i whisper. In a louder voice, he asked, "What did I just hear?"

"What? I didn't say I don't know how to cuss, just that I don't like to," I said as I glanced over at Tama'i who was standing there in shock with a helpless look on his face. I looked back at the woman who was quickly turning an alarming shade of purple and hissed, "If I ever see you again, I'll kill you where you stand. Do you understand me?" She nodded frantically as she clawed at my arm to help clear her airway. I pushed a little harder as I said, "If Archer gets so much as a hangnail, I'll fucking end you, bitch. Same thing will happen if you mutter a word about our little chat today."

The second I let her neck go, she gasped for air and bent forward at the waist in obvious pain.

Cydney picked a purse up off the sidewalk and pulled the wallet out before she tossed it back to the ground. Once she had the wallet open, she pulled the woman's driver's license out and slipped it into my back pocket before she threw it at the woman's feet.

Wren, one of the most even-keeled women of our group but also the one with the most violent temper, grasped the woman by her hair and yanked her up so that they were eye to eye. "She's not the only one you'll have to contend with, bitch. We know your name, and we can find out everything about you in seconds and then make it our mission to shit on every corner of your life until we're bored and decide to start at the beginning and do it all again."

As the woman frantically nodded, tears and snot streaming down her face, I warned, "If you ever hurt another child, we'll find you, and don't think I won't keep track. Got me?"

"Yeah," the woman said through her sobs. "I'll move away. I'll never . . . I promise. I'll be . . . I'll go away."

"Do it right the fuck now," Wren ordered before she smacked the woman's head on the bricks behind her and then tossed her aside like garbage to land at Cydney and Bella's feet.

Bella leaned down and smiled at the woman before she said, "It's so sad that you're clumsy enough to trip and fall like that, isn't it? That's what the cops are going to think if they ever ask you any questions, right?"

"Yeah. No cops. I'll just go. Right now."

"Run," Cydney ordered menacingly.

The woman scrambled to her feet just as Cydney kicked her purse closer to her. She bent and picked up her wallet and the purse before she sprinted across the street to the parking garage, her sobs echoing loud enough for us to hear them where we were standing by the hospital.

"Who was that?" Wren asked calmly.

"BAC and heatstroke," I said simply, knowing Wren would remember the patient I was talking about but not willing to give his medical information to everyone.

"Oh, that fucking bitch," Wren said as she started across the street.

"Down, girl. It's a small town, and you know she won't leave. We'll run into her sooner or later," Bella promised as she grabbed Wren's arm. "As a matter of fact, considering y'all's reaction, I think we should use the info on her driver's license and hunt that bitch down."

"I'll drive!" Cydney said cheerfully.

"Are you ready for this?" I heard my dad ask from nearby. I spun around and found him standing there next to Tama'i with Cydney's father, Grady, and Uncle Bird behind them. "Marrying my little princess will come with some challenges, Tiny."

"Princess?" Tama'i choked out. My dad and the other men laughed, and without missing a beat, Tama'i said, "You know, you're right. She is a princess. I thought I was in love with Cinderella, but I just found out she's more like

Thugerella, and I'm here for it. That was sexy as hell."

My dad grimaced and looked at Tama'i before he said, "And now I have to kill you."

I ignored Dad's irritation and threw myself at Tama'i. He caught me in his arms and spun me around as he kissed me soundly.

"Hi, Lalelei," Tama'i said with a grin the second he pulled his lips from mine. "Looks like you've had a pretty boring day."

"Just the usual," I lied with a shrug. Tama'i let me slide down his body until my feet were on the ground, and I linked my hand with his before I said, "Let's go upstairs so I can officially introduce you to another of our mild-mannered and well-behaved friends."

"I can't wait."

TAMA'I

The women who had been so keyed up downstairs were much calmer when they filed into their friend's hospital room. Apparently, they had connections here because I knew there were signs plastered everywhere that stated no more than two visitors at a time, but when we got into Zoey's room, there were already three people - her parents and a man who looked a lot like the woman in the bed.

He stood up and strode over to us, and Amethyst squeezed my hand before she let it go. The man stuck his hand out and said, "I'm Zane, Zozo's twin brother, and I can't thank you enough for what you did for her . . . for our family. You have my . . ." The man's eyes filled with tears, and he cleared his throat before he finished with, "You have my eternal gratitude. I can never repay you for the gift you gave us by saving my sister."

"I hate that it happened to her, but I'm glad I was there to help," I said honestly.

"Thank you," Zane repeated before he tugged my hand to pull me in for a quick hug with a few hard slaps on the back. When he stepped back, his eyes were clear and his posture was strong again, and I was glad to see it. He looked over at Amethyst and then down at her hand before he said, "Is this new information?"

"Yes."

"She's gonna shit."

"Stop talking about me like I'm not here," the woman in the bed croaked. "I hate that."

"Yes, my queen. Anything for you, my queen. God, the drama with this one, right?" Zane asked sarcastically.

"Piss off," the woman said with a half-smile.

Amethyst took my hand again and led me closer to the bed. Once we were beside her friend, she leaned over her and paused for a minute before she said, "You look like shit."

"The last time I saw something that looked like you, I flushed," the woman croaked. She smiled up at me and through her swollen lips said, "Whenever you're ready to take out the trash and get a real woman, I'll be waiting."

"I'll keep that in mind," I joked and then laughed when Amethyst's eyes narrowed at me in mock outrage. I could tell that she was trying to lighten the mood with her good humor, so I went along with it and shrugged before I said, "A man's gotta keep his options open."

"Just for that, I'm not going to introduce you as my fiancé," Amethyst said petulantly. "Zozo, this is my casual acquaintance, Tama'i."

"Fiancé?" Zoey asked with a gasp. When Amethyst nodded, Zoey scoffed and said, "Of course he is. I damn near get killed, and she steals my knight in shining armor. How shitty is that? Typical Amy."

"She is a drama queen, isn't she?" Wren asked.

Cydney rested her hand on Zoey's leg and squeezed it gently before she said, "Always with the drama. You know if you weren't such a puss, you'd be up walking around by now."

No one pointed out that the police officer's leg was in some sort of contraption that held it over the bed, but I knew they were just trying to avoid that elephant in the room.

"Wren lost her temper and threatened to kill someone in the parking lot," Bella tattled. "You should have seen it."

"Amy got her first!" Wren argued. "Why is it always my fault? You were there. You watched it happen!"

"I didn't see shit," Cydney said with an exaggerated shrug. "Did you see anything, Amy?"

"Nothing."

"Lies! Y'all are a bunch of lying hags," Wren said petulantly. She sat on the edge of the bed by Zoey's feet and looked at Cydney before she said, "I like what you've done with your hair."

"You do? I haven't had it done in a few weeks but . . ."

"There's one out of place," Wren said as she reached toward Cydney's face. She touched her top lip and said, "There. I got it!"

Zoey snorted and then started laughing silently as Cydney stared daggers at Wren.

"No matter how old they get, they still act like wild animals," Carlie, Zoey's mother, said through her laughter.

Her husband, Sam, agreed and said, "You ladies should take this shit on the road."

"I will as long as Cydney never gets to drive," Zoey said firmly.

"Ditto," Amethyst agreed with Zoey. "I'm not riding anywhere with that crazy heifer."

"She drives like a maniac," Bella agreed. "I think she learned from Terran."

"Or Griffin!" Wren said cheerfully. "Koda is almost as bad."

I thought I remembered that one of the wild little boys was named Griffin - Amethyst's cousin's son or something. There were so many that it was hard to keep track.

"Oh my God! I saw Koda at the clinic today. You would not believe what he did this time!"

"Oh, I love Koda stories," Zoey said cheerfully. "What did he do now?"

"I swear, Ruf and Hawk should get punch cards at the clinic and the emergency room. Buy nine x-rays and get the next set of stitches free or something," Wren said with a laugh. "You should have seen Ruf's face when he brought him in this morning."

"What happened?"

"He decided to propose to his little girlfriend during lunch at school and put the ring he chose for her on his finger. Of course, his finger swelled up around the bolt that he stole from Ruf's junk drawer, and we had to figure out how to get it off without hurting him."

"Can you imagine what kind of woman he'll snare one day?" Bella asked.

"I think our parents probably said the same thing about us when we were kids," Amethyst admitted.

"Actually, it was just last week," Carlie chimed in, causing everyone, including the badly injured woman to laugh.

Her entire demeanor had changed since the women arrived - her face wasn't nearly as pale, and she was smiling with a twinkle in her eye. Obviously, good friends were the key to healing.

We hadn't been there long before Zoey started yawning, and when the nurse came in to check on her, the girls said their goodbyes and filed out. There were lots of insults about Zoey being lazy and getting her ass out of bed, which she threw back at them by saying she looked better with a bruised face than any of them did on their best day. After hugs and kisses, I left the room with the women I'd arrived with.

We made it almost to the elevator before I heard the first sniffle, and by the time the doors opened, one of the ladies behind me was crying openly.

I looked over at Amethyst and saw tears on her face, but before I could ask what was wrong, she said, "She looked so small in that bed."

"And her face. Oh my God. I just wanted to hold her," Bella said through her tears as she walked ahead of me into the elevator.

"It was so hard to see her like that because she's our number one ass kicker," Cydney whispered. "She looks so frail."

I barely had enough time to process what Cydney had said and wonder how Zoey was the 'ass kicker' of the group when I'd just seen Amethyst go off on a woman and threaten to kill her. Honestly, I couldn't imagine what Zoey was bringing to the table.

"Thank you for saving our friend, Tiny," Wren said in a voice choked with emotion. "You're the best."

"You are," Amethyst cried as she threw her arms around me. Suddenly, I had not just the woman I loved in my arms, but three other women who loved her, too, and all of them were sobbing.

When the elevator doors opened on the ground floor, I saw several men I recognized as some of Amethysts's extended family standing with Hawk, Phoenix, and Crow. In a split second, they took in the scene in front of them and then scrambled away, going off in all directions before the women spotted them.

On a regular day, I wasn't really a violent man, but I had just added at least five names to the list of people I was going to kill the next time I got angry, and at least three of them had the last name Forrester.

TWENTY ONE

I love to insult people, and with you and the other birdbrains around, it's always a target-rich environment.

Text from Amethyst to Crow.

AMETHYST

"Talk to me, silly girl. I know there's something wrong, and it's starting to worry me that you won't share," I said as I walked past Cydney who was sitting at the kitchen table with a sad expression.

"You've got a lot going on right now, Amy. I'm fine. We'll catch up when things calm down."

"I don't know that they will anytime soon," I admitted. "Everything's been a whirlwind."

"Isn't that the truth?" Cydney said softly.

"It's been just over a month since we had our first kiss, and he's moving in with me!" I said, a tinge of mania in my voice. "Am I crazy? I'm crazy. No, I'm not. Look at our parents."

"They'd agree that you've always been at least a little bit crazy," Cydney said sarcastically.

"You know what I mean, Squid. I know it seems wild when you look at my situation from the outside, but just think - my parents' love story is legendary. Your parents' love story is just as nuts. We've watched and learned from them our entire lives, and their example shows us just how good things can turn out when you take a chance."

"You're right. My mom was a single parent and pregnant with Tad when she met my dad, and they've been happy together for years and years."

"Exactly. My mom had known my dad for a little while, but she moved in and started raising us within weeks of starting to talk to him."

"That's just crazy, but it worked, and they're still so in love that the sweetness gives me a toothache every time I'm near them."

"It can happen for me, and someday, it will happen for you too."

"Yeah," Cydney said hesitantly. "I just hope I get the happy ending my mom has."

"So, he's moving in this weekend since his brother-in-law will be home on Tuesday, and he's got friends coming in today who are bringing all of his stuff and staying for a week or so. I'm not ready at all!"

"What do you mean you're not ready? Your house is always clean because you're a germ freak who refuses to wear her work clothes further into the house than the laundry room."

"I see some really gross stuff every day, and I don't want to bring all of that in here. I'll be thanking myself for that habit when me and Tama'i have kids."

"Yep."

"Holy shit. I just said it out loud."

"That you and Tiny are going to have kids? Look at the man. Who wouldn't want to birth his spawn?" Cydney winced and said, "Okay, maybe not, because he's a really big guy, and his genetics are probably off the charts."

I sat down with a thump and said, "That's terrifying."

"Childbirth itself is terrifying, but with the size of that man, it would be a horror show. His kids are going to come out doing arm curls and bench pressing Buicks."

"He's so hot when he does that."

"He bench presses Buicks?" Cydney asked in shock.

"No, goober! I mean he's so hot when he's working out and all sweaty. His muscles start to ripple and the veins pop out. He's a phlebotomist's wet dream."

"Only someone in the medical profession would notice *or* say something like that."

"True," I conceded as I stood up again. "I need to check and make sure that the bedroom is cleared out before they get here."

"Didn't you already do that twice?" Cydney asked.

"But I just want to . . ."

"You're procrasticleaning."

"What the hell is that?"

"It's when you have to be up moving around doing

shit that doesn't need to be done because you're trying not to think about whatever it is that's upsetting you."

"Oh."

"Exactly. Get another cup of coffee and sit down before you wear a path in the hardwood."

"Do you want a cup?" I asked as I looked at the mug of tea in front of her. "Since when do you drink tea? What are you, British?"

"I'm fine," Cydney said, but her voice was less convincing than it had been earlier when she had said the same thing.

I had already asked her what was going on three or four times, but Squid was the kind of woman that kept things close to her vest until she was good and ready - she had always been that way.

"Did you ride over here?" I asked as I glanced out the front window. I saw a box truck pulling up at the curb and squealed. "Oh no! Tama'i's not back but his friends have already arrived. I need to call him. Will you get the door for me?"

"Sure," Cydney said as she pushed her chair back.

I grabbed my phone and called Tama'i, and he was out of breath when he answered. It took everything I had to form a coherent sentence because all I could think about was how sexy he must look right now, covered in sweat with his muscles bulging . . .

"Your friends are here."

"They just called. I'm getting on my bike now."

"See you in a minute. Ride safe."

"Love you, Lalelei."

"Love you too."

"This is the best meal I've had in ages," Dice, one of Tama'i's friends who had arrived with all of his belongings, said as he leaned back in his chair and patted his stomach. "I'm pretty sure I have a food baby."

Cydney choked on the tea she'd been sipping all evening and started sputtering. Tank, another of Tama'i's friends who had joined Dice on the drive to Texas, gently patted her on the back as he handed her a napkin to wipe her mouth. She gave him a weak smile and then excused herself and walked toward the bathroom.

I watched my friend go and then rejoined the conversation as my brother Lazlo told the guys about Gamma's diner and all of the goodies she had there.

"You'll love my Gamma," I assured Dice and Tank. "I'll call her tomorrow and see if she's got a free evening for me to bring y'all over so you can taste her cooking."

"Tutu is my one true love," Dice said sincerely. "Someday, I'm going to marry that woman."

"He keeps threatening me with that, but Tutu's not quite on board yet," Tama'i insisted.

"She told him if he didn't marry me, she'd find his high school science teacher and turn him into Tama'i's new grandpa," I told the guys. They were still laughing when Cydney sat back down at the table to finish her food.

"Have you met Tutu?" Dice asked Cydney.

Cydney shook her head, and I said, "Squid and the girls haven't gotten to meet her yet, but they're gonna love her."

"Squid?" Dice asked.

"It's my childhood nickname."

"You've got a road name. That's awesome," Tank said.

"Squid's a biker," I boasted. "She even belongs to a club here in town."

"Oh, really?" Dice asked.

"It's an all female MC that her cousin started," Cydney explained.

"With Squid's help," I added.

"It's too bad you guys don't have your bikes with you. The scenery around here is beautiful, especially in the early morning and at sunset," Tama'i explained.

"Is there a place we can rent one?" Tank asked.

"Let me make some calls. I might be able to find motorcycles for you to borrow while you're here," I said, sure that my dad or some of his friends would loan one of their motorcycles out to a family friend, especially since they were seasoned riders.

"That would be great," Dice said happily. "Maybe you and your all-female MC can show us around."

"My bike is out of commission for a while," Cydney said sadly.

"It is?" I asked. "I wondered why you didn't ride today since it was beautiful outside."

"I can't resist," Dice said as he reached for the bowl of fruit salad I'd made to go with dinner. "I've gotta have some more."

"You're gonna be fat for the reunion show," Tank teased.

"Fuck them," Dice muttered as he stirred the fruit with the wooden serving spoon. "It won't matter because hearts all over are going to break when they find out Tiny is spoken for."

"Whatever," Tama'i said as he rolled his eyes.

"I'm serious. The amount of fan mail your man got was insane, Amy. You'll have to beat the women off with a stick."

"I'm more of an aluminum bat kind of girl," I muttered.

The men laughed, and Cydney gasped. "That's where I know you from! The TV show!"

"And you didn't recognize Tiny?" Dice asked.

Tank laughed and said, "It's not like that big bastard blends in."

"I knew I recognized you from somewhere!" Cydney exclaimed. "That's crazy."

"When do they want to film?" Tama'i asked.

"Sometime next spring," Dice said with a dismissive wave of his hand. "We'll see what comes of it."

"Amethyst hasn't seen a single episode," Tama'i said with a laugh. "Not one."

"Technically, I have," I admitted. "I started watching them during my lunch breaks at work."

"Apparently, it's good television. You wouldn't believe the amount of drama they can stir up just for filming," Tank said with a grin. "Shit. I watched it and was surprised at how they spun things to make it look more interesting."

"Years ago, our fathers were involved in a reality television show about their clubhouse and the garage," I explained.

"I've met Tucker Martin," Tama'i boasted.

"No shit?" Dice asked. "Here?"

"He's part of their extended club family," Tama'i explained.

"His paint work is flawless. That man is a true artist," Tank said in awe. "I'd love to meet him."

"He sells actual paintings at the same gallery that carries Dub's stained glass," Tama'i said. "He was at Dub's wedding."

"How did I miss that?"

"Oh, I don't know, because it wasn't his wedding," Tama'i said sarcastically.

I picked up my phone to text my dad to see if he could find some bikes for the guys to ride while they were here and asked, "How long can you stay?"

"We'll be here for a week," Tank explained. "At some point, we need to ride up and say hello to Okie, but we were hoping you'd be able to join us, Tiny."

"I'd love to. Let me look at my schedule, and we'll arrange that."

"Until then, will you lovely ladies show us around town?" Tank asked.

"I work from nine to at least four everyday, but Squid's hours are more flexible," I explained. "Squid, can you and some of the girls show them around while I'm working?"

Tank smiled at Cydney and said, "I can't think of a better tour guide than a beautiful woman who knows the area. Would you mind showing me around?"

"Sure."

"Are you free tomorrow morning? I'll spring for breakfast."

"Actually, I *am* free tomorrow."

"It's a date."

I smiled when I realized that Cydney may have just met the man of her dreams - a big, tattooed biker with a heart of gold. That was all we'd ever dreamed of, and I'd found mine - now it was her turn.

I looked over at Dice and saw him watching Tank and Cydney's interaction and wondered which one of my friends I could set him up with.

Tama'i leaned closer to me and whispered, "I can see the wheels turning, Amy, and let me just say that Dice is not the kind of guy you want to hook up with your friends."

"You never know, I've got some crazy friends."

"I like your friends, Tama'i. They're hilarious," I told him as I tucked my braids into my silk bonnet as he prepared to brush his teeth.

He and I had spent enough nights together that we had developed a steady routine, doing the dance that couples seemed to do when they got ready together. We had the same sort of routine in the mornings, and it made my heart flutter to realize that there would be a lifetime of moments like these in my future.

"They're good guys. If they weren't, they wouldn't be my friends."

"I think Dice and Wren would be cute together," I

said as I picked up my own toothbrush and got ready for my turn at the sink. Tama'i couldn't talk, but he started shaking his head. "Not Wren? What about Gracy? How old is Dice, anyway?"

"No," Tama'i mumbled through a mouth full of toothpaste. Once he'd rinsed, he reached for the hand towel and wiped his face before he said, "I roomed with Dice when we lived at Pop's compound, and let me just say, there's not a woman out there that can - or should - put up with him."

"Wren was raised with three wild ass brothers. I'm sure she can handle him."

"I said no, Amethyst."

"Oh, you did, huh?" I asked as I put my toothbrush in my mouth to stop me from snapping at him even more.

"You heard me."

I saw red until I noticed the glint in Tama'i's eyes and realized he was teasing me. By the time I finished brushing my teeth, Tama'i was leaning against the doorframe, apparently aching for a fight.

"Are you trying to start an argument?" I asked as I leaned against the counter and crossed my arms over my chest.

"Yep."

"Why would you do that?"

"Because when we argued last week, the make-up sex was wild and fantastic," Tama'i said as he pushed away from the doorframe and walked closer to me. He turned me so my butt was against the counter and then reached down and lifted me onto it. I hissed when my bare legs hit the cold marble, and Tama'i smiled as he said, "If memory serves, it was right here in this exact spot where we made up."

"Maybe," I hedged, trying not to smile.

"That was the first of what will probably be many arguments, but if they all end up like that one, I'm willing to risk your fire."

"Fire?"

"Honey, you have very expressive eyes - especially when they get red and start glowing." I scoffed, and he said, "Although, when your head started spinning, it kind of freaked me out."

I pushed at his shoulder. "Shut up."

"I'm serious. I wondered if I needed an exorcist or a fallout shelter. I've been through some shit in my life, and that was the most terrifying thing I've ever seen."

"Well, then I suggest you not make me that mad again."

"You stuck me with a needle!"

"You didn't even know I'd done it until you saw it in the trash can."

"You got me while I wasn't expecting it, and that's just crooked."

"And I'm gonna do it again in three months because I want you to live a long and healthy life as my husband."

"It wasn't fair."

"Why are you complaining, Tama'i? You got a blow job out of the deal!"

"Yeah, but still."

"Okay, let's try this a different way."

"Does it include you tricking me?"

"No, but it includes this mouth you like so much only going near Mr. Happy every three months when it's time for your shot. How about that? You take your shot like a good patient and instead of rewarding you with a sucker, I just suck on you."

"Your eyes are getting red again."

"Then you shouldn't provoke me and make them that way."

"You shouldn't trick the man you love."

"I want the man I love to have many healthy years ahead, Tama'i. I want him to be around to be old and gray and tired with me after we have our grandchildren over for the afternoon. Then I want him to snuggle up on the couch with me while we reminisce about him and his goofy friends talking crap in a tattoo shop and making all the girls lightheaded."

"Nobody got lightheaded."

"You're gonna get lightheaded when I tell Tutu that you're being a turd and she smacks you with her flip-flop."

"You wouldn't."

"I could tell her to only make your favorite food every three months and only if you take your shot like a good boy."

"That's cruel."

"So is starting a fight with me on purpose. Are you gonna do that again?"

"Oh, I'm gonna, just so I can make up with you over and over."

"For the rest of our lives?" I asked, all anger gone now as he moved his hips against me, nudging me in just the right place that made all thoughts other than the orgasm I knew was coming my way disappear.

"Yes. For the rest of our lives."

"I love you, Tama'i."

"And I love you, Lalelei. I'll love you forever."

EPILOGUE

AMETHYST

I wiped my mouth with a hand towel and stared at my reflection for a few seconds while I got my mind straight for my day. I had back-to-back patients scheduled until almost five o'clock today, and considering there were *always* at least three walk-ins, that meant I would be here until at least six - and Tama'i and I had dinner plans at six-thirty.

There was a tap on the door, and I was shaken from my thoughts. I turned and opened the door to find True standing there with a grin.

"How ya doing?"

"Shut up."

"Let the games begin! We've already got a walk-in, and I know you're gonna want to see him first."

"Betty White!"

"That's a new non-cuss word."

"Well, she was a comedy goddess, and I think that's better than blasphemy," I explained.

"I like that. Anyway, your walk-in is in exam three, and your first scheduled well-check of the day is getting his diaper changed in exam five."

"On it," I said as I turned back to the sink to wash my hands. Apparently, my day was going to start off with a bang. I needed to get my thoughts together, although that had been harder to do for the last few weeks with everything happening so quickly. Between the holidays and planning for the wedding, I'd been busy almost every waking hour. It was starting to take a toll on me.

However, we had a trip to Vegas scheduled soon, so if I could just hold out until then, I'd be nursing one of those seafood buffet food bellies poolside with the girls soon.

The thought of shrimp this early in my morning routine made my stomach flip, but I knew I'd enjoy it when we had our vacation along with plenty of time to sleep and relax. In the last few weeks, the thought of that had been like a beacon in the distance, drawing me closer and giving me hope for the future.

I tapped on the door of Exam Three and opened it to find one of my favorite patients and his mom.

"Archer!"

He smiled at me even though his cheeks were wet with tears and said, "Doctor Amy, I hurt my hand."

"Oh, no," I said as I walked closer to where he was perched on his mom's knee. I pulled some gloves out of the box on the wall and smiled as I pulled them on and asked, "What happened, Mom?"

I sat on the stool and rolled closer as I reached out to take the bandaged hand he was clutching close to his chest.

Archer's mom burst into tears and wailed, "It's all my fault."

Archer, seeing his mom's distress, started crying, too, as he sputtered, "I fell down, and Mom started crying."

"He was running across the yard to get to the car and he tripped, which shouldn't have been that bad, but he started screaming, and when I got over to him, I realized he was bleeding."

"Was there glass or . . ."

"It was the water park!"

"You were at the water park?"

"No, there's a broken sprinkler head in our front yard," Archer's mom said before she sniffed and took in a shuddering breath. "I should have fixed it last week when I realized it was broken, but when I went to the store, they didn't have it, and I didn't have time to go to another one, and then it just slipped my mind, and now . . . and now . . . now he's bleeding!" she wailed.

"I know it's early, but I think it's time," I said as I stood up and cocked my hip toward Archer. "Reach into my pocket, buddy. I think we all need a little pick-me-up."

Archer reached into my pocket, and his tears instantly stopped when he realized what he held in his hand. He pulled out a sucker and then, at my instruction, pulled out two more. By the time he was clutching them in his hand, his mom had managed to pull herself together and unwrap them as I looked at his injury.

To take his mind off of what I was doing, I asked, "What's new in your life, Archer? Has anything exciting happened this week?"

"My dad is getting married!"

I glanced up at Archer's mom, and she smiled before she explained, "Archer's father and kindergarten teacher are in love and planning to get married next year."

I let out an exaggerated breath and laughed before I said, "That's really good news."

"Isn't it, though?" she asked, understanding my relief.

"Is my hand broken?" Archer asked.

"No, but it looks like you're going to need some stitches, honey."

"Stitches? Do I get a shot? I don't want a shot!"

"I've been hearing that a lot lately," I said under my breath before I smiled at my patient. "Lucky for you, I've got a few tricks up my sleeve to make this a little easier."

"What are you going to do?" Archer asked.

"Well, every patient is different," I choked out, thinking of how I got my future husband to take his shots every three months. "But I've got some cherry-flavored medicine that will help."

"And no shot?"

"You'll get a shot, but the cherry stuff will make everything go a little bit easier."

"Can I have some?" Archer's mom asked.

"I'd put it in a squirt bottle and give everyone who walks through the door a swig, if I could."

"Would you take some?" Archer asked.

"I can't right now, but maybe the next time you're here," I lied.

"You're my friend, aren't you, Doctor Amy?"

"I am, Archer," I said as I pulled my gloves off to prepare for his stitches. "You can always count on me."

"What else can I do to help?" my mom asked as she put the last plate on the table.

"Will you go see how Tama'i is doing at the grill? I need to know how long before he's finished with the steaks."

"I can do that," Mom said cheerfully. She winked at me and then turned toward the door as she said, "I'll be back in just a second."

"Are you feeling okay, afa'fine?"

"I'm doing much better than I was the last time you saw me."

"I was worried about you," Tutu said sadly. "Your light was dim, but it's bright again now."

"I was going through a rough patch," I admitted. "But as soon as the morning sickness started to wane, I was back to my old self."

Tutu stopped stirring the pot on the stove and slowly turned her head to look at me. "What did you say?"

Tama'i who had been standing in the doorway, ready to watch the show, walked up behind his Tutu and said, "Tomorrow is Valentine's day, and I managed to do what you asked so you don't stop feeding me."

"But in about six months, you'll have another mouth to feed," I warned.

"You're having a baby?" Tutu asked. When I nodded, she dropped the spoon and swept me into a hug. When she started crying loudly, Tama'i wrapped his arms around both of us, enveloping us in his warmth and the strength that we both admired so much.

"Don't cry, Tutu. You know how that upsets me even if they are happy tears," Tama'i said, trying to console her.

Tutu sniffed and lifted her head off my shoulder. I could see the twinkle in her eyes when she said, "I'm not crying happy tears, Tama'i. I'm crying tears of terror at the thought of another wild boy like you running around and making me crazy."

"You know you're gonna love it."

"Maybe," Tutu hedged as she leaned into his chest.

Tama'i winked at me and mouthed *"I love you."* over his grandmother's head.

"Now I get to go out on the patio and tell my Gigi and Pop that I'm having a baby."

"Is that why you wanted all of us to get together tonight?"

"Partially, but I really wanted all of us to come together for dinner because I love the fact that my family is your family now and vice versa."

"That's the way it should be, afa'fine."

Tama'i leaned over and gave me a kiss before he said, "And that's the way it always will be."

THE END

Check out Cee Bowerman on Facebook. You can also find information about the author and her books on www.ceebowermanbooks.com.

COMING SOON

I'LL STAND BY YOU, SPRINGBLOOD, BOOK 3
COMING SEPTEMBER 2024!

Aksel Nilsen and Anastacia Yeamans have known each other for years - well over a hundred, to be more specific. When they come together, anger turns to lust until they start to argue again. Since they met, their fights have only been rivaled by their passion, but something changed the last time they were forced to be around each other. Aksel and Stassi have started to realize just how much they appreciate the other, even when they're not in the bedroom.

Through the years, Stassi has always known that Aksel is someone that she can count on, and Aksel has secretly looked forward to their encounters. However, there are forces at play that could very well put an end to the push and pull of their relationship and cut off the bud of romance before it has time to blossom.

Stassi's unique abilities are coveted by a madman, and unfortunately, he's got someone almost as powerful in his arsenal who seems to be gunning for her. When fate takes them full circle, back to the place they met, Stassi's life and freedom will hang in the balance. Aksel will rescue her once more and then have to decide whether he'll stay by her side or move on like he's always done in the past.

Come with Cee Bowerman as she revisits Springblood and the unique individuals who hide in plain sight as they live and love among the rest of us mortals in the third book of the Springblood series.

About the Author

Cee Bowerman is proud, lifelong resident of Texas. She is married to her own long-haired, tattooed biker and is the proud mom to three mostly adult kids - a daughter and two sons. She believes in love, second chances, rescue dogs, and happily ever after.

Cee received her first romance novel along with a bag of other books from her granny when she was recovering from surgery at 15. She has been hooked on reading romances ever since. For years, she had a dream of writing her own series of stories, but motherhood and all the other grown up responsibilities kept getting in the way. Luckily, with the support of her family and the encouragement of her son, she purchased a computer and let her dreams become a reality.

Made in the USA
Columbia, SC
29 August 2024

41277704R00178